FALLING
under

Also by Lauren Dane

Opening Up

FALLING
under

LAUREN DANE

FOREVER

NEW YORK   BOSTON

Forever
Hachette Book Group
1290 Avenue of the Americas
New York, NY 10104

www.HachetteBookGroup.com

Printed in the United States of America

RRD-C

First Edition: August 2015
10 9 8 7 6 5 4 3 2 1

Forever is an imprint of Grand Central Publishing.
The Forever name and logo are trademarks of Hachette Book Group, Inc.

The Hachette Speakers Bureau provides a wide range of authors for speaking events. To find out more, go to www.hachettespeakersbureau.com or call (866) 376-6591.

The publisher is not responsible for websites (or their content) that are not owned by the publisher.

Library of Congress Cataloging-in-Publication Data

Dane, Lauren.
    Falling under / Lauren Dane. — First edition.
        pages ; cm. — (Ink & chrome ; book 2)
    ISBN 978-1-4555-8626-4 (pbk.) — ISBN 978-1-4789-0452-6 (audio download) — ISBN 978-1-4555-8624-0 (ebook)
    I. Title.
PS3604.A5F35 2015
813'.6—dc23

2015017113

Very few people are fortunate enough to be able to have their dream job. Despite the long hours, the deadlines, the business itself, I am one of those lucky people. A big thank-you goes to all of you who make it possible for me to do this. My husband and family, my agent, my editor, the art department, editors, marketing, sales, bookstores, libraries, and every wonderful one of you who have told someone else about my books.

Most of all, this one is dedicated to readers because you all rock.

FALLING
under

CHAPTER
One

Carmella Rossi held the truck door open for Ginger, who hopped down with a happy look. Carmella understood, she wanted to dance around for joy now that they weren't at her mother's house too.

Medication had been delivered for the next three days—it wouldn't do to let her have any more than that. She'd just use it all and then not have enough and eventually end up in an ER somewhere trying to get pain scrips to get her through.

"Some people's mothers make pies," Carmella told the dog as they headed up the steps to the front porch.

Her key was in the lock when she and Ginger both paused at the throaty growl of a motorcycle approaching.

Duke Bradshaw. The hottest neighbor in the history of hot neighbors.

Considering the morning she'd just had with her mother, it was a nice treat to see all that long, hot, inked man get off a motorcycle and amble to his front door.

"Totally the best thing about this entire neighborhood," Carmella murmured.

Ginger got in front of Carmella and sat. Ever protective and also sort of hot for Bradshaw just like her human was.

Carmella looked to the front door. "We should go in. Come on. It's weird to wait out here like weirdos." Not like it wasn't weird to have a full conversation with a dog.

Ginger made a doggie snort but shook, her tags jingling merrily as she followed Carmella up to the front door.

And that's when Duke Bradshaw pulled not into his driveway, but Carmella's. That caught her attention as she unlocked to let Ginger inside. But the man brought Ginger bones from time to time so the Manchester terrier had no intention of leaving Carmella alone to greet the big, bad, tattooed biker who lived next door.

"Jeez, dog, he's on his motorcycle. He's not carrying bones in his pocket." Not that she was unaware that he quite frequently *appeared* to have something pretty hefty behind that zipper of his.

His bike was beyond gorgeous and the sight of it never failed to make her heart beat faster. Flat, matte black. No chrome at all. It was a custom rebuild of a 1963 BMW. It was understated and classic while still being really sexy and super masculine. It also sounded like sex—low and throaty, the bass of it settled into her belly in much the same way his voice did.

He keyed the bike off and pulled it back on the stand before sliding one long leg over. He wore a half helmet bearing the logo of his shop, the T and the S swirling together looking sharp and badass.

His attention seemed to settle on her like a physical thing, freezing her to the spot.

And then he smiled and every erogenous zone—including a few she hadn't known existed until that moment—did the wave.

"Just the person I was looking for." Duke hung his helmet on a handlebar and headed up the steps toward her, still wearing black wraparound sunglasses and his jacket.

She wondered—not for the first time—if he ever wore them while he had sex. Would you be able to see your own reflection as he fucked you?

Proud at the calm in her voice, Carmella smiled like she hadn't just been imagining riding his cock while he wore sunglasses so she could watch herself.

"Me? Did Ginger get into something?" She gave a look toward the dog, whose normally erect ears were even perkier at the approach of the guy with the bones.

Duke bent to give Ginger a scratch behind the ears. "Nah. She's a sweetheart. It's her owner I'd like to talk about."

There was honey and lazy afternoons in his voice. Charming. He tucked the sunglasses into his shirt pocket and his pale green eyes took her in. Laugh lines only made him more attractive.

He had a tiny smattering of gray at his temples but it worked with the gold and caramel tones of hair that was closely trimmed at the sides, long and thick at the top. He had some sort of nouveau rockabilly thing happening.

Her fingers itched to reach out and touch.

"Um." She shook her head, disgusted with how flustered he always seemed to make her. He'd been her neighbor for going on two years so there was no reason to get fluttery, but every single time she spoke to him, he seemed to turn her into a twit.

Ginger barked and Carmella pushed the storm door open. "Sorry, where are my manners? Come in."

She let the familiarity of her front entry calm her a little as she bent to free Ginger from the harness and leash.

Duke's hand landed on her elbow when she stood again. "Here, let me help you with your bags."

She shrugged free of the totes slung over one shoulder, repressing a shiver as his fingers brushed the side of her neck. Carmella thanked him as he hung them on the peg.

Removing herself from the temptation to touch him or his leather jacket, Carmella stepped back with a smile. "You have excellent manners. Your parents did a good job."

"The army gets most of the credit for that." Again the grin.

"Want some iced tea? I was just going to make more." Of course, she'd been pondering whether or not to add a big dollop of whiskey to hers, but those were easily changed plans.

"Sure."

He placed his hand at the small of her back as he followed her through the house and into her kitchen. Which really threw a wrench into her plan of trying not to think about this big, tall, broad-shouldered man right behind her.

He took up a lot of space. His scent seemed to push itself ahead of everything else, the electricity of his body seemed to hum from him on a frequency she wanted a lot more of.

Duke was a toucher. Not in a creepy way at all, but he frequently brushed his fingers over her forearm, or a shoulder when they spoke. In another man she'd have said something or made enough of a movement away that her *don't touch me* would have been clear. But she *liked* it when he did it so she allowed herself that sensual treat.

She pointed to a stool at the kitchen island. "Have a seat and tell me what brings you here at eleven in the morning."

Ginger kept staring at Duke lovingly until Carmella sighed. "Ginger, leave the man alone." So easy. Give her a bone and she'd love you forever.

"Aw she just wants some attention. It's okay, I've got some." Duke leaned down and gave Ginger enough scratches and rubs until she made a groaning sound of joy and fell over on her side.

Carmella wanted him to do something to *her* to make her create that sound too. And she bet he could. With any combination of his hands, mouth, and that roll of quarters he carried around in his pocket that was probably a cock that got shit done.

And as if he'd heard her thoughts, he flicked his gaze up from the dog to her and smiled, bringing a blush to heat her cheeks and neck.

"I have a proposition for you."

She blinked, clearing her throat as she kept her hands busy putting teabags in the mugs. "You do?" If it had anything to do with his penis, she was ready to accept.

He touched her hand briefly. "Our accounts payable person just quit. As in she's-moving-across-the-country-in-a-week-and-leaving-us high-and-dry quit. I know you did the books before for a few years and I hope you don't mind, but I called your old boss and he had nothing but great things to say about you. Asa and I would really love it if you could take over as soon as possible as our office manager. It could be a win-win for us both. You need a job. We need an employee. We pay well. We have good benefits. The hours are pretty flexible."

Ginger growl-barked and Duke's attention shifted for a moment. "Oh, and we're dog friendly so you could bring her with you if you wanted to."

"You called my old boss? He's my uncle. You know that, right?"

Duke laughed. "I did, yes. He told me several times, along with a few dire warnings that you were a good girl not to be messed with. He still had nothing but nice things to say about you. You have the experience we need. Our shop is bigger, but you understand the basics."

Her uncle's auto repair business had been a mainstay in North Seattle for thirty-five years. When the economy took a hit, he did too. And though things had begun to recover, he hadn't ever been the same. It'd been hard to compete with the quick-serve corporate repair places, and in the end, after a few health scares, he'd taken it as a sign to close up and retire.

"He's family, so he *has* to say nice things about me." He was her mother's brother, and more of a parent to her than her mother had ever been.

A job would be really good. She'd decided not to stay on when new management took over her uncle's place after he sold it, fairly sure she and the new owner were a bad fit. Her unemployment was enough to keep the lights on, but not much more. She had savings, but preferred not to touch that if she could avoid it.

Duke's smile was one of the sexiest things about him, she realized as she nearly poured boiling water on her hand instead of in the pitcher.

"You know the industry. We're nice guys, I promise. We bring in food every Friday. Free soda in the fridge and ice cream bars in the freezer. I did mean it about the dog friendly thing. One of our guys has a Jack Russell terrier. Xena, as in the warrior princess? She hangs out a few days a week. She'll love Ginger. What do you say?"

Carmella should say that being in routine, close quarters with Duke Bradshaw was bad for all her promises to stay away from bikers and grease monkeys and the like. It wasn't that she couldn't see his appeal. No, it was the opposite.

He was pretty much a total package. Tall, he stood well over six feet. He was handsome. Like really handsome in that rugged, works with his hands way, which in her opinion was the best kind of man. Duke wouldn't be thrown off by hard work. If something broke, he got it fixed. Broad shoulders, work-strong muscled arms and legs. She'd seen him in enough T-shirts to know he had detailed ink on his arms and belly. A really flat belly too. He moved with confidence, like he always knew exactly where he was going and how to get there.

Duke was at ease with himself. That sort of confidence was a sensual punch to the gut. She knew she wasn't alone in liking him. Friends were often at his house on the weekends and in the evenings. Never so rowdy she considered calling the cops. Always cleaned up afterward.

He owned his business. Owned his home and a number of vehicles. At times he had a slow as molasses delivery with a hint of New England. And then he'd say *right on* like some sort of Zen surfer.

No matter what he said, he said it and made her hot and wet and tingly.

On top of all those things? He had an amazing ass.

She was beyond any ability to deny his appeal. If she could have ticked a bunch of her favorite man-type things and that was rendered human, it would look a hell of a lot like the guy in her kitchen just then.

And none of that erased the fact that she couldn't afford a man like him. Her mother would love him, which was Carmella's general meter for acceptability in a gentleman companion. The more Virgie approved, the less suitable the guy would be. She'd loved Carmella's ex-husband too and look where that had gotten her.

But he wasn't there asking her to nail him. He was offering her a job. And damn if she didn't need one of those. The number he'd rattled off as a starting salary was higher than her old job. She needed the benefits and the income, and he was right—she was familiar with the industry so it would probably be pretty easy to get started.

But she had a crush on the man. If he was her boss, that would complicate things. Not like he'd made a single move her way in the time she'd lived next door to him, though.

"Wow, you're doing a lot of thinking in there." He tapped her temple and she smiled.

"Not thinking gets a girl caught in too many dead ends." She paused. "You said you needed me right away?"

He nodded. "The sooner you can start, the better. Even if it's just a few hours here and there until you can start full time."

"All right then. Sounds like you have a new office manager."

CHAPTER
Two

Motor oil, metal, rubber from tires new and ancient, the bite of new paint, and the buttery tones of leather—these were the scents that greeted Duke as he pushed open the side door of Twisted Steel on a gorgeous July morning.

Their logo, mounted high on the wall across from the main doors, caught the sunlight on the sharp edges of the letters. He'd seen it thousands of times and yet every time it moved him still.

He'd created this place with his hands, his heart, and his mind. He and his best friend Asa had started their custom build business in Asa's cousin's garage. Just scraping by as they created a reputation and saved every damned penny they could.

He looked around their space. They were open six days a week with Duke and Asa still part of every single project.

They continued to build—both reputation and footprint. Ground had been broken on the construction of a brand-new showroom nearly twice the size of the one they had now. A gleaming, soaring space where they'd show off current work and greet potential clients.

They didn't get where they were by slacking and neither man planned to lose what they'd fought so hard to achieve. Which was why Duke was there at six thirty on a Thursday morning to finish a project due to be delivered the following day.

The bounce in his step, though, was entirely due to the fact that their replacement office manager was starting in just a few hours. Just thinking about Carmella Rossi made him smile.

Asa was already in their break room pouring himself a mug of coffee when Duke walked in hoping to find some caffeine. He held up the carafe before putting it back. "Just made a pot. Better get some before everyone else gets here."

Duke grinned as he put his saddlebags away in one of the lockers lining the back wall. "Right on," he said, grabbing his mug from the dishwasher on his way over.

Duke lifted his coffee mug in salute as Mick came in with a huge box of bagels and every kind of topping you could want. "Figured that since we have to go over the schedule, we should carb load," Mick said.

They had a lot of finish work to do, which meant the rest of their crew would begin to show up soon enough. The custom leatherwork on the doors had been a week behind its due date, which put the entire project's schedule at risk. And then there'd been trouble with the headers.

Mick, the third in the Twisted Steel hierarchy and the master of their build schedule, had dealt with each setback patiently and efficiently, which left Duke and Asa alone to fall into the work.

"Another reason I'm glad to have you around," Duke said as he helped himself to one of the few rye bagels. Mick understood what it meant to have his mojo interrupted so he often played offensive line to protect the headspace Duke liked to fall into when he got his hands on any machine.

Mick had a large whiteboard calendar he rolled over, along with the laptop and the ever-present notepad he kept in his back pocket, and they had some breakfast and coffee while going over the schedule for the next week.

"We probably should have included Carmella in this meeting," Mick said. "I'll get with her soon to see what her preference is. I think it's good for her to sit in a few times at least to get a feel for how we work."

All the guys had been thrilled that Carmella accepted the job, especially knowing she did the books and managed the office for her uncle's business for years.

Kismet, Duke thought.

"Makes sense. Did you crash here in your office or did you manage to make it home?" Duke asked Asa, who'd still been there when he'd finally left.

Asa rolled his head on his shoulders, a few cracks in his spine as he did. "I slept next to my woman. I'm getting too old for sleeping on couches. And I'm really too old to pretend I'm not way more comfortable at home with PJ."

Eight months after Duke's closest friend had moved in with his girlfriend PJ, there were still brawls and races, and plenty of working until all hours, but the heart of Asa's life had settled and it looked damned good on him.

Duke was happy with his own life, but he had to admit sometimes he felt a twinge of yearning when he saw Asa and PJ together. Their connection was so clear, that sense of partnership so tangible it made Duke begin to think being with someone for the long haul was not only possible, but something he might want too.

"I'm going to get to it," Duke said, standing and gathering his stuff, his head already in the hybrid 1934 Ford at his workstation.

Duke and machines had a thing. A hot, steamy affair. He touched them and they obeyed. As it should be. He couldn't remember a time when he didn't fix things, but he did recall the moment he understood it was more than a thing he did out of necessity but something he did because he loved it.

Which was a good thing because the Ford was pretty much a

rebuild. The parts had taken forever to drum up and even then they had to machine a lot of their own stuff and repurpose a different Ford engine when the one it came with nearly blew up.

That's when Duke had taken over the project. The guys they employed at Twisted Steel were all great. Skilled in their trades and consistently turned out fantastic work.

But this persnickety '34 wasn't going to submit to anyone but Duke. So, Mick kept people away from Duke, enabling a mind-set Asa referred to as "the machine whisperer."

There was no need to hammer home who was boss. No, Duke was a chill dude for a reason. Machines didn't give a damn how much you needed them to work. They didn't worry about breaking down. Moods were irrelevant to whatever Duke wanted to fix so he always figured he might as well keep his act together instead of losing his shit.

Instead, they responded to patience and determination.

A little bit of magic, some luck, lots of skill, and endless patience and the '34's engine had a rumbling growl. And when they finished up, the car would be one of their best builds yet, bringing them enough cash—and attention as the customer was a car enthusiast with connections at several magazines—to continue to make their mark as masters of their craft.

Asa stopped by, interrupting Duke what turned out to be two hours later. "Carmella just arrived. Let's not scare her away with our bad manners the first day."

"Especially as I pretty much ambushed her when I made the job offer."

Twisted Steel had been in a bind and Duke was not even the tiniest bit embarrassed at how fast he took it up as a chance to be around her more.

She walked in, impressed by the place immediately. Sure it was a shop; she'd been in them on a regular basis pretty much her entire life so there was always a sense of homecoming. But some shops were shitholes. Most were in the middle somewhere.

Twisted Steel, though, was special.

It was clear they took pride in what they did and the product they created.

"Morning, Carmella."

Hello, tall, dark, and handsome. Hazel eyes took her in. Long, dark hair was tied back to expose one hell of a face. Tawny skin with ink peeking out here and there. He wiped his hands on a cleanup rag.

Asa Barrons. The other owner of Twisted Steel. He held out a hand and drew it back. "Sorry, I was just dealing with a funky carb. Let's just pretend I shook your hand and then I won't get you dirty."

Too bad. She bet he could get a girl really, really dirty. Carmella knew PJ Colman, Asa's girlfriend. PJ looked *really* happy every time Carmella saw her since getting together with Asa.

Instead of saying it and getting fired her first five minutes on the job, she smiled. "Hi there, Asa."

"We're glad to have you here. Let me take you to the office so you can meet Lottie."

She followed him back to the administrative area that overlooked the work floor via a wall of glass. A petite woman with thick-rimmed glasses looked up.

"Lottie, this is Carmella, she'll be taking over for you."

Lottie waved as she came over and pulled Carmella into an unexpected hug. "Hi! Come on over and put your bag away. Asa, get back to work. I'll get Carmella started after some coffee and a tour. Don't worry, I won't scare her off."

"Okay then. Again, welcome to Twisted Steel, Carmella."

Asa left and Lottie snorted. "They're nice guys to work for. I'm bummed to be leaving." And then she pretty much told Carmella her entire life story as she showed her where to stow her coat and other stuff.

"This'll be your desk unless you want the other one. They, the guys I mean, use whichever desk you won't be using a few times a day. I like this one because that one is right under the vent so it's freezing in the summer and hot in the winter. Plus from here you can keep an eye on the floor where everyone works and the front door too. We don't get much street traffic. They do have open hours for the showroom but there's a receptionist over there so you don't have to deal with any of that stuff. They only see clients by appointment. Asa and Duke have offices just through here." Lottie indicated two side-by-side offices. "They see clients for consults usually over in the showroom, though."

Sweet baby Jesus, how did this girl even breathe around all those words? Lottie was like a hummingbird, flitting all around, talking at hyper speed.

"Let's go out and meet everyone. They're finishing a job right now so I'll warn you they might be short and a little punchy. They'll deliver tomorrow and then there'll be a huge feast here." Lottie paused and looked Carmella over. "Good, you're not wearing heels. I tried that when I first started. You'll find your-self running around too much for heels."

Ha. Heels in a shop? Not likely. She liked not breaking her bones too much for that.

She followed Lottie out but Duke was already approaching, smiling. "You're here. Good. Come on so I can introduce you around." He put his hand at her elbow and drew her away from Lottie, who didn't even stop chattering for half a beat.

Despite Lottie's warning, no one was anything less than friendly and welcoming to her.

Twisted Steel had a great crew. The Ford they were finishing up was stunning work. She walked around it, pausing here and there to appreciate the craftsmanship on every level.

"This is sweet," Carmella said, meaning it.

Duke grinned. "I can't lie, it's fucking gorgeous. I'm glad it turned out so well, but damn, I'll be sorry I can't keep her." He polished up the chrome of a side mirror.

He charmed her, this man who looked at his work through the eyes of a little boy.

He straightened, looking all around her at floor level. "Hey, where's Ginger?"

"She's at home. First day at a new job so I figured I'd bring her in next week. Just the mornings probably. She's too social and would be in everything if I had her here all the time."

"Well, it's up to you, but she's welcome."

Carmella thanked him again and got back to work.

She spent the afternoon getting a quick and dirty education on how Twisted Steel liked its books handled. Carmella figured once Lottie was gone, she could apply some discipline and things would be a lot smoother. The other woman was sweet and friendly, but it appeared there was a lot of pestering of the crew over things like time sheets and invoicing.

Carmella liked to run a very tight front office so she'd have to see just how much change the folks at Twisted Steel would tolerate.

At quitting time, Lottie patted Carmella's hand. "It's time to clock out. You can work pretty much your own hours. I do eight to five but you can do nine to six or whatever. They're here late all the time but there's stuff you need to do during regular business hours. I'm sure you'll get it all. It's not like you're new to this or anything. I'll see you in the morning. I need to go home and help pack. John, that's my husband, he says to thank you for jumping in so fast to help." She smiled brightly up at Carmella. "We'll go through payroll together first thing. Friday is doughnuts and bagels in the morning and they're delivering that 'thirty-four so there'll be more food after that too."

Carmella asked her question quickly while Lottie appeared to be breathing instead of speaking. "Do I need to pick them up?"

"Nope. They'll be delivered here first thing. Duke takes care of all that. Just come hungry."

As Lottie and Carmella started to leave, Duke looked up from his work and jogged over to the doors. "Hey, how was your first day?"

Lottie answered, "She's a natural. She's gonna be great though I do hope you guys miss me at least a little."

Duke put his arm around Lottie's shoulder. "Of course we'll miss you. It'll probably be way quieter around here, that's for sure." He winked and Lottie laughed.

"See you in the morning." Lottie scampered out and Carmella let out a long breath.

Duke laughed. "Yeah, she's got a lot of energy. Sort of a tiny female Tigger sometimes."

"I hope you guys don't get disappointed. I don't think I have the stamina to talk that much. Plus I like breathing now and then."

He laughed. "You'll do fine. I have no doubts. Thanks again for pitching in. We're a family here as you'll come to find out. Lottie needs this move, but she's leaving the place in good hands."

"I'll do my best not to let you down," Carmella said with a smirk. "I'm excited to see the finished project and the customer's face when he sees it for the first time."

"Best part of the deal other than the check." Duke stepped back. "I'll see you in the morning. Drive safe."

It was good to have a job again. Being worried about money sent her back to a place she hated to go. A place where her helplessness wasn't something she could get around.

A good-paying job gave her independence. It gave her the ability to make her own choices. And that meant she'd always be in charge of her destiny. She'd do whatever it took to keep from depending on anyone else to survive.

While dinner cooked, she played ball with Ginger for a few minutes and tossed some clothes in the washer. She'd sort of been on summer vacation schedule, though having to deal with her mother's appointments got Carmella out on a regular basis.

The stability of gainful employment and a real schedule would benefit mother and daughter both, Carmella hoped. As she settled at the dinner table, Ginger joined her, lying over Carmella's feet.

"I think this is going to work out, Ginger. If I can keep from thinking with my pink parts, that is. Something about Duke Bradshaw makes me want to fall on my back and open my thighs wide. He's a menace."

Ginger gave Carmella a growl-bark that Carmella figured was a canine version of *girl, me too*.

The paperwork she'd filled out had included a retirement plan. A *retirement* plan! They matched a percentage of the total she put into it monthly. It wasn't that she'd never thought of such a thing but it had always seemed like something other people had and she never would.

And they liked dogs. Really, she wondered when she'd find out they were all in league with Satan or something. The place seemed so awesome she was sure there'd be another shoe dropping at some point.

Unless she found out something horrifying, she'd take this news as wonderful and let herself be hopeful instead of hopeless.

CHAPTER
Three

Duke made himself promise not to watch Carmella all morning long. A difficult promise that only worked out partway because there was no denying he liked to look at her.

It was impossible not to. She was everything he loved about redheads. To say she was curvy wouldn't have done justice to just how juicy those curves were. It wasn't just the banging tits and that sweet ass, but the way she dressed. Confidently, sexily, mindful of what she looked good in, and she worked it.

Damn did she ever. Not blatant. She wasn't a sex bomb that way. But the heat was there, just beneath the surface. Hints of it had driven him nuts over the last few years of living next door.

But when the morning break came and she'd come out of the office and had hustled into the break room, he'd managed to sidle up next to her.

She smelled really good. Flowers and spice. Not overpowering at all. In fact, he only smelled it when he was right next to her. Just a bit of it here and there. He wanted to tell her that, but he was her boss and so he didn't.

Carmella had her hair held back from her face with a navy blue band. She wore a blue and white polka dot blouse that dipped in the front but didn't even approach inappropriate and navy blue pants with flats. Even so she came off as tall. Statuesque. Like one of those Italian actresses his old man used to love back in the day.

But she wasn't. Standing next to her, he realized just how petite she was. All that tall stuff was the way she made him feel. Damn.

Her makeup was pure forties with dark-lined eyes that brought out just how blue they were. Freckles danced over her nose and cheeks and her lips were shiny.

"Redheads should wear red lipstick more often."

It was out before he could stop himself. Another thing a boss probably shouldn't say.

Her mouth was so lush he wanted to lean in and bite her bottom lip. Currently it curved up at one edge as she smiled. "My grandmother taught me that red lipstick is revolution in a tube. Nothing else so cheap and small can make you feel so much better after you use it."

He laughed. "Your grandmother sounds wise in the way of things."

"She was pretty fantastic in her day. She passed a few years ago, but her best lessons have stayed with me. So, how goes the Ford?"

"Want to see the final product?" He wanted to show off. Wanted her to see what he did and find it impressive.

Her eyes lit up. "Yes. I'd love to. I figured because you had the tarp over it, you wanted to do a reveal all official like."

"Mainly to keep the dust off as we cleaned stuff up. Asa is going to move it to the showroom in a few minutes. Come on down."

She followed him, and when he drew the tarp off, she gasped, clasping her hands in front of her body. "Wow." She circled the car slowly, taking in all the details.

He swung the driver's side door open and she hummed. A

sound so carnal and greedy it shot straight to his cock. He licked his lips and swallowed hard. A woman who'd make a sound like that over a car was the ultimate aphrodisiac.

"Tell me what you've done," she murmured as she continued to take in all the details.

"The car had been sitting under sheets in a barn for at least forty years. The undercarriage was a ruin. There was a family of mice living in the seats. The frame was about sixty percent salvageable. I rebuilt the rest. The client wasn't that big a stickler on it being stock. Which was good since it would have been next to impossible. We updated the engine. Asa designed the rims. Client wanted suicide doors so we built them from the original."

She pointed to the custom work they'd done on the inside of the doors to echo the seats. "This is beautiful. You guys have made a piece of art."

Duke grinned and Asa strolled up, pleased by the compliment as well. "Wait until you hear the engine."

Her eyes were bright, her smile big as she stepped back. "I can't wait. The paint? Obviously not stock, but wow the deep wine color, so sexy."

"That's all Penelope Jean." Asa's expression softened at the mention of his incredibly talented girlfriend. "Client saw this color on a pillow. Brought it in for us to see. PJ created a custom color from that."

"It's fantastic." She moved out of the way as they pushed open the bay doors, prepping to move the car next door to the showroom. When a client picked their car or bike up, it was a big deal and Twisted Steel made it that way.

The lights would be on it just right, highlighting it for delivery. They'd had this moment many times but every single time was special. Every single customer reacted differently.

"So what's next for you guys?"

"Two projects. A 'forty-seven Chevy two-door coupe. They want a custom rebuild so this will be crazy fantastic. The other is a trike. One of our signature builds."

"Can't wait to see—"

Asa started the Ford and the air was filled with muscle. All the normal talking silenced and then applause and whistles broke out.

Twisted Steel was about to deliver another winner.

When Lottie had told Carmella they brought in a feast when a project was delivered, she hadn't been kidding. The post-delivery celebration had also turned into a good-bye party for Lottie.

They'd closed the shop and headed into the back, where pizzas, salads, sodas, beers, sweets, and hoagies waited.

PJ showed up, coming straight over to give Carmella a hug. "Asa told me they'd hired you. How are you? You look like you're ready to bolt. I promise they only look like bad boys."

Carmella snickered, patting PJ's arm. "Believe me, I know the difference. It's just...well I'm new and this is a good-bye party. I don't want to intrude."

PJ shook her head. Asa came up behind her, sliding an arm around her shoulders. "Ha. No intruding. This is a welcome party for you as well as Lottie's going away. Let everyone get to know you. Have a few beers. Relax."

So, Carmella went back into the break room, now burgeoning with people and food, and couldn't help but smile at them. Duke leaned against the far wall, the neck of a beer dangling between his fingers as he listened to something Chick, one of the metal fabricators, was saying.

Lottie buzzed around hugging people, trying not to cry.

PJ handed her a plate and Carmella grabbed a bottle of cream soda. Two slices of loaded pizza later, she found herself squeezed in between Duke and Asa as they argued about just where they found a part. Duke insisted it was in a junkyard in Concrete, Washington, and Asa was saying it had been in Macon, Georgia.

It was clear the two men shared a deep friendship, which she liked a great deal.

"How did you two meet?"

"We served in Iraq together," Duke said.

Asa made a sound. "Duke saved my ass in a firefight. Three of our guys were killed. I was pinned down. I'd been shot four times and was bleeding like a stuck pig. He tossed me over his shoulder and ran for it. He saved three of us that afternoon."

Duke waved it away with a blush. "You do what you gotta do. They'd have done it for me if the situation was reversed."

Asa rolled his eyes and kept talking. "He does that. Like he's shy. Which he totally isn't. But he still saved my life, and after that, I figured he had to be pretty okay."

"We came back stateside and Asa lived out here. I floundered awhile back East until I finally gave in and moved out here. The rest is what you see."

"Well that and a lot of work I expect. I like that story," Carmella said.

Asa and PJ ducked out, leaving Duke and Carmella alone. "So you want to go out for a beer after this? I mean, a group of us are heading out."

Oh, how she wanted to. It'd be so nice to make a few really bad choices and end up with that hot man meat in her bed.

And yet, it was always the morning after that got you. "I'd better not. I have plans for the morning." A trip over to her mother's apartment to dole out pills and listen to complaints.

"Has Ginger been inside all day?"

Damn, it was nice that he thought about that. "No. I have a doggie door. I went home for lunch too. She's fine. Don't let her con you with those big *no one ever feeds me* eyes. She'd eat the chrome off a bumper if you let her."

He laughed and she had to stop herself from leaning closer to get more. He had a good laugh. A really good laugh. God.

She wanted to step away but her back was to a wall and he stood in front of her. He stared at her—at her mouth—for long moments before he seemed to snap out of it.

"Okay. Well, next time then. We do lunches here on Fridays but we often hit the bar up the street for beers after work. Everyone's happy to have you here, I know they'd love it if you came out with us."

Maybe later. Once she'd managed to get some walls built between her libido and the man in front of her. Right then she wanted to push him back on the table and scramble aboard.

On top she'd have him spread out below her so she could dip down to kiss him as she rode his cock. He'd have access to her nipples, to her pussy. She had no misperceptions about him. A man like Duke would know how to make a woman come. Quite ably. Most likely more than once.

She'd snuck enough looks at his lap to know he was packing something thick.

She loved a thick cock.

She nearly moaned at the thought, catching herself only barely in time.

"I should be going. Unless you need help cleaning up?"

He shook his head, still standing really close. Close enough that all she could really see was him. He blocked the rest of the room with those wide shoulders of his.

"We'll get it. Everyone works their tail off for us, we can clean up the mess. I'll see you Monday then. Have a good weekend." He stepped back and she gulped in some air.

"You too." She waved her good-byes and allowed Lottie to hug her and wished her luck.

As fast as her feet could take her, she cleared out and headed home before she did something monumentally stupid like take Duke up on the sensual promise in his gaze.

She had a good job. With benefits. And a retirement plan. She could not—would not—fuck her boss, no matter how fat his cock was or how nice of an ass he had.

Nope.

But that didn't mean she couldn't think about it when she was alone in her shower with her detachable showerhead. Which she planned to do in an hour or so.

CHAPTER
Four

Carmella was grateful she had work to dive into after the nightmare weekend she'd had. Her mother had been kicked out of one of her favorite urgent care clinics. The police had called Carmella to pick her up instead of arresting her.

So Carmella'd been over at her mother's, keeping her fed and entertained long enough to finally sleep her way out of the manic state she'd worked herself into.

Which meant Carmella had finally fallen into her own bed somewhere after one in the morning and had gotten very little rest.

Normally she'd go in later than seven, but despite her exhaustion, she'd woken up at six. So, she accepted it, showered, ate some breakfast, and headed to her new job.

The office was now hers. Carmella would need to make her own way there. Figure out what she liked where. She'd need to find a way to handle all the people who worked at Twisted Steel as well.

She cast her gaze over the shop floor below. She'd worked in garages her entire adult life. When her father had been around, he'd been a mechanic at her uncle's shop.

Those guys down there worked hard and played harder. They

were all of a type. Asa with his taciturn super-amped-up alpha male energy. Duke, the laid-back guy, good with his hands. There were shop guys, long beards, backward-baseball-hat guys, big, quiet beefy dudes of indeterminate purpose, and yet they knew more than most anyone when it came to machines.

Carmella took her attention away from the shop floor and went back to setting up her office. The Friday before, Lottie had taken home a big box of shiny things, pictures, dolls, buttons, and all manner of busy, sparkly crap that people tend to gather over years at a place.

That had all been picked clean so the slate was totally blank. Carmella wasn't one for sparkly little bits of crap. It wasn't as if she would have been able to keep anything anyway as a kid, so she never developed that habit.

But she liked pictures, so she'd brought some of them from home and had begun to set things up the way she liked them best.

Carmella wasn't a Nobel prizewinner or anything, but she knew numbers and shops and that world. It had taken a while to get there, but Carmella liked what she did. And she had zero problem being proud of it.

Duke had wanted to go next door all weekend long to visit with Carmella. He told himself it was about making a new employee feel comfortable but really, he just dug her.

But he'd been out late working at the shop, and it wasn't until she walked in Monday morning looking ridiculously adorable that he was able to be around her.

Of course, he got sucked into a crotchety engine and swept up in making it right again so he lost track of time until Asa spoke.

"You can stop looking at the door. She came in a few minutes ago," Asa said as he walked over carrying a fender.

"I know when she got here." Duke liked the earliest hours at Twisted Steel, when it was just him and his machines. There were a few others who liked it when it was quiet and Duke wondered if Carmella was one of them.

"Before you go moon at her, let's see if this fits."

"I don't *moon* at anyone." Nevertheless he pulled his head out of the engine he'd been elbow deep in and helped Asa get the fender into place.

They machined it at the shop, which took longer than ordering one, but that was far more expensive. This client was happy to wait for something that met her exact specifications and Asa, the weirdo, seemed to love that sort of excruciatingly boring work.

"She's our employee. It'd be stupid to moon at her." Duke wasn't sure who he was trying to convince.

Asa raised one brow and went back to sliding the fender into place.

After a little bit of to and fro, they managed to get it lined up so Asa could then secure it.

"I'm not going to lie. After the last two times I was beginning to wonder if this fender was cursed."

"I love how you'd chalk it up to a curse instead of owning your shit," Duke teased his perfectionist partner.

Asa flipped Duke off as he examined his work.

Duke kept on, cleaning up a little. "If I can get her running by the end of today, I think we should be able to deliver at the end of the week probably. For now, I'm breaking for some coffee."

He not only grabbed a cup for himself, but one for Carmella too, bringing it up to the deck where her workspace was.

"Morning."

Carmella wore her hair in some sort of braid wrapped around her head. It should have looked ridiculous, but it didn't. It exposed the beauty of her face. Big blue eyes, those damned freckles he couldn't stop thinking about, her lips, glossy with a little makeup but not too much.

The blouse she wore was nearly the same color as her eyes and it skimmed over her curves lovingly but was entirely appropriate for work.

"I brought you some coffee." He should have invited her into the break room. There was cream and food and stuff in there. "Or if you wanted sugar or milk, we could have a cup in the other room. Have you had breakfast yet?"

Her smile was patient but amused at the edges. "I have sugar right here." She pointed at the coffee station she'd placed in her office. "I may be what's termed a caffeine junkie so I like to make my own half-caf brew so I can drink it all day and not act like a bee in a jar."

He had to pause to think for just a moment about all her parts jiggling as she bounced around the office. "'Scuse me for saying so, but that might be fun to see."

Carmella laughed. "I'm glad to hear my hyperactivity would be appreciated."

Duke leaned his butt against the empty desk, tipping his chin at her. "You've done some work in here." Not a lot, but certainly she'd claimed the office. Some of the furniture had been rearranged and he noted the baskets neatly marked with each employee's name along with one for invoices and the like.

"How are you settling in today?"

"Not too bad. Moved some stuff, made labels."

"Your eyes just sparkled when you said you made labels. I'm a little nervous," Duke said. And sort of turned on. Huh.

"I like things in their place. I like knowing things are where they should be when I have to find them."

"Right on."

"Okay, you need to tell me where you're from with that accent of yours. Before that, though..." Carmella nudged him toward a pink pastry box. "Go on. Cherry popovers. There are more in the break room, but I kept these three back. I'll share one."

"I think the better question is what kind of planet you came from bearing all that red hair and pastry too," Duke said as he leaned over her, taking a deep breath as he grabbed his pastry.

"I might smell like window cleaner," she murmured.

That might make you even fucking hotter. He managed not to say it out loud, but damn, who knew?

"Was it that bad in here?" he managed to say, like he hadn't been sniffing her and she didn't know it.

"Nah. I just figured since I had everything off the desks when I moved them, they may as well get a bit of a wipe down. I hope you don't mind that I rearranged things."

"This is your domain. Do whatever you need. But don't forget there's a floor full of big-ass burly dudes who would happily move heavy stuff if you asked. Me included."

"I'll be keeping that in mind. Mainly it was just desks so it wasn't a big deal."

He didn't like the idea of her moving stuff. Or maybe he liked the idea of doing it for her. Duke wasn't that alarmed by the wanting to take care of her part. He liked to make things easy for people when he could. But this was . . . odd. Far more intense than he usually felt about women he dug.

The phone rang and she grabbed it, her voice going soft and sexy. Duke stood, dumbfounded by the way she effortlessly stepped into the job.

Carmella was an adult. A woman in charge of herself. So. Fucking. Sexy.

"I don't even know what to do with him, Ginger," Carmella said later that night as they took a walk around Green Lake after work. "He's really hard to resist."

Ginger barked and kept walking alongside.

"You like him too. I know."

Duke flustered her in ways she wouldn't have allowed in anyone else. It was his rhythm. He took his time. With every word. With every step. And yet he didn't come off lazy so much as totally enjoying every moment.

He was intense the same way watching a big wave safely from the shore was intense. And right then he looked at her like he wanted to spread her on a cracker and take a bite.

It didn't matter that she was fully clothed, when Duke looked at her, Carmella felt naked. And it wasn't predatory. He wasn't being lecherous. It left her exposed and a little off balance.

She never did find out where he was from with that surfer boy drawl with a hint of Northeasterner flavor to his words because the day was flat-out crazy after that.

Maybe she needed to stop even thinking about this whole thing. The man was her boss. It was such a bad idea to let herself get tingly.

"I need this job. Men are plentiful if I should find a need for one. I can keep all my dirty thoughts to myself. I'm not a toddler. I have self-control."

The path was full of people out enjoying the warm evening walk around the lake so a few people gave her a look as they passed, but mainly no one seemed to care that she was talking to herself and her dog.

Which was good because by the time she'd made her third go-round, she was ready to head back home, feeling a little more solid in her *you can look but not touch* plan.

Mostly.

CHAPTER
Five

I don't know if you like racing or not, but Twisted Steel has a team and we're headed out tonight. I wanted to invite you," Duke said as he poked his head into her office.

Ginger, who'd been draped over Carmella's feet under the desk, nearly broke something at the sound of Duke's voice.

Seeing her, he grinned and knelt. "Hey, gorgeous girl."

Ginger was so excited she shook, making her little bark growls of joy as he scratched behind her ears.

"Unfortunately I think it might be too noisy and dangerous for you," Duke told the dog.

Carmella loved racing and had been out to the track a few times to watch the Twisted Steel team. It was pretty nice to be invited in person, though.

"I just might be there." She needed to check on her mother first, and be sure all was well before being out, but it sounded like just the thing.

Duke gave Carmella a lopsided grin and she got a little faint.

"Ginger, you want to hang out with me awhile? I need to root around out back for some stuff," Duke asked her dog, and obviously Carmella too.

Ginger barked, wagging her tail so hard her entire rear end vibrated.

"No one compares to you, Duke. You've spoiled her." Carmella winked and Duke blushed.

Blushed.

"Well, I'll be back shortly," Duke said as he left with the dog and she tried to pretend it didn't make her all fluttery. It wasn't a date. Carmella had noted the people who worked at Twisted Steel also hung out socially a lot. Duke was just involving her like everyone else.

Her first week there had been mainly about learning the ropes and getting people in line with her way of doing things. Asa and Duke left the office stuff to her, which she approved of. The other guys quickly adopted her system of what invoices went where and of what they needed to call to her attention so it wasn't as hard as it could have been.

The work was something she knew. Her first real job at the age of sixteen had been helping out in the office at her uncle's shop. He'd pushed her to go on, attend college, go out and be something more than his accounts person.

But that wasn't what she wanted. Some people had a calling or whatever, but she liked her job. It was a way to get money to pay her bills and that was fine. She didn't need to be fulfilled by her job.

Though she did need to be fulfilled by her life and that part was a work in progress. Which was one of the reasons she planned to head out to the track that night.

PJ strolled in as Carmella was in the break room grabbing some iced tea.

"Hey you," PJ said as she came over to hug Carmella. "What's up today?"

"Just grabbing something to drink. How are you? Down here working or dropping something off?"

"Doing some detail stuff for a motorcycle build."

"The bike with the hand-tooled leather accents?"

"One and the same. I put in little bits and pieces from the seats and other leather work. If I do say so myself, it's pretty cool."

PJ was an artist with her work in much the same way Asa was. They both loved cars and clearly loved one another and it made Carmella happy to see her friend doing so well in every way.

"Excellent. I'll need to go look at it later before I leave for the day."

"You going to the track tonight?" PJ asked with faux casualness.

"I was thinking about it. Duke just told me about it a few minutes ago."

"Oh, he did?"

Carmella rolled her eyes. "You're so transparent."

"Please. He's ridiculously adorable. And the track is *full* of hot guys if you're inclined otherwise. Plus Asa will be all involved with his car and stuff so it'll be nice to have you there."

"I've been before," Carmella said. "Craig and I have seen you a few times."

PJ waved a hand at that and the mention of Carmella's cousin, who was part of PJ's crowd. "That's different. Now you're there with Twisted Steel. There's food and beer and soda for everyone."

"Like a cool club?"

PJ leaned closer. "They now have ice cream too. They're making root beer floats at our tent."

"Oh, really cool club." Carmella laughed. "You don't have to sell me. I love the track and I love ice cream so I'm delighted to combine those while I look at hot men."

"Well now." Duke stepped back into the room, the skitter of Ginger's nails sounding quickly as she came over to check on Carmella.

Her face heated and she wanted to apologize and hide under

the desk and burst out laughing. Maybe she could fake something medical and run out of the room.

Instead she squared her shoulders. "Thank you for returning the dog."

"She's always happy. Being around her makes you happy too. She's an excellent dog."

"Carmella is coming tonight. To the track, I mean. I finished the bike if you want to take a look." PJ looked around Duke's body. "See you tonight!"

"She's happy a lot too." Duke propped his butt on the edge of her desk so she was unable to pretend away the snowy white spots on his jeans where the denim had worn thin.

He had fantastic legs. Long and lean, like a swimmer or a runner.

"Where'd you go?" he asked softly, almost a tease.

She flicked her gaze from his thigh to his face and got caught up there. The bits of gray mixed in the darker caramel at his temples and a bit in his beard. His eyes, gracious, it was the way the lashes fringed the pale green that made them so gorgeous.

Currently his mouth was working a cocky grin and it worked because he was hot as fuck and he had every reason to be cocky.

"I haven't gone anywhere," Carmella answered, though she knew that wasn't really what he'd been asking.

"You were thinking. Arguing with yourself maybe?"

Well, she'd been thinking about his thigh and his cock and she should have been arguing with herself to stop that but she didn't bother.

"I bet it was about sex given that blush."

This was bad. So stupid. Bad. Wrong. All those things, but man, he smelled really good and he made her feel...lighter. As if he saw her without all the baggage she carried around. It was nice he didn't know Carmella in that context.

Freeing.

And it was really fucking cool to have a man this handsome and charismatic clearly find her attractive and engaging enough to flirt with. They had some major chemistry between them, and while she knew she needed to run screaming, she let herself breathe in a little deeper to sniff him.

"Could be. Or it could be about laundry or grocery shopping." She smiled and he laughed, standing once more.

"I'll see you tonight. Since you'll be looking at hot men, I expect you'll find me."

He sauntered out, whistling.

Damn, that ass.

PJ had been right. It was different going to the track now. It had hit her as she'd gotten dressed after work. Tonight she changed into an entire new outfit, whereas when she'd gone before with her cousin, they'd just headed out in whatever they'd worn to work that day.

She wanted to look nice for the people she worked with. Probably Duke more than everyone else. Carmella rolled her eyes at herself in the mirror after she checked her lipstick.

It was just *flirting*. She could flirt and enjoy herself and not end up like her mom. She was twenty-six years old, far from dead so why live like it?

Carmella had written all that down in a journal and needed to look at it from time to time. But it was true.

A lifetime of caretaking her mother as her mother had deteriorated had kept Carmella wary of most personal relationships. Which had only been underlined when she'd realized her ex was pretty much a carbon copy of every dick her mother had ever been dumped on by.

But it was lonely either having one-night stands or time with her hand and showerhead. Working at Twisted Steel made her happy and she'd decided it was all right to live like a young woman and let herself enjoy herself.

Within moderation, of course. But Duke was attractive and sexy and they had a nice back-and-forth and it made her feel *alive* and something more than a caregiver.

So she took off, glad for the warm, dry evening, and when she'd pulled into the lot at the track, she'd parked where the other people who worked at Twisted Steel had.

PJ had just been getting out of her car when she caught sight of Carmella.

She gave Carmella a hug and tugged her toward the covered area the Twisted Steel folks hung out at. "So glad you're here. Asa and Duke came together so I don't expect to see him for a while."

"I'm here for root beer floats."

"Me too. And rings."

Both women were greeted happily, and before too long they both had a root beer float and a basket of freshly made onion rings on the bench between them as the first racing heats began on the track.

Duke raced in their fastback. Carmella *loved* the sound of the engine and bet Duke did too.

"I met Duke before I met Asa and I remember thinking how gorgeous he was. He's a ridiculous flirt and women seem to swoon and sigh in his wake. But he's not a jerk or a pig," PJ said to Carmella.

"He's the kind of gorgeous that makes a girl forget everything else." He *really* knew how to flirt. "I feel like a total amateur around him," Carmella admitted.

"But you're having fun." PJ's brow—the one with the piercing—rose.

"God yes, it's fun. Still, on a scale of one to ten, being here and letting myself flirt with him is a bad idea in the eleven or twelve range," Carmella admitted to PJ.

They surged to their feet as Duke raced over the finish line.

"I hear you. So much." PJ's gaze roved over the crew at the fast-back, looking for Asa, who stood out with his hard-edged good looks.

Once she found him and he'd looked up to wave their way, PJ turned back to Carmella. "But what's the worst that could happen? It's just flirting. Even if it was more, it's not the end of the world, right?"

Carmella couldn't nurse any grand notions for anything happening with Duke beyond harmless flirting. She knew the score. Knew what Duke was. "I know you and Asa have this amazing thing so you're love's cheerleader. But I'm Duke's *employee*. If things go wrong, I could lose my job." Her healthcare, her benefits. Her freedom to make her own choices on her own terms. "I can't afford it."

PJ cocked her head. "Do you really think Duke would fire you if you two made out and then moved on? He only looks like a bad boy but he's truly a nice guy."

"I think it's dangerous territory. Regardless of what he is or isn't."

"Sounds like you've been there," PJ said. "I'm here if you want to talk about it. Or anything else."

"Thanks." Carmella realized how much she'd missed having close friends. "For the record, I don't think he's a bad guy. Or that he'd misuse his power to hurt me. But I can't rely on that. People depend on me."

PJ thought about it for a bit. "Fair enough. It's still early days with all of us. You'll come to trust what you think in time. In any case, if you lost your job, know I'd snatch you up in a hot minute to work for me at Colman Enterprises."

Carmella goggled at her. "What?"

"What yourself, Carmella. You have the magic. Lottie was good at her job but it was a little loosey-goosey in the office. She let stuff slide. They were all used to that and you came in and you're tightening things up, organizing. It's two steps instead of four to do things now. You have a way with the guys at the shop. I have a thriving business and you'd be the perfect person to keep it that way. So. I'm just saying that if you wanted to go a little further than flirting, and if Duke was terrible and fired you, you'd still have a job."

Carmella let herself relax just a little. Options were always a plus. Not that she planned on flipping on the red light and having Duke over for several bouts of enthusiastic sex at the suggestion she had a job somewhere else.

"Thanks. It's never a bad thing to be wanted." Carmella's gaze slid from PJ to where Duke had just gotten out of the fastback and was talking to Asa.

His helmet was under his arm and he stood in that lanky way of his, all loose and warm. It was deceptive.

She'd seen a glimpse here and there of what lay beneath. He didn't miss much and she had her doubts he was more than two seconds away from springing into action at any given moment if he needed to be.

"No lie." PJ patted her arm. "Now, I'm going to head down to the pit when Asa races. Because it's really hot. You should wander over to where Duke is staring at you. Say hey. Be neighborly."

Neighborly. Right. Well, he was her neighbor. But she wanted to ride him, not take over a cake. Maybe she could take over a cake and ride him.

Hm.

Or she could feed him cake as she rode him. He would be so inventive. The way women he was involved with had looked at him over the time she'd known him told her the man had to be a champ at sexytimes.

So of course now all Carmella could think, as she locked her attention on him and she found herself headed his way, was of Duke, naked and covered in sweat. And some frosting.

"Nicely done. Congratulations," Carmella said as she reached him.

"Thank you kindly." They began to walk toward the crowd. "Not too many people get to drive cars really fast and call it work. Turns out I'm pretty lucky."

They hadn't gotten very far before his friends had started to gather around him, plenty of them women looking at his marvelous ass, just waiting for his attention.

But instead of going with them, Duke took Carmella's elbow. "Walk with me."

She nodded and let him steer her away from the crowd and toward the quieter area on the other side of the tents housing food and beer.

"Now then." They paused at a bale of hay with some fabric on it. "I can hear myself think back here." He'd had a light jacket under an arm and he spread it over the hay and the cloth. "That'll be easier and probably warmer."

"Thanks." It was such a gentlemanly, old-school thing and perfectly Duke.

Duke sat close enough that their thighs touched. "I didn't expect to see you in the stands tonight," he said.

"I'm sorry," Carmella said automatically.

"Hey." He took her hand. "What for? It's a good surprise. I knew you were coming, but it was cool to see you up there watching me race. You apologize a lot."

It kept the peace.

She shrugged. "I'd say I'm sorry, but, uh . . ."

He laughed and kept her hand. "If you step on my toe, or scratch my door, you can apologize. But not for being there looking so damned good when I got out of the car after winning a race."

"Oh. Okay." Carmella clamped her lips against another automatic apology and he noticed, grinning.

"They have burgers here and all, but I'm all out of patience for people and fried food at the moment. Want to escape the madness and grab dinner? I've had this totally weird craving for some pancakes and eggs. You in for breakfast for dinner?"

She should say something about how this was odd because they worked together. But he went out with people at the shop all the time, right? So it was cool.

Plus, breakfast sounded really good.

"All right. I'm pretty hungry."

"I rode in with Asa, you got room for me in your car?"

Boy oh boy, how she went from zero to totally over her head with this man in such a short period of time she wasn't sure other than his near-perfect charm.

And she guessed she'd get to know him better as they drove to breakfast in her truck. "If you don't mind dog hair."

It was like watching this all happening on-screen as he helped her to her feet, called out his good-byes, and steered her to the parking lot.

"Thing is, Carmella." He paused like he needed to taste his words, savor them even after he'd given them to her. She found herself leaning toward him, wanting more.

One corner of his mouth tipped up and she walked past her truck and had to backtrack. She knew her blush was bright pink. "Oops. I guess I wasn't paying attention."

"'Seventy-seven Ford F150. I've been flirting with your truck for the last year."

"It was my first car," Carmella told him as he took the keys, and unlocked her door.

He slid in on the passenger side and handed her keys back. "Just like I was about to say back there. There's no dog hair in this truck. You're too fastidious for that."

"There's a blanket behind the seat where Ginger hangs out."

He hummed what was probably agreement. But it sounded a little like a come-on. A tiny bit like a sex sound.

She turned the engine over and pulled slowly out of the lot.

"So this was your first car, you said?" Duke continued once she got on the road.

"Yeah. Craig and my uncle bought it for next to nothing and then they cleaned her up and gave her to me for my sixteenth birthday." It enabled her to get to a job. A job she could keep and pay the rent. If her mother went into one of her dark times, Carmella would have a way to earn a living. Or as her cousin had told her, to come to their house, where she was always welcome.

"It's handy having lots of mechanics around, huh?"

Headlights shone around him, casting him in shadows that only made him more attractive. More mysterious.

"It's *very* handy." A car meant everything and it was the one thing she always knew she'd have access to once she started working for her uncle's shop. "I was assuming you meant Beth's to grab a bite?"

"Sounds perfect." He leaned back. "You're pretty close with Craig, huh?"

"Craig is three years older than I am and the youngest of four brothers. I was like the little sister in the group. He's always been my protector."

"Right on."

"You have to tell me where you're from," Carmella said. "The accent is killing me."

"New Hampshire until I was fifteen. Then California. Then Iraq for longer than I cared to be there. When I got out, I ended up out here."

Duke's family, newly upper middle class, had ended up in a four-bedroom house with a pool, just three miles from the beach.

He'd found a community with the kids he greeted at the beach every morning. There were girls to kiss, waves to surf, and beer to drink.

After the isolation of his life in New Hampshire, Southern California had embraced him and given him a place to fit.

And then, like a dumbass, he'd enlisted and it had all gone in a totally unexpected direction for about ten years.

"I'm glad you made it back here safe and sound. I hear you saved Asa's life more than once," Carmella said.

Asa needed to stop sharing those stories.

Duke grunted to give an answer and then wanted to change the subject. He liked the way Carmella drove. Liked, too, the way this truck was taken care of and kept up. So many people threw things away long before they were worn out. This truck was a perfect example.

"We can hook you up with snow tires when winter hits."

"Random. You're very random." She whipped into a space with the ease of the Zen parker.

"I am. I'm also impressed with your parallel parking."

"I used to deliver pizzas in the summer and over holiday breaks. You gotta be good or it takes too long." She gathered her things, neatly avoiding his compliment as he had her comments about the war.

Inside, they settled in at a scarred table and ordered.

"What about you? I know your uncle's shop had been open a long time. Did you grow up here too?" Duke asked.

"Seattle born and bred. Went to Ballard High School. I grew up about three miles from my aunt and uncle. They still live in the same house."

His chocolate shake arrived, along with her cranberry juice, and shortly thereafter, the food.

"I don't need snow tires, by the way. I have a set. I just show up and my uncle or Craig puts them on. The guy who bought the shop from my uncle promised my family we'd all still be able to get our work done there."

Duke frowned. Inwardly, of course. This was her family. Naturally they'd put on her snow tires.

"Okay. Well, remember Twisted Steel does that for all our employees too. Might be more convenient to come to work and have it done while you're there. I'll even volunteer to load them into the back of your truck so you won't get your clothes dirty."

"What about *your* clothes?" One of her brows slid up. Every time she did that, he wanted to lean in and press his lips to it.

She tucked into her heaping plate of food and he followed. "My clothes are made for moving tires into the back of pickup trucks," Duke said.

"Fine with me. I like to watch you all heft stuff. It makes all those tattoos and muscles flex."

He grinned but found himself annoyed that she'd look at anyone's ink and muscles but his.

"Right on. I'll remind you come winter."

"It's not like it snows that much."

"You do realize you even eat neatly?"

"What is your fascination with my neatness?" Her expression was teasing, amused so he knew she wasn't offended.

He was fascinated by everything about her.

"I like precision. You're precise. It's good to be around." That wasn't a lie. Duke found deep comfort in people and things that worked as they should. She exuded an effortless sense of being utterly capable. She'd taken over Lottie's job but Carmella had tightened everything up, put everything where it should be. Demanded they all do the same.

She made a sound, one of those women things that's sort of a hum but not quite so you didn't know if it was good or bad.

It made his cock hard in either case.

"I like that." She nodded. "Precise is a good thing. Hang on a second. I need hot sauce."

Carmella turned to the group sitting next to them. A rowdy bunch of dudes making lots of noise, eating lots of food.

She cleared her throat and Duke watched, amazed as to a one, they all gave their attention to her.

Her smile—the one she gave the guys at the shop—said *good, boys* in that tough fifth grade teacher way. And they all wanted to help her.

"Can I borrow your hot sauce for a few shakes?"

Two bottles were thrust her way and they all waited, watching her as she chose one and shook it over her food before recapping it and handing them both back.

"Thank you."

Christ. She'd made them so happy, like big goofy dogs she'd played ball with a few times. It wasn't that she used her sexuality or even her gender to manipulate anyone. She had this authority that guys like him seemed to snap to attention at the sight of.

She was efficient. Orderly. And yet he knew she had a sensual side. He'd seen glimpses of it living next door to her over the last two years. That was the side he wanted more of.

Not that he had any complaints about this side of her either. Duke liked Carmella. Liked being around her. Wanted a hell of a lot more of her.

That pleased him, and as he liked pleasure a whole lot, he couldn't figure out why he should deny himself.

They finished up and the table of dudes waved and called out their good nights.

"You're magic," Duke said as they got back to her truck.

"I am?"

"You're really good with people."

Carmella waved it away. "Do you want me to take you home or

back to the shop?" she said, changing the subject once she got the car started.

"My bike's at the shop so there is best."

There was more small talk on the way over to Twisted Steel, but before too long he found himself having to get out of her truck and leave her.

"Thanks for dinner. I'm planning on sleeping the moment my head hits the pillow and dream sweet, carby dreams."

It was one of the silliest things he'd ever heard her say. He *really* dug that.

"Right on. I'll be doing the same. See you tomorrow."

"You too. Drive safe."

She pulled away as he watched, waiting until her lights had faded off until he turned to head inside.

CHAPTER
Six

Sitting on his back deck in the late evening light, Duke watched her. Like a weirdo, he knew, and yet, he didn't move.

Carmella had her windows open as she cleaned her kitchen. Her hair was wrapped up in a bandana and she wore a tiny pair of cutoffs and a T-shirt as she scrubbed a counter.

It would be a lie for Duke to claim he hadn't looked before. In fact, it was just last year when he'd been out watering the strawberries on his deck. He turned and caught sight of her through a gap in the curtains.

Her skirt had been tossed up over her ass as a guy fucked her from behind.

Her hands gripped the same counter she cleaned just then. That moment, the look on her face, the pale skin on her thighs where it had met stockings, had never left his brain.

He hadn't been able to see her face when she came. Her hair had tumbled free, obscuring her features. But he hadn't needed to see her face because her back had arched and she'd pounded the counter with her fist.

He hadn't ever told anyone about it.

But Duke knew without a doubt that was when he'd begun to crave Carmella Rossi in earnest.

He wanted to be the man fucking her from behind. And it didn't matter that there were fifty reasons not to.

Her music was turned up loud as she worked. She did *not* have a lovely singing voice, though her body made up for it as she danced while cleaning.

He wasn't sure what made him hotter, the cleaning or the body. Which was so weird. It wasn't like he'd gotten wood when he saw anyone else clean things. But whatever it was, when Carmella did it, it drove him out of his mind.

He found himself making sure to go to his office through hers just in case she was wiping something down or organizing something. Lottie had run the place like, well, like her personality. Fast and loose. Stuff got done on time mainly and all, but Carmella was different.

Carmella kept them all in line and everyone allowed it. The guys didn't complain when she put something back into one of their in-boxes asking for it to be corrected. They did it.

Duke wasn't entirely sure what her superpower truly was, but certainly, she kept the beasts he and Asa employed obedient. And then money arrived faster, also a plus. Bills were paid quickly, also a plus.

Everyone in their community knew her, which was also helpful, including twice when he'd been running all over for a part and she found it in three phone calls.

"I shouldn't do this. I should get up and get on my bike and ride over to Asa's. Maybe see if Mick wants to hang out. There are more suitable women out there." He said this out loud as if his dick had any plans to obey.

Duke looked down at his phone. He could call Asa and ask his friend to talk him down. Except now that Asa was in love, he seemed to think Duke should do things like romance their office manager.

Really, it was all Asa's fault.

He got up and headed next door.

*   *   *

Carmella answered her door to find Duke standing on her porch with a six-pack and some chips.

He held them aloft. "I was thinking we could hang out and have a beer and some snacks."

She smiled, even as she looked down at herself. "Uh. I'm sort of messy. I was cleaning the kitchen."

He walked in without saying anything else, but once he got to her kitchen, he turned back. "You look fantastic."

Ginger had already abandoned her nap at the sound of Duke's voice and deposited herself at his feet.

"So easy," she murmured to the dog as she joined them in the kitchen.

"Glasses or the bottle okay?" He indicated the beer with a tip of his chin.

"Bottle is fine. There's an opener in that drawer there." She pointed. "If you're hungrier than just chips and dip, there's leftover baked ziti. I was just thinking about some dinner."

"Leftover ziti? How is that even possible? Was everyone sick? I promise if you made me baked ziti, I'd eat every last bit." He cocked his head and looked extra hot.

She put a hand on her hip. He was so totally full of it. "Actually, I made a smaller one for myself and took two to a big family dinner. It's my uncle's favorite. But I brought home coconut cake and some other stuff."

Carmella bent to look in her fridge because he was standing so very close and she was getting giddy. Giddy was bad. Giddy ended up being the last time she slept with her ex. Though to be fair, it had been fantastic.

This man was a giddy nuclear reactor and it made her girl parts want to be so stupid.

And then he bent to peer into the fridge at her side. "Jesus

Christ. Carmella. Baby, this is the most organized refrigerator I've seen in my entire life. I'm in awe."

She was so surprised and weirdly flattered, Carmella turned to look at him and ended up whacking her forehead to his so hard she saw stars against her closed eyes.

Firm hands took her by the upper arms and helped her stand though she wobbled a little. "Honey, are you all right?"

"Ouch," Carmella managed. "Sorry. I got you pretty hard."

Duke laughed as he moved the hand she'd had over her forehead and replaced it with a bag of frozen berries. "My go-to is corn usually, but you don't have any. That should help. I'm okay. I have a very hard head. That's totally true so stop it with that look of yours."

"You have a go-to remedy for head bumping?" Carmella sat at one of the stools at the island. "And what look do you mean?"

"Works for busted knuckles, black eyes, the usual sort of lifestyle-related injuries."

Carmella winced when she raised her brow at him. "Lifestyle-related?"

Duke shrugged. "What can I say? Ass kicking and fisticuffs seem to be a regular part of my life. And the look I meant is the one you're wearing right now. The one you give that makes everyone feel like a wayward boy who craves your approval."

"I have that look? Really?" How awesome! She clearly needed to use it more.

"You do. Why do you think we're all so obedient to your paperwork rules?"

"Because it's efficient and makes money move back into the shop more quickly?"

He laughed again and then moved the bag of fruit to kiss the sore spot.

They both went very still.

His muscles tightened, the tension radiating from him made

her dizzy. And probably crazy, but needing to soothe. So she slid her hands up the wall of his chest, not to restrain or hold back, no matter how much she told herself that lie.

Once she touched him, she knew it to her toes that everything had changed.

"Damn it," he snarled and then kissed her. Only, no. He took her mouth, owned it, and had his wicked way with it.

Who knew this laid-back dude with a Boston twang who also sounded like a surfer could kiss like this?

He nipped at her lips, licking and sucking as he kissed her. His tongue, holy shit, his tongue slid into her mouth and then, sinuous against hers, danced along until she jutted her hips forward in response.

Thank god she'd been sitting because there'd be no disguising that.

He stepped back, breathing a little heavily, his pupils huge. Carmella touched her lips, pressing a little to keep the sensation awhile longer.

"I should apologize but I can't because I'm not sorry. I've wanted to kiss you for at least the last year. In case you're curious, it was a billion times better in real life than my imaginings."

A year?

Carmella swallowed hard, beyond flattered and flustered and definitely interested.

"Say something, baby, because I'm getting nervous."

Carmella found that statement so startling and silly she snapped out of her kiss-induced haze. "You *nervous*? I doubt that very much."

Duke's expression was *aw shucks* and *I want to bone you* at the same time. "I don't get nervous about too much. But you bring it out."

"You don't need to apologize. I'd probably be really annoyed if you did." Or to be nervous. Hell, he made *her* jittery and nervous all the time so it was slightly hard to believe she made him that way.

"I'm also not going to say I think it shouldn't happen again either. I'd like it to happen again. A lot. I'd like it to be happening right now, to tell the truth," Duke said.

The giddy was back, but it was sweeter. He made her laugh. He didn't take himself too seriously and he was one hell of a kisser.

But there was no denying the possible problems between them. "You're my boss."

"I am. That's obviously problematic."

He stayed close. Ginger looked up at them both, not making a sound.

"I'm going to go ahead and kiss you again. Because I don't want to talk about work and I really want that mouth."

Duke pressed against all her lush curves as she stood. But she was short. Really short and he didn't want to stoop.

So he picked her up and put her on the island facing him before stepping between her knees.

"You're very short." He kissed her chin.

"You're freakishly tall." Carmella tipped her head back, allowing him access to her throat.

He nibbled across her jaw and then up to her ear. The bandana she'd been wearing slipped off, dropping to the counter as her hair bounced free. He buried his fingers in it, using the purchase to tip her face and kiss those lips.

Carmella might have been quiet at work, but she demanded everything he had to offer, kissing him back with a deceptively lazy pace. Really what she did was seduce him moment by moment until all he could think about was kissing every inch of her.

She tasted like oranges. Smelled like them too. As he pulled away, breaking the kiss, he gave a quick look to the spot on her forehead she'd whacked into his so hard. It would be fine, probably not even a goose egg.

"How are you feeling?" he asked.

"I'm hungry."

"Is that sexual innuendo?" Duke teased.

"Oh, when I want you to make me come, I'll let you know. I'm not delicate when it comes to sex. However, I meant food. For now."

Coughing to cover up the way he nearly choked on his spit, Duke helped her down, trying to figure out why he was so turned on by pretty much everything about this woman. "You should take some pain reliever when you eat. Just in case you get a headache."

"Is *that* sexual innuendo?"

"Ha! Sit down at the table. I'll rustle us up something. It's the least I can do after nearly splitting your head open."

"You cook too?" He *was* really bad for her.

"I do okay." He ducked his head.

Carmella didn't argue any more because she really wanted to watch him move around her kitchen.

Other than her family, she'd never had a man make her a meal before. It was especially nice when that man was Duke Bradshaw in his jeans and T-shirt, padding around quite competently.

"I can't for the life of me figure out what you were cleaning in here because this is the most orderly kitchen I've ever seen in person," he said as he slid the ziti into the oven.

"It's stress relief sometimes. Or I'm working through something and mindless activity helps. Ironing, laundry, that sort of thing." And when she was growing up, it gave her some measure of control and comfort in a world full of chaos.

"I get that. I like to do physical stuff when I'm stressed too. Racing, as you know."

"Fistfighting." She raised a brow and he waggled his brows.

"I freely admit we're a brawling bunch. But we're all consenting adults."

Carmella was familiar with that type of man. Which was why she should run the other way when he came near.

Easy enough to think, harder to do. She hadn't been so hot for someone in years. It addled all her defenses.

"That ziti will take a while." Duke looked her up and down and in her head, she told him that they should leave well enough alone and not complicate things with sex.

Instead she found herself saying something else entirely. "Probably about half an hour given that cantankerous oven."

"I can do something with half an hour." Like kiss and kiss those lips of hers. "That's not enough time for what I plan to do to you when we get naked finally. But I can work with it."

She laughed and he really liked how it looked on her. More often than not she had a more serious or thoughtful expression. Pride warmed his belly that she'd opened up to *him*.

"You're very sure of yourself." Her voice had gone lower, throatier.

Now that he'd had a taste of *this* Carmella, Duke was pretty sure he was going to want a lot more.

"When it comes to the inescapable fact that you and I are going to end up in bed, hell yes. For now, I think we should head into your living room, settle on the couch, and make out awhile."

Carmella thought about it for a moment and then stood, giving him a fantastic view of her body as she swayed from the room.

He double-timed it to catch up, nearly tripping over the dog, who, once she was assured everything was fine, headed to her bed in the corner and curled into herself with a sigh.

"Your dog is a trip," he said, settling on the couch.

"She doesn't know she's not a person. Don't tell her," Carmella said as she sat next to him.

"Her secret's safe with me." Duke stared at Carmella's mouth until she licked her lips and made him groan. "I need that." He tipped his chin in her direction and she gave a cockeyed expression in return.

"Come get it," she murmured, knowing exactly what she was doing. It flipped switches he never knew he had.

He slid an arm around her, pulling her to his side, and did as she'd bid, wasting no more time getting his lips on hers.

Duke cupped her cheeks a moment, brushing his thumbs down her temples as she made a sound. This sort of moan that verged on a purr of delight. He sucked it into his mouth, tasting her as he did.

Taking his time, he nipped at her lips, licking them to take away the sting. Each time he did, she arched, pressing into his teeth a little more.

He bit a little harder and that purr deepened. He pushed his control back into place, wanting to see just how much pain Carmella liked with her pleasure.

He licked and kissed down the line of her neck, abrading the pale, velvet soft sensitivity of her skin there with his beard and the edge of his teeth. She shifted, pressing closer, her pulse thundering against his lips when he kissed her just below her ear.

He bit the lobe, sucking it into his mouth, and then whispered, "Someone likes it a little hard."

"Mmmm."

How she managed to make it sound like an order as well as an answer, he wasn't sure. But he liked that too.

She slid her fingers through his hair, tugging him back to her mouth and he was only too willing to comply.

With one easy movement, he banded an arm around her waist and pulled her into his lap, facing him.

"Yeah, this works," he murmured into her mouth and she nipped his bottom lip.

Perfect. He slid his hands up her sides, over her generous, luscious curves, as the music still played in the other room.

They kissed like this, her body against his, the heat of her pussy against his cock as she rocked back and forth against him, for long, lazy minutes as the scent of the pasta rose and her taste settled into his system with deep roots.

By the time the buzzer on the oven timer sounded, he was beyond hard and drunk as fuck on her.

Ginger barked twice as Duke resisted Carmella's efforts to move, not wanting to lose the heat of her. The dog jumped up and licked them both and then got down.

"Ginger says playtime is over," Carmella said as she got off his lap.

"See if I bring her a bone anytime soon," Duke said, a total liar because he really did love that dog of hers.

They moved together in her kitchen, setting the table and getting the food out before sitting down to eat.

She jiggled a switch and then had to duct-tape the door closed on the oven. "What's going on?" Duke asked.

"It's old and temperamental. The landlord tells me he's replacing it, but that doesn't appear to be too high on his list. It works. It just needs some extra love."

He frowned, making a mental note to take a look at it later on.

The first bite of the pasta told him everything he needed to know about Carmella Rossi. "This is magic," he managed to say in between bites.

"Everyone has one or two things they make really well. Baked ziti is mine."

"Your mom teach you? Mine isn't such a great cook, but I learned enough to get by."

A shadow crossed her features for a brief moment. "My grandmother. She taught me how to cook. She was good at everything, and when I'd complain, she'd say she had a sixty-year lead on me and when I was old like she was, I'd be great at lots of stuff too." Her smile told Duke that Carmella had a great deal of affection for the woman.

After they finished, he watched her wash dishes from his side of the kitchen, while he put things away in her fridge.

She had such an intense look on her face—a little dreamy, a little driven—that it was impossible not to keep his gaze from returning to her time and again.

Quickly enough, though, they were done, she let the dog outside to do her business and turned to him, her back leaning against the archway to the kitchen.

"Maybe you should give me a tour," Duke said.

Suddenly Carmella was shy. Her one bedroom couldn't be anywhere near as nice as the house he owned next door.

"Why are you looking at me that way?" He stepped close enough to brush some hair away from her face with a fingertip.

"What way is that?" What was she going to say? Confess her weirdness about the house or go for sexy to change the topic? Like it was any contest.

Carmella took his hand and pulled. "Not a big tour. You've seen the kitchen and living room. The backyard."

"That's just for this flat, right? Or do you have to share with the downstairs guy?"

"He has a patio out in front of his place. The back is all mine and Ginger's."

"He's odd. The guy downstairs, I mean." Duke walked down the hall with her.

"He's quite shy." Carmella pointed to the bathroom and then opened the door to the bedroom.

"Is this where the magic happens, Carmella?" Duke stepped close, crowding her until her back met the wall.

"Sometimes. Sometimes it's out there too. Magic can happen in lots of places."

"Do you realize how hot it makes me when you're like this?"

"Like what?" Carmella asked, a little breathless at his proximity.

"You're a woman who knows what she likes and isn't afraid to demand it."

Not when it came to sex. At least with sex, she was in charge. She made the choices about who and when. If or not. A hard-won gift of self-confidence when it came to that one very essential thing.

She wanted the man in front of her. Wanted the heat coming off him in waves. Wanted his taste, his touch, his scent all over her.

This greed for him was stupid and selfish but she was going to keep him anyway.

"Take your shirt off," she said.

"Right on," he said slow and honey sweet with a smile that sent her blood rushing straight to her clit.

And then he reached down, the muscles in his forearms cording as he grabbed the hem and yanked the T-shirt over his head.

She shoved her hands in the front pockets of her shorts to keep from touching him just yet.

On his belly, he bore the tattoo of some sort of insignia she recognized as being connected to his military service. A fist, knuckles first.

"Knuckles up." He brushed his fingertips over it. "Our patch."

Carmella nodded, past words at how fucking hot he was standing there in her bedroom. The late afternoon sun cast the bedroom and hall in a warm, golden glow. It hit the caramel notes in his hair, the bits of gray at the temples and shot through his beard. One curl hung toward the front and he worked it a little.

"Okay, I can't deny the appeal of that little look there." Carmella fanned her face and then yanked her shirt off, tossing it to the side.

"I . . ." Duke indicated her breasts. "Wow."

"I didn't know you'd be seeing me undress today. So I must confess I'm wearing all my daily, non-going-to-have-sex stuff."

"You have non-going-to-have-sex stuff?" He crept close enough to slide a finger beneath one of her bra straps. A shiver stole over her skin as she let herself fall into this thing they were making between them.

The slow build of attraction and sexual chemistry that had been building bit by aching bit until it had spilled free.

"I clean up nice. If I'm going to be seen naked or getting naked, I bring out the big guns. Lace. Some silk. All the colors of the rainbow. You know the drill." Carmella had been aiming for saucy, but he hooked the strap and pulled it down her shoulder, leaned down, and licked the skin.

A helpless moan of entreaty broke from her lips then, sending saucy straight out the window.

"I'm finding this plain cotton pretty damned hot. Who needs lace when your skin is covered in poppies and freckles?" To underline it, he bent to kiss the freckles over her shoulder as he traced over the garden of orange flowers inked over her back and side.

"You're trouble." A tease, yes, but also the truth. While Carmella couldn't deny how flattering and sexy the stuff he said to her was, it would be suicide to take him too seriously.

"I'm not," Duke protested and then snorted. "Well, maybe I am sometimes. Usually for a good reason and usually with someone else who is also trouble."

That grin he tossed her way was a panty dropper. Stepping back, Carmella spun her finger in a circle, urging him to turn.

Hoo.

Across the very wide, sun-kissed muscles of his shoulders, *Twisted Steel* scrawled in old-school tattoo letters. On the left shoulder, a black-and-gray half sleeve. A screaming skull with pops of red where the petals of a rose had been inked as if they'd fallen.

His jeans hung low, the top bit of his boxers showed now that his shirt was off. For some reason, this only made him hotter. Like the wide shoulders that led down to a tapered waist. Here and there, small tattoos dotted his torso.

Duke Bradshaw was a man very much at home in his skin. He *knew* she liked what she saw. Preened a little. His confidence was beyond erotic.

"Whad'ya think?"

"Oh, there's your New Hampshire showing." She liked that as much as she liked that surfer dude drawl. Especially loved it when they combined in a way that suited him perfectly. "I think you're wearing pants."

Duke unbuckled his belt and got rid of his jeans, along with the boxers and his socks.

Powerful thighs and rock-hard calves weren't that much a surprise, though no less a delight to look at. An ass that called out to be gripped, urging him on as he fucked her hard and deep. Yes, lawd.

And then, as she came around him, his cock. Hard enough that it stood up, nearly tapping his belly, curved just a smidge to the right. Fat. She only barely managed not to sigh happily at the sight.

"Now I think, *lucky me.*"

He tipped his chin. "Make me lucky too then, Carmella. Get naked."

*   *   *

She was the most beautiful thing he'd ever seen. Carmella Rossi in her plain white cotton panties and bra, now naked except for the beautiful orange poppies on her back, sweeping down from one side to the other.

Honest-to-god dimples at the small of her back to each side of her spine led to the curve of hips he couldn't wait to sink his fingers into. On her forearm, an old-school anchor tattoo with a smattering of nautical stars.

Without her bra, Duke had much easier access to her breasts, which, like the kiss, had been even better in reality than he'd dared imagine.

Perfect.

"Lucky doesn't even approach how I feel right now." He stepped to bring them skin to skin, his arms sliding around her, hers around his waist, her cheek to his chest.

So. Good.

She licked over his nipple, then dragged her teeth across until he broke out in shivers.

"On the bed. I need to be horizontal with you all spread out for my enjoyment."

Carmella closed the door before getting in bed. "If not, we might have company."

Duke wanted her all to himself so he had no problems with that. He got on the mattress, crawling up her body on all fours, kissing his way to those magnificent tits.

Licking over the left nipple, he blew over it, watching it tighten. Several times before she tugged on his hair.

He looked up from what he was doing. "Yes?"

Carmella rolled her eyes. "You're killing me."

"I know. And you interrupted me." He caught the other nipple between his teeth, settling against her, making a space between her thighs, his cock sliding against the wet heat of her pussy.

"Carry on," she said, a little breathless.

There was something irresistible in ruffling her feathers. She was normally so unflappable that getting a reaction from her was unbelievably hot.

He teased, biting and licking her nipples until she writhed against him, and that's when he kissed a trail south, over one of her hips and across her belly to the other.

She had a faint scar there and he kissed it as he moved on, spreading her thighs wide and pushing her up the bed a bit so he could get comfortable.

It was full daylight, sun streaming in through curtains sheer enough that if someone was standing outside her bedroom they'd be able to make out what was going on. But Carmella wasn't shy. Not about this. He looked his fill at her pussy, slick, dark with desire, and then he took a lick and was lost.

He held her up to his mouth, serving himself, his hands splayed over her ass and the backs of her thighs. He ate her cunt like a starving man, devouring each one of her moans and gasps along with the taste of her body.

When she flew apart in his arms, he continued to push her higher and higher until she spun into another climax on the heels of the first.

Carmella gave a long, satisfied sigh as she opened her eyes to find him digging through his pants until he held a condom aloft with a triumphant grin.

"Glad to see you were prepared, but don't go wrapping your cock up just yet. I haven't even gotten to play with it."

Laughing, he jumped back into the bed, rolling to bring her atop his body. "This is a mighty fine view. You can play with it inside your pussy because I'm dying to get inside you."

She blushed, one of the big bouncy curls of her hair fell forward, the sight filling him with tenderness.

Carmella fell to her hands at either side of his head so she could kiss him long and slow, licking over the swell of his bottom lip as she drew away at the end. In the other room, the Sneaker Pimps' "6 Underground" began to play and he molded his palms against her breasts, her nipples at his palm.

She got flustered a few times, which made him feel very smug until she angled his cock and backed herself up against it, taking the length of him inside her in one movement.

"Not so smirky now, I see," she murmured with a sly look.

An intensely fantastic rush of pleasure had taken him beyond words so he tugged her nipples until her eyes went glossy.

She tightened her inner walls, sending stars to the edges of his vision.

"This is the best contest I've ever been part of," he gasped out.

"I never had any idea I was so competitive." Carmella sat straighter, now undulating herself against him, keeping his cock deep.

"Gold star. Blue ribbon. World champion." Duke let go of one breast long enough to give her the *you're number one* symbol and then grab her, flipping them both so she was on her back and he on his knees between her thighs.

Which only took him deeper into her heat.

Carmella thought she had never enjoyed sex more when he flipped them over and took over, fucking into her body over and over. But that was before he hooked her knees over his forearms, grabbing her hips and pulling her up his cock until her nails dug into his skin.

She hung right on the very edge of it being too much. It hurt and felt unbearably good all at the same time.

He growled, all that slow, easygoing long gone. This Duke was stripped down to the alpha male he was beneath all that suave cat stuff on the surface. And it was way too late to run the other way because damn and whoa he was good in bed.

And he made her laugh.

Right at that moment, though, he was so impossibly thick inside her pussy, so deep and so close to orgasm. The light in his eyes had gone from ferocious to dreamy and his growl had died, his mouth in a line of concentration.

Carmella was warm and soft, wet and open for him so she gave over to the pleasure of watching him come.

The muscles on his neck corded and his gaze cleared, locking onto hers as he pressed against her, coming as he kissed her senseless.

CHAPTER
Seven

Carmella, smiling, bearing a bag of food she'd made for her mother to eat over the course of the week, let herself in, calling out as she did.

"Mom, you here?"

A growl prefacing a stream of high-pitched barking sounded, answering her question.

Virgie had a dog of her own. A perpetually cranky dachshund her mother carried around like a baby and spoiled rotten. She was barely tolerant of Carmella but was absolutely horrible if any other dogs were around.

"I brought you some food." Carmella headed toward the kitchen, poking her head into the living room as she passed by.

"Thank you, sugar," her mom called out.

Carmella unloaded the food into the cabinets, fridge, and freezer before heading to drop a kiss on her mom's cheek and sit across from her.

In her day, for a brief, shining time, Virginia Hay was a great beauty. She liked to tell a story about how at sixteen she ran off to Hollywood to be a star but that in the end, love saved her from that crazy famous life she'd have had.

Virgie liked the fragile flower bit. Maybe it was just an act, way back in the day. Maybe there was a time when Carmella's mother had strength and courage. A time when she hadn't been content with letting herself be taken care of—and sometimes ill-used—by people.

"I put your pills in the keeper in the cabinet. I'll be here tomorrow at ten to take you to the doctor. I'll call you when I leave work so you can be ready."

Her mother shrugged to say time was something that never really bothered her.

"Remember I'm not at Salazar anymore," Carmella said. "I have less ability to come and go as I please." Though Carmella had no doubt that if she needed the time to take her mom to a medical appointment, Twisted Steel would give it to her.

Still, she'd prefer not to involve relative strangers in this situation so she'd go in early and take a long lunch to get her mom to the doctor's and back without shorting Twisted Steel any time.

"I promise I'll be ready."

At Carmella's look, her mother's mask slipped a little, giving a glimpse of the lost girl who lived in her mother's skin.

For as long as Carmella could remember, her mother made promises and broke them. Carmella believed honestly that her mother truly meant to keep her promises when she made them. She just never followed through.

"How's my brother?" Virgie asked, lighting a cigarette.

Carmella sighed. "Put it out. You're going to aggravate your lungs."

"You're no fun," Virgie said, meaning it. But she put the cigarette out.

"Someone has to be the grown-up." Carmella hated herself when she allowed her mother to get under her skin and goad her.

"That's boring too. You're too young to give up on life, Carm."

Carmella gave the dog a look, like *for real?* The vicious little snausage snorted a little. Even she couldn't make excuses for Virgie's bullshit.

"If you want to know how Uncle Carl is, you should call him yourself. I saw him yesterday. He and Aunt Maria just got back from a trip to Lake Chelan. Both were tanned and rested. They asked about you." Her uncle loved his sister, even if he also understood how fucked up and toxic Virgie could be at times.

They never liked Carmella's dad, or any of the placeholders Virgie brought around. They had called her on her bullshit when she'd waltzed off for several days, leaving fourteen-year-old Carmella at home.

Virgie didn't get why her older brother, who'd spoiled her when she was a young girl, would make her do *boring* stuff like take care of Carmella every day and have groceries in the house.

Love was one thing, but he'd long since given up hope that she'd ever rise to the occasion and be a good mother. Or a halfway responsible adult. He resented the way that impacted Carmella's life and future because she was the one her mother leaned on.

He saw it as Virgie stealing her daughter's life and he hated it.

Over the years, especially after Carmella's grandmother had died, it had driven a wedge between the siblings and Carmella had done her best to stand between her mother and uncle to keep the peace.

"Must be nice," Virgie complained. "I never go on trips. Not that my brother ever bothers to invite me along."

Carmella didn't rise to the bait. It was a long road with no real destination. Just hours of listening to Virgie bitterly blame all her failures on other people. Or crying because she let them all down and knew it. Sometimes there'd be promises to be better, but usually it just went on and on until she wound down or Carmella left the room.

"I made you some enchiladas, some baked ziti, and chicken salad. Bread for sandwiches is in the bread box. I even put some presliced tomatoes, onions, and lettuce for toppings in your veggie drawer. I'm making pineapple upside down cake this weekend. I'll bring some over for you."

Virgie started to push the point about Carl, but let it go. "You don't have to do all this. I won't starve if you don't bring over food. Get out. Live your life. Date, for god's sake. You want to be old and alone?" Empty words. Even if having to take care of her mother *had* obstructed her life, her mother would still need taking care of so there was no use examining it too closely.

"I'm not any more interested in this discussion than I am the one about Uncle Carl." Carmella tried hard not to be offended or hurt that her mother actually believed she could get by without other people constantly cleaning up after her.

She usually failed, but it was a work in progress.

"At least tell me you're not a lesbian."

Carmella stood, bending to kiss her mom's cheek. "I'll see you tomorrow. Don't forget. I'm calling you before I leave."

"You never answer when I ask you," Virgie said, unbelieving that anyone would simply think the question was stupid and irrelevant.

Carmella could mollify her by giving an answer, but she wasn't going to.

"I only ask because I care." Virgie's tone was wistful. Carmella realized her mother was high on meds and on the verge of melancholy. Another thing to bring up with the doctor.

"I love you. Don't forget to eat."

Even as she drove away, the guilt pulled at Carmella. The niggling idea that if she lived with her mom, things could be better for Virgie. It wouldn't be enough. Nothing Carmella could do would ever be enough. So she'd help but from a distance, from her own house.

*   *   *

The shop was already buzzing by the time Carmella found herself making the third pot of coffee in the break room. She didn't have to do it. No one expected her to. But it got her up out of her seat and walking around and she often strolled through the shop on her way back to see what people were working on.

It was really an excuse to look at shiny machines and peek at Duke and quite often it included doughnuts as well so there was no problem with that as far as she was concerned.

She hadn't been at work since they'd slept together. Well, since they'd fucked three times was a more accurate way to say it, she supposed. She wasn't sure what to expect, but Monday at Twisted Steel was pretty much the same as every other day.

As she neared the door, Asa rolled in with an empty mug and a searching look.

When he saw she had just made a pot he grinned her way and looked far less scary and much sweeter. "You're my favorite person today."

"They go with the doughnuts PJ brought in a few minutes ago," Carmella said.

"Just one of the many reasons I keep that woman around."

That and Carmella figured PJ was the only one capable of keeping a guy like him in line.

"Morning, Ms. Rossi. How are you today?" Duke asked as he sidled next to her as she was leaving to head back to her office.

"I tracked down that crankshaft you said you thought the shop had ordered. *Seven* months ago, actually. You paid in advance." Carmella frowned. It hadn't been a cheap part. They'd prepaid and then no one had bothered to push past the bullshit to get to the person who could make something happen.

"How'd you manage that? They claimed we never ordered it so we tracked it down elsewhere. Damned big chains," Duke said.

"I'm revamping and organizing the filing." Lottie might have been able to make sense of that hamster's nest of paper shoved in drawers, but if that crankshaft situation wasn't a rarity, they were losing a lot of money just from sloppy record-keeping.

Duke stood very close. Close enough she could smell his skin. Just under the cotton of his shirt she'd marked his back. He'd made her come so hard, she'd dug her nails in. He seemed to find it sexy, but Carmella was still a little embarrassed about it. Not more than she was aroused knowing they were there.

She made herself stop thinking about coming and focus on answering his earlier question. "I found some notes. It's a long, boring story. Do you want me to get our money back or the part sent?" Carmella asked as she headed for her desk.

"First tell me what they told you when you informed them you had proof of payment," Duke said, leaning a hip against the counter before continuing. "Because if they were assholes, I want the money back. Also, they dicked me around when I called so I'm dying to know how they took it when they were proven wrong."

They had been dicks, though probably less so because Carmella had dealt with crap like that from people for so long it didn't even faze her anymore. She didn't take it personally that they had asked for proof of payment. But it had been pretty delightful when she'd been able to slap back after being given the runaround for nearly a week.

Carmella smirked. "After I sent over everything I had, including a timeline of what happened to their fax machine every day, twice a day—along with e-mails—I was finally able to connect with the correct person. They had a fax machine so they deserve to have me send them all that paper. Who has a fax machine anymore? Anyway, when I was finished with him, I was offered overnight shipping of the part this week, or a refund. I said I'd get back to them because obviously we had to get the part else-where at significant cost."

"It was only twenty bucks more, I think." Duke's pleasure was all over him. Carmella loved to look at him when he was in a good mood. He seemed to give off waves of calm.

Carmella made herself a cup of coffee from her own stash. "He doesn't know that. He screwed up and acted like a clown. Maybe you need the part for a project, maybe not now. But you might need a part from them in the future and this could be an anom-aly. They need to make it right, however you decide to do that. And then the relationship can be reset however you want it to be and they realize they'd better pay attention if you give them another chance."

Duke said, "You're pretty perceptive." She had a way with under-standing people.

"It's not that hard to understand, really." She blushed as she shrugged like it was nothing.

She looked fresh and lovely, a green blouse and black pants, her hair held back with two enamel barrettes.

He'd seen her naked.

Knowing they were alone, he risked a whisper. "How are those bruises today?"

He'd left fingerprint bruises in the flesh of her hips and ass. Duke was a man who liked to hold on when he dug in to fuck and her body was perfect. He'd been a little worried about her reac-tion, but she'd given him a smirk and said she liked knowing he'd been there and had a good time.

"They're nearly gone. I bruise easy but heal fast. I need to take my lunch early." She bent to grab her things. "I'll be gone for more than an hour, but the phones are going to route to the showroom and I handled everything pressing."

"What are you doing later?" He hadn't meant to ask so quickly. He'd wanted to be smooth, bring it up naturally.

"Tonight later?"

Duke nodded.

"After work, PJ and I are meeting up and going for a walk around Green Lake with Ginger."

"After that? Come over for a beer on my back deck. Bring Ginger. I got her a new chew thing."

She smiled. "Okay. I've got to run now. I'll see you later."

Carmella dashed out and he pretended not to watch her longer than he'd have looked at anyone else he worked with.

Which didn't work, because Mick and Asa knew him better than anyone else, and before he could get his door closed, both were standing there with coffee.

"Break time. You can share with the class just exactly what it is you've done to and with our lovely Ms. Rossi," Mick said as they came in and made themselves comfortable.

Duke could ignore them. Which wouldn't last. They'd bug him until he gave in. He joined them, kicking his feet up on his desk as he looked them both over. "I have done lots of things with Carmella. Just now she was letting me know she'd be taking a long lunch but came in early to make up for it."

Mick looked to Asa, who shrugged.

"Fine, fuck you." Mick flipped Asa off and turned back to Duke as they both laughed. "So, what's the deal?"

"I've had a thing for her for a while. It's fine. Nothing crazy. She's not going to set anything on fire or slash my tires."

"So, the whole don't date where you work rule is out the window?" Mick's grin was more open than Duke had seen it in a very long time. He was healthy. By all outward appearance he was happy. The ghosts of his time in the military still lived in him, Duke knew, just like he had plenty of his own in residence.

"I can't seem to abide by any rules, apparently. It's counter to my constitution." Duke smirked. "It's stupid. She said so herself. I'm her boss. It's harder for her than for me. I just have to take extra care to make sure our personal stuff stays away from work." Because he wasn't letting go.

"If you say so," Asa said and lifted one shoulder. "PJ is very protective of Carmella so don't fuck up and make me deal with it. I like my woman happy."

"Considering how she gets when she's mad, I don't blame you," Duke said and they all laughed because PJ was so sweet until she got mad. The woman had a temper that was impressive and a little scary to behold.

Duke liked that PJ was protective of Carmella. It meant she thought Carmella was worthy of her energy and affection.

"We on for drinks tonight?" Mick asked.

"I have a prior engagement." With his deck, some beer, and Carmella.

"Everyone is going to know you two have hooked up. You may as well bring her to the Ditch with everyone else. Craig drinks there, so it's not like she'll be a total stranger."

Duke knew Mick was right. But it was early days yet. She didn't hang on too tight after they'd had sex. She didn't get in his face, or seem to have any real expectations of him.

She had no way of knowing whatever it was in her pheromones set off all his bells and whistles. A little taste of Carmella wasn't going to be enough. Not by a long shot.

CHAPTER
Eight

Carmella liked PJ Colman immensely. The other woman was so much fun. So smart and vibrant. She needed more of that sort of energy and influence in her life.

"I'm glad you mentioned this," PJ said as they started out. "I need the break sometimes. Work is crazy. My man is bossy. My family is...well, anyway. How are you? You've been at Twisted Steel a month now. What do you think? How are you liking it?"

"A month yesterday. I have to admit I was a little nervous at first. I worked for my uncle for my entire life, you know? How would it be with people I'm not related to? But as fancy as Twisted Steel is, it's a shop. It turned out to be just fine because I know shops. Everyone's been nice. They bring me treats and let my dog hang out."

"Yeah. And there's Duke to look at."

Carmella burst out laughing even as a blush heated her cheeks. "My workday *is* full of hot men covered in ink who bring me baked goods and obey my orders."

"Look at you neatly avoiding the Duke topic. Should I back off totally?" PJ asked.

"We had sex," Carmella blurted out loud enough that the people passing by on the path turned to look.

PJ waved and they kept going. "I knew it! We saw him yesterday afternoon and he was all goofy. Well, even more goofy. And lots of lady-type people were all over the place and he couldn't be bothered."

Carmella found herself very satisfied by that information.

"I told Asa this morning that something had happened between you and Duke recently. He said Duke was always weird and to leave it alone." PJ snorted.

"Which you promptly ignored," Carmella said, but she laughed.

"He's my friend. You're my friend. I'm in love, so as Asa likes to tell me, I want everyone to be happy."

"Love? We had sex. I hope to have more. But he's my boss and it's already complicated."

"Like I told you," PJ said, "you have a job with me if things go bad. Asa will kill me because he, Duke, and Mick think you're perfection in that office. But whatever. I hate the idea of you feeling like you *have* to do one thing or the other."

"Thanks." It actually *did* make it easier to throw a little caution to the wind and keep seeing Duke. "So, things are good with you and Asa?"

"We've been living together six months. I keep wondering when it will get sucky, but he's pretty awesome. This is it. The real thing."

Carmella didn't say much. She didn't believe in the real thing. There were people you had good click with. But this concept that one person could be trusted not to dash your heart and mind on the rocks for all time? She didn't think it was possible.

But that didn't mean she wished anything but happiness for PJ and Asa. If forever existed, they deserved it.

They walked and talked as Carmella got to know PJ better and opened herself up as well. It was nice to have a friend she saw regularly. It made her feel normal. Normal was kind of nice.

Finally, they went their separate ways after making plans to hang out later on in the week and Carmella headed home, where she was going to obsess over what to wear to Duke's house.

Carmella pulled up and saw Duke out in his yard. Great, because she was sweaty and fresh from exercise and he looked fucking fantastic.

She'd expected him to stay over there so she could duck in and change, but nope. He waved, heading over.

"Is he kidding with this?" Carmella murmured to the dog. "I'm not ready yet," she called out, hoping to keep him at a distance.

But Duke Bradshaw went where he wanted, which was taking the keys from her hand and opening her door for her all while he talked to the dog.

"It's cool. Take your time. Though." He paused to look her up and down, that smile of his making her all tingly. "You look just fine right now. Fine enough to lick. You smell good." He bent to sniff her.

"Dude!"

He laughed. "What, darlin'?"

"I am *stinky*. I've been exercising. My hair is frizzy. Why do you have that giant toolbox?"

"Pick a topic, darlin', any topic at all," Duke teased. "You smell good. Like woman and work and sunshine. Not stinky at all. Your hair is adorable. The toolbox is because I'm taking a look at your oven."

"What?"

"Your oven is broken. I'm pretty good at fixing things. I think at the very least I can replace the spring on the door so you don't have to tape it."

She was speechless for long moments, and when she spoke, it was around a lump in her throat. "Oh. Thank you."

"It's my pleasure. Ginger and I are going to hang out in the kitchen while you clean up. Even though I'm just dandy with how you are right this moment."

She knew she blushed. "So full of it." With a wave and another thank-you, she headed down the hall to her room.

It bugged Duke that she always seemed so surprised when people did nice things for her. It meant she wasn't used to it.

She took care of her things. Which told him she scrimped and saved for them and couldn't easily afford the hit of having to replace something major. Duke remembered that time in his life. Remembered the time his mom took a second job to pay for a new furnace. Remembered, too, the way they'd all slept in the living room with the woodstove going until they could afford that new furnace.

Duke didn't miss winters in New Hampshire. And he sure as fuck didn't miss being that on the edge.

It made him want to spoil her.

Ginger watched as he worked. "This part is pretty easy. I had a feeling it was the spring." Apparently he was going to talk to the dog too. "Now I need to figure out what's causing the problem with the heat. Don't be offended when I'm quiet."

Duke lost himself in the task, looking at the oven from a few different angles. He knew enough electronics that it wasn't so difficult once he found the problem and began taking things apart.

That's how Carmella found him some twenty minutes later. He looked up from his place on her floor, struck by how much he enjoyed the energy she gave off.

"I found the problem. I don't have the part I need, but I got the info and I'll grab one for you. I put the old one back so you can use the oven until I get the new one installed. It still works. The door was a spring. I had a few I thought would work and they did."

Duke finished putting everything back together, aware she'd come to kneel nearby to watch what he was doing.

"Thanks," she said when he finished. "Is the part like a two-hundred-dollar thing or a five-dollar thing or what?"

There was an edge to her tone. Just a little one. He'd been right to assume things were tight for her.

"It's a common part. I looked it up on the Internet earlier today. I can get the part via Twisted Steel at our cost. It was thirty-seven bucks that way. Retail, that could be fifty or more. Shouldn't your landlord pay you back? I'll keep the receipts so you can send them to him."

"He's been blowing me off for months. If it were totally broken, he'd do something. Probably. He's not a monster or anything. I asked if it was under warranty. I figured I'd just have it done myself. He said he got them secondhand. So it's not like you fixing anything screwed that up. Thirty-seven bucks is fine. Three hundred and I'd have to wait. Thank you again."

He stood, pulling her up his body, getting a better hold by bending his knees, grabbing two handfuls of her ass, and lifting.

"My. You're very strong." Her voice bordered on that purring thing she did. Duke's cock liked that very much.

Carmella wrapped her arms around his neck and her legs around his waist. The play of her muscles as she did spoke to her strength. She was fire. So very lovely to look at. Ferocious, he bet, when necessary. Dangerous. Orderly. Usually. But Duke bet she could be unpredictable too.

He kissed her as he deposited her ass on the counter again; this time there was no crack to the skull to be worried about.

Still, he promised her some romance. Back deck. Stars and beer. "We should go over to my place. I promised you beer. I have food too." He spoke around kissing across her collarbone, through the thin material of her blouse.

"We will." Carmella slid her fingers into his hair, tugging him to her mouth. He kissed her and forgot what he'd been planning to do before.

"Are you trying to distract me?" he teased.

"I'm trying to nail you."

Startled, he paused a moment before he burst into laughter. "My fragile flower." He nipped her chin.

"Fragile flowers get trampled. Can't afford to be fragile."

But there was something distinctly vulnerable about Carmella. Something that called out to him. Spoke to him. Made him want to soothe and defend.

He didn't say any of that.

He needed to seduce the trust out of his skittish redhead. Slowly and surely. She was wary. Enough that Duke was sure there was something in her life—past or present—that had left some deep scars.

But he wanted her to open up. Wanted her to look at him with the same unguarded pleasure she did only very rarely now.

So he'd take his time and do a lot more showing than telling.

He unbuttoned the front of her blouse, exposing a far fancier bra than she'd had on a few days prior. Navy blue against her skin so pale she seemed to glow in the golden, end-of-the-day light flooding the kitchen.

Another flick of his wrist and the front of the bra came open, her breasts bared to his gaze. His touch.

"You requested nailing?" Duke murmured as he took her right nipple between his teeth, tugging until she arched on a yes. "Handy you have a skirt on."

"I'd never leave such a thing to chance."

Of course not. That made him so hard his skin seemed too tight. He stepped back as she wriggled free from one leg of her panties all while getting his belt, jeans, and boxers out of the way, his cock in her fist in what felt like forever but was more likely to have been less than a minute or two.

He hated to stop her, but he had to bend to grab the condom in his pocket. Knowing he'd be inside her shortly was finally enough to work up the nerve to move.

"Stay right there." Duke kept one hand on her hip, not wanting her to fall, and grabbed the condom with the other, ripping it open with his teeth and rolling it on.

"Hurry."

She was slick and hot, ready for him. But he lowered his mouth to her pussy, replacing his fingers. Her gasp and the way her grip tightened in his hair only drove him harder. Need beat at him in waves as he floated on her taste.

He wanted his scent all over her skin. His marks on her body. He wanted to drive any thought of any other man at any other time out of her head.

She tightened against him, straining as orgasm hit her, he kept going for a few more seconds before standing, sliding into her pussy. He'd planned to fuck her hard and fast, but once he'd gotten all the way inside, he had to stop, still, and concentrate to push back climax.

He'd masturbated in the shower just an hour before and he still had such whisper-thin control when it came to her.

"So good. You feel so good." He kissed her as he began to move in hard, deep digs. She drew her knees up and he braced his hands on the other side of the narrow counter, bending over her body as he did.

"Just so you know, I'm going to be having you again. We're going to relax and have some food and then we'll get to it." He kissed her when she stretched to meet him halfway. "For now I think you need to finger your clit. Make yourself come around my cock."

She swallowed hard, her pupils going wide. But she did it, a hand sliding between them.

Her pussy tightened, inner walls fluttering as she began to stroke.

"Soon I'm going to watch you masturbate. You're so pretty when you come."

Carmella's breath caught as she heated even more.

"Not going to last much longer when your pussy does that." He gave her a quick kiss. "Don't make me wait."

He went to his toes each time he slid all the way inside, crushing her hand between them, and in a few more breaths, Carmella let out a strangled moan and came, slick and fast all around him.

There was no way he could have held back at that point. No way the sweet, tight squeeze of her body could be denied.

"Yes, yes, yes," he murmured and came, holding her fast against him, heart hammering in his chest.

Carmella had come out of her shower and heard him in her kitchen. He'd done something to make life easier for her and who wouldn't like that? It was pushy, but not in a creepy way.

When she'd entered the kitchen to find him on his knees, his love for fixing things lighting his expression, she'd let herself admit she was more than flattered. More than appreciative.

That he'd taken the time to not only fix the oven but do all the research it took to get him that far was something no one other than her family had ever done. Her ex had been useless. A pretty, lazy con artist who led with his dick because his brain was far smaller.

Duke's behavior fed that part of her that wanted to be worthy. She *knew* that was dumb, but sometimes a tiny voice said it anyway.

And then he'd looked so happy that he'd fixed it and had been so sexy and had grabbed her and kissed her and, well, did all that.

He was so good at sex. Carmella knew she'd be sleeping well that night.

They sat on his deck, the stars beginning to sparkle overhead. A beer dangled from Duke's fingers while Carmella ate even more lemon curd cookies.

"You need to move those away from my reach," she said, watching Ginger happily gnaw on the new chew thing Duke had for her.

"I don't think so. I like watching you enjoy them."

She turned, one brow sliding up. "Are you saying I eat too much?"

He burst out laughing, leaning over to kiss the top of her head. "A man'd be a damned fool to say, much less believe, such a thing. No, darlin', I like your expression when you're doing something that brings you pleasure. Fucking is my favorite, but I'll take what I can get."

He was so charming it made her slightly desperate. He was a lot like the charismatic men she grew up around. Most of *them* were fucking idiots who couldn't keep a job. But the men like Craig and her uncle were different. Duke was too.

But she'd be a fool to think too much more of that.

Instead, she would enjoy this. The heat between them. The way he made her feel when he touched her. It was new, exciting. At that precise moment she was satisfied. Happy.

That was more than enough.

"Tell me, did you always love to fix stuff?" she asked him.

"It was necessity at first. We didn't have much so we had to fix things or go without. My mom would deny it now, but she was an excellent plumber when I was a kid."

That's how Carmella had started sewing. Hand-me-downs from Craig and things from the thrift store were the bulk of what she wore so she had to figure out how to repurpose things. Her aunt had given her a sewing machine for her thirteenth birthday.

She still used it. The thing was a workhorse and had been repaired more than once. But Carmella knew it, and it loved her as much as she loved it.

Duke spoke again, capturing her attention. "And then I realized I wasn't only good at it, I loved it. Machines are rad puzzles I loved to solve. I still do."

"Wow. That's nice. I'm glad you do something that makes you so happy. I bet your family is proud of you."

He paused a little longer than normal and she cringed that she'd asked and hit a nerve. "I'm sorry. I didn't mean to pry."

He snorted, reaching out to take the hand finally empty after shoveling cookies into her mouth so busily. He kissed her palm. "Sweet. I want you to pry. It's fine. Please don't apologize. My parents came up very blue-collar so they take financial security and respectability really seriously after working their asses off to be well-off at last."

There was a slight edge of something in his tone. Regret maybe? Bitterness? And when he continued speaking, it was gone, the smooth, laid-back veneer in place once more.

"So, as you might have guessed, they think owning a business like Twisted Steel is unstable. They wanted me to go to college and get a good job like my younger siblings have done. But over the last two years or so things have gotten a little better."

Part of her, just a small part, thought, *They don't want you to be like me.* But she knew *Duke* didn't believe that so it was easy enough to let go of because a far bigger part of her was outraged that they didn't see just what their son had built.

"Nothing like a mention in *Celebrity* magazine, numerous front-page articles in newspapers, and the cover of *Time* to lend credibility, eh?" Carmella kept her tone light.

"Yes!" He chuckled. "Though they'd prefer it if I did my job in chinos and a polo shirt, at least they're finally understanding what we've built here."

"I'm glad."

"I think they're coming up here when we do the grand opening party for the new showroom in September."

They'd better. If not, Carmella might need to make a trip down to Southern California to pay them a visit herself.

"Good. They should. Going to be quite the party."

"As long as the contractors finally get it all done. I can't believe how stressful it is to have other people building stuff for you. I get how some of our clients feel now."

Carmella laughed and laughed. "Please. Asa glowers at them if they're even half a day behind. They'll finish on time if for no other reason than that."

"His grumpy attitude does come in handy at times."

"He's only hard on the outside. Now you?" She pursed her lips as she thought about it. "You like to come off soft, all laid-back and mellow. But I've seen glimpses. You're not soft."

"I was for about ten minutes back at your house after I came last."

He tried to joke it off when he wanted to change the subject. It wasn't the first time he'd done it, and like the others, she let him. If he wanted to tell her something, he would. But she understood not wanting to deal with stuff. Not being ready to think about something or just being totally over a situation that would only upset you if you if you dug back in.

"Tell me things, Carmella."

So damned charming.

"Like what?"

"Get to know you things. Like, what do you do as a hobby?"

"I sew. I read. Watch movies. Oh, I love to scour garage sales and used bookstores."

"I didn't know you sewed. Though the shelves jammed with books at your house and the way you always have a paperback and your digital reader with you were pretty big clues you were a reader. Sexy."

Carmella leaned back, looking up at the sky as the last of the purple had bled into black. It was warm and the air smelled like freshly cut grass and the blooms on someone's rosebush.

"Sewing is sexy? That's a new one."

*   *   *

Duke looked over at her, all relaxed, eyes on the sky above. She had a smile on her mouth. One he'd never seen her give anyone else. Or hell, in public.

"I meant reading. But to be totally honest, the idea of you sewing makes me hot too."

"Color me surprised."

He laughed. "Can I confess something to you?"

"Uh-oh. Let's hear it."

"It turns me on when you clean stuff. And probably when you would sew too. When you set the office in order and that sort of thing, it's so unbearably hot. It's all I can do to get through the day because it makes me hard."

She turned her head to look at him. "Maybe everything makes you hard."

"Well, certainly it doesn't take a lot to get a little tingly. My cock is always happy to tingle a little. But this is different. Anyway, it's hot. I'd watch you sew any day."

"All righty then." She didn't sound horrified in the least. "I'll try to be less orderly at work so you don't have to go through that."

"Darlin', it's sweet suffering. I promise you that." He paused. "While I'm confessing things, I should also tell you I saw you getting fucked from behind in your kitchen. It was over a year ago. But... I can't apologize because it was hot and gorgeous and I've wanted you ever since."

She gave him a raised brow. "I know you did."

"What? Wanted you?"

Carmella sat straighter, tucking her legs beneath her. "I know you watched. I knew you were there."

Surprise arced through him. "You did?"

She laughed. "I did. Are you shocked?"

"Not shocked. Surprised? You keep me on my toes. I guess I didn't expect you to be so..."

"Filthy? Dirty? Turned on by knowing my hot inked neighbor was watching me get fucked? Are you scandalized I got off on a little exhibitionism, knowing it was you watching?"

He swiveled in his chair to face her. "What a constant surprise you are."

Carmella tsked. "And this is good or bad? What exactly did you expect that makes me so surprising? Hm?"

He found himself sweating, cock throbbing in time with the pulse hammering in his head. "It's good. Really good. I didn't know you before. Not really."

She laughed, but there was an edge to it. "You don't know me now either."

"Working on that part. But what I do know, I like enough to want more."

CHAPTER
Nine

W hat are you doing on Saturday?" Duke asked as he caught up
with her after work the following Wednesday.

"I have some stuff to do early on, but I'll be free by ten or so."
Carmella was getting used to his attention. He wasn't obvious
while they were at work, which she appreciated. But he brought
her in treats every day. Just that afternoon he'd brought in a new
mug for her desk.

Wonder Woman. Her favorite.

He really was sort of perfect, which made her even more wary.

Not enough to stop seeing him. She hadn't been this happy in
a very long time. A new romance, her mother was having a good
period, her new job was more like home—all things that filled
her with a sense that things were looking up and she was content
to imagine they'd remain so.

"Mick invited us to spend the afternoon out on his boat. Asa
and PJ will be there too. I figured we could take some lunch."

Carmella paused at the door to her truck. A group date thing?
She tried not to show any panic.

Duke opened it and she got in.

"You look like I just said I was a cannibal."

That was enough of a shock to make her laugh. "Well, you *are* pretty good at eating my pussy."

His smile got very cocky. Making him even harder to resist.

"I am, huh? Well, I'm happy that's the case 'cause I sure do like eating it. As for the boat, we're seeing each other. Asa and Mick know. Obviously PJ knows. It's just a fun thing so we can all hang out. Nothing more than that."

It was weird that he understood her so well. "Uh, sure. I've only been on a boat a few times. Mainly ferries. But it looks fun." She could even do the lunch as a thank-you.

"Good. You sure you can't come to the track tonight?" He got a little closer and she snapped her seat belt like it kept him back, which it didn't.

"I have errands to run." Pills to drop at her mom's place. She wanted to check in with her aunt and uncle too. "It's not like I won't see you tomorrow."

"I like it when you watch me race."

He gave her a look so potent that if it wasn't her mom waiting, she'd have canceled and given in, heading to the track.

"I like to watch you race too. Luckily, you do it all the time."

"Fine." He winked and she rolled her eyes.

"You really don't like it when you don't get your way, do you?" she asked.

"Not when what I want is more time with a certain gorgeous redhead I know."

"You're so full of it."

He kissed her right there in the parking lot! And she didn't stop him.

"I half expected you to whack me upside my head for taking liberties with your mouth in a public place. But then I remembered you like the idea of being seen and I took my chances. Because your mouth is worth it." Duke's voice had gone huskier, whiskey rough instead of honey smooth. It never failed to send shivers through her.

"You're using your sex voice. Also this is work, not you peeping like a perv through my kitchen windows." But Carmella smiled a little as she said it and his answering grin told her he took it as the tease she meant it to be.

She liked getting to know him. Really liked what she found out with each new thing. Again the perfect stuff made her a little jittery.

"You bring it out. The perv in me and the voice."

Before he did anything else to seduce her, Carmella pushed him back enough to get her door closed without hurting him. "Have fun tonight. Win all your races and try not to break anything or get a black eye."

"Aw, gorgeous, you know I can't make promises like that. I will win, naturally. As for not breaking anything or getting a black eye? Well, I'm not superhuman. Drive safe. I'll see you later." He squeezed her hand quickly and stepped back enough for her to pull the truck away.

Duke had worked outside most of the morning. It'd been a gorgeous Saturday morning and he needed to trim the hedges around his front steps. It also, not entirely coincidentally, gave him a view of Carmella's little driveway spot and her front walk.

He wanted to see her. Had stopped pretending otherwise a few weeks before. And if he could sneak in some fantastic sex before they left to spend the day on the boat, even better.

He also wanted her to share with him about what her errands consisted of. She was rarely still when she wasn't at work. He knew she was close with her uncle and cousins and she mentioned her mom living in the area too. But she didn't share much more than that and he was hungry for details.

Hungry for her trust. For her to let him in a little more.

People told him things. All the damned time. So much so it got to be annoying. But she wasn't that way. Carmella listened more than she spoke. And he liked that. She was thoughtful.

But he wanted *her* to tell him things too.

And when she finally pulled up in her driveway, he was moving to her before he'd registered it.

Ginger wasn't with Carmella, which surprised him.

"Morning. Can I help you with anything?" he asked her as he opened her door.

Carmella smiled his way, turning her face up for a kiss. He tried not to show how startled he was. Because he dug it so hard. She wanted a kiss and he'd damn well give her one. He craved that again. Wanted her to turn to him, expecting affection. He took his time, needing to remind her what a good choice it was.

And got all tangled up in her. Her taste, the way she felt against him. She hadn't even gotten out of her truck yet and he had to wrestle back his urge to lay her back and taste all of her.

He made himself back up instead.

"Uh, I didn't need any help with anything, but I sure appreciate your idea of assistance," Carmella said, a little breathless.

He took up at her side as they went into her house. Ginger was already waiting at the front door, happy her human was home.

"How'd you get out the door without your partner?" Duke asked.

"She was way happier here with her chewie and a patch of sunshine to sleep in than visiting my mother and her vicious little furball."

"I really can't blame her. But being around you is just as nice."

"I have boobs, which you seem to appreciate like Ginger appreciates sunny patches for naps." Her expression made him so damned pleased.

"You're quite the comedian today." Duke stole another kiss.

"Errands are done. Gorgeous man in my house wearing an *I want to fuck you* face. Going out on a boat with friends on a beautiful summer afternoon. I have a lot of wonderful coming my way. What's not to smile over?"

"Put that way, yeah. Indeed." Duke pulled her close, hugging her for a bit until the dog kept head butting him to get his attention.

"She's jealous." Carmella bent to scratch Ginger's ears.

"If she knew what I planned to do with you, she'd run the other way." Or watch. Carmella had to shut the bedroom door because the dog often sat looking at the two of them as if they were absolutely crazy.

"Maybe. She sort of looks that way all the time, though," she said.

Ginger snorted a little bark and then, after assessing Duke and his lack of treats, went off to do her thing elsewhere.

"About that *I want to fuck you* thing. That's accurate. Totally."

Duke used his body to move her back to the couch. He eased her down, lying against her but not with his full weight. The windows were open, letting in some light, but the couch was low enough that while they reclined, they weren't visible. But he knew Carmella had a thing about maybe being seen.

Duke was beginning to realize that he got off on making her hot. He loved watching the Carmella she showed to most people fall away and she gave him a side of herself he knew she rarely trusted anyone to see.

A secret, dirty Carmella that was all for Duke and goddamn if that didn't make his fucking day. He got off on it in a way that shot right through his body.

"I'm going to have you," he murmured against the skin of her neck. "And later, when we get home from being out on the boat all day? I'm going to have you again."

She hummed her assent and he managed to get her shirt off while only breaking his mouth away from her skin for the barest of moments.

More. More. More.

Her bra fell away under his fingers, allowing him access to her breasts. He buried his face, breathing her in for long moments.

"If anyone came to the windows now, they'd see us, here on your couch. All spread out for me. Your lips swollen from my kisses, eyes glazed."

She made a sound that seemed to tear through him. A moan full of need and pleasure. Her nails dug into his shoulders, urging him closer.

He licked over her nipples, going from one to the other. Then over the silk of each rib, down across her hips. Her ink stood out, the color of the flowers vivid against the cream of her skin. Feminine and sexy. Like Carmella herself.

"Carm, baby, I just want to spread you on toast and eat you up."

"You don't even need the toast. I'm low in calories," she said, a tease in her tone.

"Leaves me more room to gorge on you without wasting any time on bread. I like the way you think." He didn't bother with the skirt she wore, as he dropped to his knees in front of her. Drawing her panties down her legs and off, he reversed his hold at her ankles, sliding his palms up her legs as he pressed them apart at the thigh, exposing her pussy. "Mmm yes. Right there."

Duke dove in like a starving man and Carmella loved it. Loved the way he seemed to revel in her, in every single part of her, of her taste and the way she looked. She could easily get used to a man treating her like that all the time.

Which was stupid as well as dangerous. You went getting used to it and it hurt a hell of a lot more when it ended.

He held her wide, palms hot against her inner thighs. His beard scratched the sensitive flesh around her pussy and the pleasure pain of it was just on the verge of being too much.

Her skin felt too tight. Ready to burst with all the pleasure building up as he sucked on her clit, tickling the underside with the tip of his tongue. She arched against his hold and he kept her in place. Heat arced through her at that, at the ease of his strength.

Not once did he let go, licking and sucking relentlessly until climax hit her so hard all she could do was feel until she finally went limp, breathing hard.

The rip of the condom wrapper and he gripped her hips. Before her eyes were all the way open, he'd pulled her down as he rested on his knees, his cock thrusting into her pussy so hard she saw stars.

Carmella leaned back against the couch, giving herself balance so she could thrust back at him each time he moved. Though they both clearly were hot for the other, their frenzied movements clicked into synch after several breaths. And she let it.

Outside, she heard the drone of a lawn mower, the hum of other machines all the neighborhood dudes paraded out the first sunny day and played with at all hours until they had to admit the grass wasn't going to need cutting until spring.

Anyone could hear Duke when he came. He tended to keep his sex talk quiet, but when he came, he could be loud. So could she, for that matter.

Neither of them spoke as he fucked her slow and deep. Each thrust sent her boobs bouncing, which seemed to delight him anew. She had no real complaint about such a thing.

In the kitchen, Ginger's collar jingled as she got some water and then the flap of her doggie door opened, letting in a little more noise from outside. Carmella's heart beat even faster as she heard her neighbor outside.

He rarely came over, but he could. Anyone could.

And Duke knew how wet that got her. And he worked it. For her.

Her orgasm was slow to build the second time around, but he adjusted her weight to reach between them and circle her clit with his fingertip in time with his thrusts.

"So close," he muttered as he sped up.

Mail hit the door slot, falling onto the floor in her entry, and

Carmella cried out, leaning in to bite his shoulder to keep quiet. Orgasm claimed her again, and with a snarl, the grip he had on one of her hips tightened as he came hard.

He continued to fuck into her slowly before pulling out, helping her sit on the couch and leaving quickly to deal with the condom before returning, flopping down beside her.

"So, welcome home," Duke said, putting an arm around her shoulders.

"You really do have the best ways of saying that. Ginger just wants food."

He flashed a grin at her before settling in again. "We have about an hour or so before we need to head out to the marina. PJ told me to make sure you had sunscreen, but to do it in a way that didn't insult you or assume you were an idiot. Those were her words."

"I think you managed that very careful feat." Carmella snorted.

"Who knew you had such a great sense of humor? Can I help with anything?"

"I need to change my clothes. You can't help with that or we'll never make it out the door. I made a bunch of sandwiches first thing this morning and some macaroni salad to go with."

"I picked up soda, water, and beer. I have a cooler we can put the food in when we're ready to leave. And what if you need help zipping or snapping or something? I'm sure I can help you get dressed."

"I'll be back out in a few minutes. Or I can come get you when I'm ready."

Duke frowned and still looked handsome. "I'm here. I'm not going anywhere. You smell good."

Carmella kissed him quickly and headed to her room to change. In the background she heard him talking to Ginger when the dog came back inside.

Really, this was the best Saturday she'd had in a really long time.

CHAPTER
Ten

"We should get moving," Duke said as they came back inside from her yard. Ginger would be staying home, so Carmella and Duke had played ball with her awhile, getting her nice and tired.

"Yeah. I'll get all the food ready. I've got it all in the fridge so I can easily tuck it into your cooler or keep it in mine." Without thinking about it, she yanked him down, tugging his shirt so she could kiss him quickly. He was so much taller she'd just found it easier to pull him to her height than to scramble up on things to get to his.

"I want to wash the dog slobber off my hands before we do."

She laughed and pointed to her bathroom. Heaven forbid a little dog spit got on his precious steering wheel. "You take that sink and I'll use the one in the kitchen."

Once he'd disappeared, she'd headed into the kitchen, cleaning up, making sure the dog had food and water and moving the picnic supplies near the door.

Duke came out a few minutes later and Carmella smiled his way. "Ready?" Her gaze slipped to his hand and the bandage on it. There was a little blood on his shirt. Her smile fell away. "Are you all right? What happened?"

* * *

He lifted the hand, a little blood showing through the bandage. "I broke the glass you have next to the sink. Sorry."

She moved to him, trying to take his hand. "Did you clean it up? Do you need stitches?"

"It's not that serious. I found a first aid kit in your cabinet." The most perfectly organized and supplied first aid kit he'd ever seen. Nor was he surprised to see it that way.

But he *had* been surprised to find all those bottles lined up in neat rows. All bearing someone else's name. He'd been arguing with himself since opening that cabinet about whether to say anything. It was her business after all and it didn't seem to affect her work or her life negatively.

But there were *a lot* of bottles. He'd seen this sort of stockpiling before and the size of that kind of addiction could land her in the hospital at best. The worst-case scenario wasn't something he wanted to think on.

So he sucked in a breath and decided to say something. "Speaking of that. Honey, you've got a whole lot of pill bottles in there with someone else's name on them."

She flinched like he'd slapped her and he knew he'd landed a direct hit. He didn't want to embarrass or hurt her, but he sure as hell didn't want to lose her either.

He tried again when she didn't reply. "What you do when you're not at work isn't my business—"

Carmella held up a hand to stop him speaking. "Those belong to my mother." She pointed to a picture on the far wall of her and another woman. "Virgie Hay."

Nausea swamped her. Shame that she'd been confronted like that. Accused in her own house. Not being able to trust him when she'd begun to truly believe he was someone to count on.

She hated few things more than feeling like a fool.

And then he made it worse. "Your name is Rossi and your uncle's name is Salazar. Look, it's fine. I don't care that you might need a boost. I'm just saying that many bottles says you might have a problem."

She blinked at him, utterly incredulous. Her first inclination was to apologize and then explain about how she had to monitor her mom, keep the pills with her so there'd be no accidents, overdoses, or days-long binges that drew Virgie into the darkest pit of her depression.

But Carmella then realized he hadn't *asked* her anything. He assumed all sorts of stuff and made her some sort of villain when he had no reason to.

Carmella was only getting to know this man and she wasn't feeling exactly eager to cut open a vein and vomit the trauma of her goddamn life to him. She didn't owe him that. He hadn't earned it.

"You're out of line," Carmella managed to say. "My mother's name is different because she's been married three times. It's different from mine because I was married too."

He gave her an expression that told her he thought she was making excuses. It sent her back to every time in her life she'd been looked at with that face. It seemed to pinball between all the worst moments until she throbbed with it.

"I like to party too so it's not like I'm judging. I just worry about you," Duke said as he stepped closer.

Carmella moved back, spine ramrod straight. She'd come into Twisted Steel and had given it her all. *They* had fistfights in the backyard and raced and got drunk and he had the stones to stand there and say all this to *her*? She showed up early, never shorted them even a minute of her time.

She went to her door and opened it. "Get out of my house."

"Don't be mad, Carm." He held his hands up in entreaty. "How can you kick me out because I'm worried about you?" He pointed to her bathroom. "I care about you and that right in there is a pill problem that's going to land you in the hospital. Or worse."

"They're my *mother's*. I told you that." Though the words came from Carmella's mouth, her voice seemed to have come from a stranger. When he didn't reply, she asked, "Are you firing me?"

He shook his head, clearly confused, and all she wanted to do was cry. Or punch his face. "Why are you so mad? What kind of guy do you think I am, anyway? Of course I'm not firing you."

She tried to tell herself it was for the best that he had no idea why she'd be upset. It was good he was being so awful. It made the break easier.

"Fine. Now get the hell out. I'll continue in my job unless you have a problem. This"—she waved a hand between them— "is over."

Duke sighed explosively. "Of course it's not over. You're being defensive."

"Gee, and why would that be? Because you just accused me of being an addict when *you're* the day drinker? Fuck off."

"I told you I don't care about the pills." Duke said this to her like it was entirely reasonable to snoop around in someone's medicine cabinet, see pill bottles, and assume their presence meant the person was an addict. Oh, and then to accuse them of it on the way out the door to a romantic day on the boat.

"They're not mine! Oh my god. Why am I even explaining this to you?" Carmella had to throw her hands up in utter frustrated disgust.

This was why having a man around for more than his cock and ability to fix things was a stupid idea.

Ginger knew there was trouble. She sat, leaning her body into Carmella's calf. Reassuring. Giving support.

"How the hell can I believe they're not yours?" Duke cocked his head, so earnest she probably could have forgiven him if he just shut up already. But it was too late. Her stomach hurt as he kept saying things she wasn't sure he could ever take back.

"Because they're not. Because I said so. Because my mother's name is on them." Because she'd never given him any reason to believe otherwise.

"Some of those meds are heavy-duty shit. You can't be drinking at all with all those pills in your system. You're going to overdose."

It was as if she hadn't said any of it. What a fool she'd been.

"Get out, get out, get out!" She was so outraged she didn't even have the energy to be horrified she was screaming loud enough the neighbors could probably hear.

He loped from her house to her porch, deliberately taking his time, and she only narrowly avoided planting her foot in his ass. But she did slam the door, locking it. On shaky legs, she stepped quickly to close her front curtains.

"You know where I am when you come to your senses," he called out as he headed next door.

Within five minutes, her phone received a text, and when she heard his tone, she blocked his number.

She was trustworthy, damn it! She took care of people and kept them out of trouble. She was a good person and he'd just made her feel like dirt. In her own home.

Having it be *Duke* who judged her, who saw her through that perception, was the worst part. Hadn't she done enough penance for everyone else's bullshit?

He was supposed to be *different*, and when you scratched the surface, he was just the same as all those other well-meaning strangers who took one look and decided who and what she was.

She grabbed her tote and leashed Ginger. "Come on, you. Let's go for a ride."

Ginger licked Carmella's nose and gave her a little nuzzle of encouragement.

After peeking to be sure he wasn't outside, she headed out with the dog to her truck. She'd had plans for romance, which had gotten shot all to hell. But she had a lunch packed and decided to head over to the Arboretum to eat her picnic anyway.

Duke got back to his house and texted Mick to let him know he and Carmella weren't going to make it to their afternoon boat trip. He wasn't overly specific, not wanting to drag all their friends into this situation.

He just needed to let Carmella cool off awhile. Of course, he realized that after he saw her truck was gone from her driveway. But it was for the best. He texted her a few times but then stopped when he realized she wasn't going to reply.

She was embarrassed most likely, but she was smart. She'd figure out he only wanted her to be safe and would come around. Couples fought. Heaven knew PJ and Asa did. And despite being a giant tool, Asa still found his way back to PJ time and again.

When Duke showed up to work Monday, Carmella was already there, as she was wont to be, studiously avoiding him. So he let that go too.

He was a patient man. She'd come around.

By day three it wasn't any fun anymore.

Every time he tried to swing through her office, she was on the phone. If he saw her heading to the break room and moved to intercept her, he always got waylaid.

She'd blocked his number from her phone, and when he came to her door the night before, she didn't answer.

Even Ginger was giving him the cold shoulder. The dog who'd loved him just a week before no longer jumped to her feet to come greet him when he entered the room.

"You going to tell me why you're so pissy this week?" Mick asked, approaching, wearing a master schedule face.

"I'm not pissy. Why are you bothering me?" Duke said in what sounded like a pretty pissy voice.

"Just checking with you. What's your timeline like on this?" Mick indicated the dozens of pieces of the '73 Duster's engine.

"I'm not Rumpelstiltskin. I can't spin gold from this shit. It's an old engine and no one took care of it," Duke said.

"Yadda yadda. I get it. You're great." Mick patted Duke's head. "Now, so like a week? A day? An hour? You complain but it never really seems to connect with just exactly how much time it takes you to fix something so make your answer time specific."

"Four days. Go away." Duke turned his attention back to all the parts spread out before him. Like a puzzle. If he focused on that, he could forget his annoyance about Carmella.

"Does this have anything to do with the way you look at Carmella and she goes out of her way not to look at you? Did you guys have a fight and that's why you didn't come out on Saturday?" Mick asked.

"I don't want to talk about it." Duke wasn't used to being the one who needed this kind of support. *He* was the one Mick and Asa came to for advice. He talked people down, defused potential friendship-ending arguments, mediated problems.

Duke liked that. And he most certainly didn't like it being the other way around.

Mick blew out a breath. "All right. At least talk to someone, man."

Duke knew a lot of people. He seemed to be the kind of person others thought of as a friend. He got along with most everyone. Knew how to listen more than he spoke.

But Mick and Asa weren't simply friends. The three of them were family. In truth, Duke trusted them *more* than the brother he was related to. Mick had reenlisted and spent a few years away from Duke and Asa. Away from the foundation of the life they'd built, of the shop. Their friend had only come home to Seattle the year before.

More than just about anyone Duke had ever known, Mick needed roots. He needed to belong. Duke needed to remember that and not make his friend feel rejected just because Duke was on the outs with his woman.

"Damn it." Duke tossed the cleaning cloth he'd been using to the counter.

"Let's go to lunch." Mick jerked his chin toward the door leading outside.

"I was in the neighborhood so I figured I'd drop in to see if you were free for lunch."

Carmella grinned as her cousin Craig came through to her office. She hadn't seen him in nearly two weeks. "I'm so glad you did. I'm free and really hungry."

The hug was something she'd really needed. Enough that he noticed, eyeing her carefully.

But before he could question her about it, she wanted to be away from work. "When we have food, we can continue this conversation. And since you're a full-time college student now, lunch is on me," Carmella said.

Instead of taking over his father's shop, Craig had decided to go back to school to get his engineering degree. The entire family had been behind the choice. Craig wanted to design aircraft. Carmella couldn't have kept the shop up. So they'd sold to one of their mechanics, who'd relaunched as a franchise in a chain store.

"Excellent."

They walked across the street to the burger place. "They're having clam chowder today." Carmella pointed.

"You always remember." Craig put an arm around her shoulders and hugged her to his side. "So, you're in a fight with Duke? Did he do something really bad? If I'm going to be punching him, I should have fries. Bulk up and all."

Carmella burst out laughing. "I'm so glad you came by. I really needed to see a friendly face."

He frowned but held his question until they'd gotten seated and had ordered.

"I thought you two were cool. What happened?" Craig asked.

"I thought we were cool too. One minute we're chilling, getting ready to spend the day on the water, and then boom he comes out of my bathroom..." Carmella jerked out of her conversation and wrenched her neck to the side.

Duke stood there with Mick, who waved and smiled.

"Go on with your story," Duke said.

"Go away, Duke," Carmella whispered.

"No. I want to hear how you're going to spin this to Craig."

"Why the hell are you speaking to her that way?" Craig demanded.

"He's got a point," Mick murmured. "Maybe let's all sit down and chat this out."

Carmella wanted the ground to open up and swallow her. The whole situation was humiliating.

She leaned out to speak directly to Mick. "There's nothing to chat out, Mick. I appreciate that you're trying to help. I'm having lunch. I clocked out if there's an issue with my work performance."

With an annoyed growl, Duke threw himself into the open chair on Carmella's side of the table and Mick settled next to Craig.

"Does he know?" Duke jerked a head at Craig.

"That you're an astounding idiot?" Carmella asked. "We all do."

Mick snickered and quieted at Duke's glare.

"About all the pills," Duke said through clenched teeth.

This motherfucker. He was really going to do this here?

Carmella wished she hadn't already drained her iced tea because she wanted to throw it in his face. Instead she kept her cool. "You're truly picking this hill to die on, Duke?"

"You're the one trying to spin it." Duke raised one shoulder, deliberately slow.

Which only made her want to hit him in the nose with a rolled-up menu. "Trying to *spin* what? What am I spinning?"

Craig rapped his knuckles on the tabletop. "I'm going to suggest someone tell me why Duke is speaking to my cousin in that tone. I'm beginning to get cranky, which makes me want to punch whoever is making her so sad."

Duke looked up at Craig's demand. "I'm worried about her and you should be too."

Carmella leveled a glare at Duke. "Stop this."

"He asked, Carm," Duke said. "I'm just answering."

"Why is it you're worried about her?" Craig asked.

There was no way this conversation was going to take place around her as if she wasn't even in the room.

Carmella said, "Duke saw Mom's pill bottles in my bathroom cabinet and has decided that I'm an addict in my ubiquitous free time."

Craig blinked several times. "Virgie's pills?"

Just hearing the incredulity in his voice made Carmella feel better. "Yes. Despite my repeating this multiple times, he's convinced I'm involved in some sort of complex scheme to get pills I'm addicted to. Because doesn't it make sense to jump to that conclusion?"

"What was I supposed to think?" Duke reached for her and she scooted away.

"I don't know. Since you never actually *asked* me and instead accused me, I guess we'll never know. What I do know is that you're out of line. You've been out of line and I don't see any point where you won't be if you keep on this way."

"Why are you avoiding the subject then? Just tell me. If it's such a believable story." Duke reached toward her again.

"*Avoiding?* I'm here having lunch with my cousin. You came

over here. Uninvited. You sat down. You're picking a fight. That's not me avoiding."

She saw her food coming and got up to meet the server. "I'm so sorry, but can I get that to go?"

Craig joined her as Duke and Mick remained at the table.

"What's going on?" Craig asked.

"I've lost my appetite. You stay and finish your lunch. You have a late class and you'll be starving if you don't."

"I'm not letting you go when you're this upset. You didn't tell him any of the details about her, did you?"

He would have known how intensely private Carmella was when it came to the situation with her mother.

"He didn't really even ask. He just accused me. I told him they belonged to my mother. I showed him the picture of her on my wall. But..."

"But the rest wasn't his business and you wouldn't have shared after he made you feel bad. I get it." Craig smiled. "You don't have to be embarrassed about it, you know."

It had been a really long road to where she stood right then. Carmella was still working on knowing things, while at the same time, truly feeling them. She worked on that part a lot these days.

She blew out a breath. "It is what it is. Despite her flaws, she's my mom. I love her. She's fucked up and I take care of her. I pretty much always have. I would have shared with him. At least some of it, if he'd *asked*."

"I think he needs a Come to Jesus. I won't hit him. Unless he deserves it. A lot more than he does now. But he's making some judgments he has no call to make."

Duke came over. "Why are you hiding over here? We should talk this out."

Carmella ignored Duke, speaking to Craig as she headed to the front, where her lunch had been boxed up. "Finish your food. Call me later, okay?"

"Definitely. Since we got interrupted, I didn't even get up to speed. I want to catch up. Come over Sunday. We'll walk over to the pub, have a pint or two." He searched her features before kissing her forehead.

"Sounds good. Use your words, not your fists. Remember that," Carmella told him with a wink.

She headed a few blocks down to a pretty little park. She wasn't ready to go back to Twisted Steel just yet and she needed to get herself back together first.

"I'm totally sure I told you to approach her slowly," Mick said when Duke and Craig came back to the table.

"She was here. I was here. We're both adults so why not just talk about it?" Duke sat, digging into his lunch.

"Because you're charging at her like a bull, Duke. Jesus. She's a nice woman. She's got good manners. You're coming at her like she's a rager with a rap sheet. This is about me, isn't it?" Mick asked.

Craig growled at them both as he ate. Duke had always regarded Craig Salazar as sort of a laid-back dude. But this was a totally different side Duke hadn't seen in the other man before.

Fiercely protective.

"Maybe you should back up and go at this from the beginning, Duke. Including this stuff about Mick," Craig said.

"It's really not your business," Duke answered.

Craig put his fork down and wiped his mouth carefully with his napkin. "Well, you see, that's where you're wrong. You *made* it my business when you came over here and terrorized Carmella until she fled your presence. So, why don't you back up and start at the beginning because I promised her I'd use my words instead of my fists and I'm already thinking about how I'll explain to her that I failed."

Mick snorted and then spoke to Duke. "You put yourself right where you are now. You found pills in her bathroom. Lots of them. In someone else's name."

He remembered that sick feeling when he'd caught sight of the rows of bottles. He'd seen the signs before and pretended everything was all right. He'd told himself Mick's life needed something to soften the edges and help him get through the day. And that had been a mistake he wasn't going to make again.

"I did. And so I confronted her about them," Duke replied. "And then it went off the deep end. She kicked me out of her house."

"I think you skipped a step or two there, Duke. You *confronted* her. And she said what?" Craig asked.

"She said they were her mother's. But there were so many bottles. Ten maybe. A few from different pharmacies. I know what that means." Duke looked over to Mick briefly.

"You don't know shit. Virgie Hay *is* her mother. Those are her mother's prescriptions. But Carmella already told you that and you didn't believe her. The only thing you would have believed was a confession of a misdeed." Craig ate awhile before speaking again. "You have some scenario in your head for what you think is going on but you couldn't be more fucking wrong. About all of it."

"So why not explain it to me?" Duke asked.

Craig rolled his eyes as he started on his second sandwich. "Because you just admitted you had your mind made up! She told you the truth and you called her a liar. And you're faulting *her* for not explaining something you'd already made your mind up about? That's stupid."

"He did it because I had a problem. For a while, several years ago," Mick said. "He came at this wrong, sure. But he did it from a good place."

"And that means exactly what? You don't know what you've poked at."

Duke liked to think he was smart. Good at things. But he'd fucked up. He wasn't sure of everything, but he knew enough to see he'd done some damage.

"So tell me, Craig. Explain it to me."

"Why do you think you're entitled? Huh? You think Carmella is this private for no reason?"

"If she wasn't so damned stingy with her life, it wouldn't have even been a problem. She shuts me out and it's my fault?"

Craig just looked at Duke as he ate, shaking his head.

"I had a drug problem. Duke knew it and tried to talk to me about it. But I blew him off and he let it go. I ended up in the hospital having to get my stomach pumped," Mick said. "He handled this wrong, but he did it because of that. He was worried. Help him out, man. He digs Carmella, and from what I can tell, with the exception of this, she seems to dig him back."

Craig sighed and shoved some more fries into his face. "She's important to me. I really dislike seeing her sad. You made her that way. I'm wary about giving you anything else to hurt her with."

Duke scrubbed his hands over his face. "I don't want to hurt her at all. Jesus. I was worried. Should I have stayed silent? And then what? In the ER when she's in a fucking coma and you all knew I saw those bottles and said nothing?"

"This right here is one of those relationship things. Your shit got mixed up with her shit and it all blew up like a shit bomb."

"You're very poetic, Mick." Duke rolled his eyes.

"But right." Mick smirked.

Craig wiped his mouth with a napkin. "If you have questions about whatever she's doing, *ask* her to explain. Don't accuse her. Don't make up your mind before she can speak. That's a surefire way to earn your exit. And believe me, Carmella can—and does—forgive a lot. Be worthy of that."

"You won't just tell me?" Duke asked. "Don't you think it'd be easier for us to work it out if I knew?"

"Take a guess. Her mother has a lot of pills. Carmella keeps them at her house instead of with her mom. It's not that hard to piece together really." Craig stood. "Don't come for her if you're not willing to do what it takes to stay. She's had enough losers in her life."

He turned and walked out, leaving Duke sighing and looking over to Mick. "I fucked up." He was only now beginning to understand it. He'd come at her all wrong. Even though it was for the right reasons.

"Yes. You gonna fix it? Or leave it be?"

"I don't know." Which was sort of true. But the fact was, he wasn't going to walk away without trying his hardest to make this right. Carmella deserved it and he did too.

Mick leaned back and looked his friend over carefully. "Look, you wouldn't have said anything to her if you didn't have feelings for her. I understand that. And I know why you did it. You need to tell *her* why you did it. And it's cool with me if you share my story. And then grovel a lot for *how* you did it."

Duke raised an eyebrow Mick's way. "When did you get wise on romance?"

The amusement in Mick's gaze dimmed a little. "Hard lessons are the ones that stick, I guess."

"You ever going to tell me about it? Whatever happened that sent you back to hell after finally coming home?"

Several years back, Mick had come out of the army and back to Seattle, where Asa and Duke had begun Twisted Steel. He'd come in as the shop manager but he'd been distracted, and then without any warning, he'd reenlisted and left town.

"Yeah." Mick sighed. "But not here and not today. Come on." He stood and Duke joined him, dropping a tip on the way out.

The year before, Mick had come back to Seattle, and though

Duke saw shadows in Mick's gaze from time to time, he'd begun to grow some roots, to really take on a leadership role within Twisted Steel.

But he'd never really told Asa and Duke what drove him off to start with, and because both had their own shit to handle, they'd given him time to tell them. Which is what they all did with one another.

"Right on. I'm here when you're ready. I guess I've got some work to do."

Mick snorted. "You better keep your strength up for all the apologizing you'll be doing."

"Fuck off."

Mick found that hilarious, still laughing when they got back to Twisted Steel. "Don't do this at work," his friend warned as they walked inside.

"I'm not a total idiot." He wanted to rush up there and hash it all out. But he knew Carmella well enough to understand she'd only be embarrassed and close off even more.

Plus, when he groveled, he didn't need fourteen people watching.

He knew where she lived, after all.

CHAPTER
Eleven

Carmella had gone back to work, keeping her head down, and for the most part, Duke had let her be.

But the man skulked around all day. Just at the edge of her attention and it made her want to cry and punch him and laugh all at once.

PJ strolled in with two coffee cups. "I bring you an offering of caffeine."

"You're my favorite. Don't tell the others, though, or I'll have to deny it." Carmella took the cup with a grateful sigh. "Thank you. I was waffling on another pot since it's so close to quitting time."

PJ dropped into the chair at the empty desk. "How are you today? We missed you Saturday."

It hadn't really occurred to Carmella, until she'd seen PJ walk in, that she'd have to say something about her fight with Duke. And since she and PJ had already discussed Duke before, it was even more natural that she would explain it.

"Ah," PJ said after taking a long look at Carmella. "There's trouble? What'd he do?"

Carmella laughed, feeling a little better. She gave PJ a brief overview, not going into a lot of details.

PJ shook her head at the end of the story. "I've known Duke a few years, pretty well for the last year and a half. He's solid. I can't imagine he's overly happy you're mad at him."

Carmella shrugged. "I'm just hoping we can manage to work together after this."

"So, you don't think you can work it out? Do you like him enough to try? Or was this your line that can't be crossed?"

"The . . . whatever it was between us isn't even that serious, for god's sake. We had sex." Carmella looked around to be sure no one was within earshot. "Really good sex. But that's it."

PJ's brow rose very slowly. "I'm not going to argue with you. Not because I agree. Because you're full of it, Carmella." She gave Carmella one of those *I'm keeping an eye on you* things with her fingers. "Just know I'm wise to that. I've seen the two of you together. But I'm not going to call you on it because you're not ready to share. Or face it or whatever. I know what that feels like. Plus I don't want to scare you away because I want sex details and you won't give them to me if we're not friends."

"You're a shit stirrer, PJ." But Carmella wasn't mad. It was sort of endearing.

"I'm an *active* friend, silly."

"So being your friend is, like, a contact sport?"

PJ laughed and laughed. "Only for Asa. I just want you to know that I like you and, as your friend, am always available when you need to talk. Or share sex details. I'll tell you up front, I'm really nosy."

"I might have noticed."

"Come out to drinks at the Ditch with me and my friends on Thursday night," PJ said. "You know most everyone already anyway. It's totally casual. Wings and beer with fun people for a few hours."

"Will Asa and Duke be there?"

"They have their boy club thing until about ten or so. Come

early if you want." PJ's smile was so sweet and full of hope Carmella didn't have the heart to say no. And she liked the group of women PJ hung out with so it wasn't a hardship to get to know them better.

And as she could avoid Duke by leaving before ten, she agreed.

They chatted awhile more until Asa caught sight of PJ and the two of them went off to have dinner.

Half the guys were still working when Carmella headed out for the night. They called out their good-byes and she waved, realizing that she'd begun to really consider Twisted Steel a home and its employees her family in a sense.

She frowned as she thought of Duke and then pushed it firmly from her mind as she headed home.

After she'd changed and started to put together a sandwich for her dinner, her doorbell rang.

"If that's Duke, I'm going to turn the sprinklers on," she told Ginger as she headed to the front door.

Duke stood on her porch, looking so good she wanted to punch him in the throat for it. This getting past him business would be a lot easier if the man was gross, or slovenly in some way.

A gray T-shirt stretched across his muscles like a caress. His faded jeans were worn at the pockets and hems. And when she opened the curtains on the window to find him there, he smiled, holding both hands up in entreaty.

"Please, Carmella, hear me out. Just give me ten minutes. I'm sorry."

Ginger barked once and walked away from the front door to stand on her human's right side. Carmella looked at him, and though she knew she should follow the damned dog, she opened up.

"Why are you here?" Carmella kept her hand at her hip, squeezing to keep from reaching out to touch him instead.

"Can we talk? Please? I want to apologize and work this out."

"Apology accepted. Problem solved." She started to shut the door—not very hard—but he blocked it with his foot.

"Not even halfway solved. I made a damned mess, so I need to clean it up. And you need to hear why."

Oh. He had this thing he did when he got bossy. He jutted his chin out just a little. Enough that she realized what a sneaky fucking alpha male he was underneath all that smooth laid-back exterior.

Damn it.

"It's over." Meaning the argument *and* their relationship, but not believing it even as she said the words.

He didn't believe it any more than she did apparently, because he managed to walk into her house, closing the door at his back. Ginger hadn't left Carmella's side, but she also hadn't so much as growled at Duke.

"I didn't say you could come in." Carmella was pretty proud of how nonchalant her voice sounded.

"I know. I'm a dick sometimes. But I aim to make you happy so I came in anyway."

She sighed, crossing her arms over her chest.

He frowned, looking miserable, and she *nearly* felt sorry for him.

He walked down her hall and into the living room, settling on the couch. She moved to the chair across the way—and out of his reach. Ginger settled over Carmella's feet, keeping an eye on Duke.

"Why are you here? I accepted your apology."

Duke's expression showed surprise, but no anger. "Okay so I'm also at the point where I can see you have a temper."

Carmella nearly snarled. If she did, it was all his fault. "I don't have a temper. *You* have a temper."

"Is that your version of *I know you are but what am I?*"

She just glared his way and he kept grinning like an idiot.

A *hot* idiot.

His grin fell away, replaced by a more serious look. "I'm here because I want this to be okay. I want us to be okay. When I said I was a dick, I was joking. I'm not. Usually."

"But you were this *one* time?"

"When you raise your brow at me like that, it makes me so hot for you."

Carmella stood and Ginger sighed, rousing a halfhearted bark at Duke. "Are you kidding me? Get out. I was an idiot to let you come in here."

Duke joined her, hands up again. "Sorry! I'm sorry. I thought it'd lighten things up. Wrong. Sorry." Duke blushed and for whatever reason it made her sit back down.

Ginger head butted Carmella's leg until she gave the dog a behind the ears scratch. "It's okay," she murmured to the dog, who settled back down.

She could punish him forever, and no one really won. She could make him go and underline the fact that she was an employee and nothing more. Or since she'd let him in, she could listen.

"Thank you for hearing me out," Duke said as he sat once more. "Like I said, I'm really sorry for the way I came at you on Saturday. I'm sorry I didn't *ask* you what those pills were. I'm sorry I didn't believe you when you told me."

In the whole of Carmella's life, she'd heard men say they were sorry more times than she could count. But when it came to actually believing any of them—with the exception of her uncle and cousins—she had a very brief record.

People said they were sorry a lot. People *meant* it far less often.

And yet, as she sat there across from Duke, she believed his words. He appeared genuinely contrite. It made her weak, that small hope. And she let herself feel it anyway.

"Can I explain? The why? I don't want you to think I'm making excuses. I'm not. But maybe once I tell you, you'll know me a little better."

Carmella knew she should usher him out. Thank him for his apology but underline they were only neighbors who worked with one another.

Instead she nodded. "All right."

"I've seen a lot of medicine bottles—like in your bathroom—before. And when I asked, I was told they were someone else's. And I let it go, even though I didn't believe it. Because it made me uncomfortable to push and pry. And then I watched Mick get more and more careless when our unit was out on patrol. You can't be careless when people are trying to kill you. He got written up a few times for not showing up, or being late. Also something you can't do when people are trying to kill you. And I *knew* he was self-medicating. I knew it and I understood it. Maybe I wished I could do it too because I hated being there. But he's my brother, you know? And he was hurting. So I kept my mouth shut and he got worse and worse until he ended up overdosing."

Carmella had felt like nothing he could have said would have excused his manner. But she'd been wrong. Because what he'd done, she realized, he'd done because he was worried.

"He nearly got booted from the army. Though in retrospect I wonder if that wouldn't have been better for him. We managed to convince everyone it was a combo between the heat and the medication. They were his pills after all. He made up some story about how he'd forgotten he'd taken an earlier dose. It was stupid and he could have died because I kept my mouth shut. I saw your collection and it sent me back there. I honestly struggled with myself about saying something, and when I did, I came at you all wrong. I'm sorry I did that. But I'm not sorry I spoke up. I like you and I'm sure as hell not going to let anyone else I know end up nearly dead because I didn't want to make anyone uncomfortable."

Carmella looked at him for what felt like forever. Not speaking, but clearly thinking.

"I should have asked you," he continued. "And I should have believed you. All I ended up doing was hurting your feelings and making you mad at me. Next time—and okay, so I'm a dude so we both know I'll fuck up again—I'll do better. I'll ask instead of accuse."

"Next time?"

Duke wanted to touch her. Wanted to kiss her. And instead, she sat out of reach, aloof and sad.

Mad at him was one thing. But sad, well, that was unbearable.

He moved to her, kneeling at her feet, and still got eye to eye. "Next time." He said it with utter certainty. "For now, I see sadness in your gaze and it tears at me. I want to make you smile. Or scream out my name as you come. Or if you want to say 'Would you like pie?' at the end of any sentence to me, I'd be okay with that too."

One corner of her mouth tipped up and his heart seemed to hitch just a little too and then the ground at his knees seemed to fall away as he realized he was falling in love with Carmella Rossi.

Oh fuck.

Wisely, he kept this to himself. She was skittish as it was and he'd made it worse. It would take a while to rebuild what he'd messed up. In the meantime, he'd seduce her into falling in love with him right back.

"Will you tell me? About the pills?" He tried to keep his hunger for details out of his voice.

Carmella licked her lips and he had to swallow hard to keep from kissing her.

Finally she spoke. "I can let a lot go. I don't care if you check out other women's asses as long as you keep your wits and your manners. I don't care if you have to work overtime on a project. I don't mind that you go out and rabble-rouse with your friends. But trust is something super important to me. I don't share my private life with very many people. And never with those I *can't* trust."

She sucked in a deep breath.

Duke saw yet another facet of what a huge mistake he'd made with her. Risking it, he slowly took her hand, entangling his fingers with hers.

"I'm a dumbass, but I *am* a good friend. And you can trust me not to reveal what you tell me if you don't want me to. I won't judge. Please tell me?"

"The truth is what I already told you. The pills are my mother's. I make sure she takes what she needs." There was a nearly desperate tone in her voice and he felt even worse.

As much as Duke wished he were closer to his biological family, he found the concept of a child taking care of a parent outside of real medical need pretty ridiculous. But he said he wouldn't judge so he tried not to.

She didn't add anything else. He wanted to know more, but he also understood he'd have to earn those details.

"All right. I'm sorry I didn't believe you before." He cupped her cheeks, relieved she hadn't kicked him out yet. "I hurt you and I hate that."

"You did it from a good place," she said, her voice very small.

"In the end, the result is the same. I was careless with you. Do you think we can get past it? I promise to be worth it and make you come lots of times to make up for my mistakes."

"Please don't make me regret this."

His heart nearly broke because she wasn't teasing.

He let go of her to make an X over his heart. "I'll do my very best. I'm a risk, but I'm a good one."

"I think we can get past it."

"Thank goodness because I was going to have to bug you incessantly with my charm to get you back and that's exhausting,"

Duke said, hoping this attempt at levity went over better than the earlier ones had.

Carmella rolled her eyes, looking down to where Ginger had worked her way between them. "What do you think?"

He fished a treat from his pocket and Ginger, to her credit, looked to Carmella for permission before she took it from his palm.

"She's adorable, but loyal." He pet the dog and then took a risk and kissed Carmella.

Just three days since he'd done that last but it soaked into him as if he'd been starving for it. A sound came from his gut, one he'd have been embarrassed making for anyone else. But he wanted Carmella to hear what she did to him, just from a kiss.

He wanted more but also realized he'd probably need to work his way back to that too. That and he found himself needing to make her better. And that should start with dinner and a beer.

"I guess she forgives me too." Duke indicated the dog with a tip of his chin.

"I'd keep my bedroom door closed when she's over there. She might leave you a present in a shoe." Carmella's smug smile made him laugh.

"I'll keep that in mind. How about you and Ginger come over to my place. Let me make dinner," Duke said. "I've got some salmon to grill. Some corn from Mick's garden. Who knew he'd be so good at growing vegetables? I have ice cream too. For dessert. I've missed you, so you should say yes."

"I guess I can eat."

He took her hand and they stood. "Come on, you," Duke called out to Ginger.

CHAPTER
Twelve

Duke had to admit he liked her in his house. She had a way of filling it, of being so together and calm he wanted to soak her in. It also meant he could smell her on his sheets, or a wisp of her in the air as he moved through the rooms.

"Can you peel and slice some cucumber? I've got fresh tomatoes if you want to use them," he told Carmella.

He hoped so, because watching her cook was as hot as watching her organize or clean.

"I can toss together a quick cucumber and tomato salad." She opened a cabinet, pulling out a bowl, and he liked that too. Because it meant she'd been there often enough she knew where it was. "Do you have vinegar?"

Duke pointed, hoping he wasn't too obvious about checking out her ass. "To the left of the sink. I think I have balsamic but I don't know what else."

She tiptoed up to look through the bottles assembled on the shelf. "Rice wine vinegar. You have hidden depths, Bradshaw."

"I do? That's good to know. Vinegar is an indicator of this?"

Barefoot, she padded across his kitchen to grab one of his knives to slice up cucumber and tomatoes, swaying as she went. Her reserve was still in place, but not nearly as icy as before.

"Among other things."

He made no attempt to hide the way he watched her as she peeled and sliced. Ginger made a little jingling sound, the tags on her collar swaying as she sniffed all the corners of each room, making sure she hadn't missed anything in the three days he and Carmella had been arguing.

"I promise you I haven't had any other dogs over."

Ginger looked up, one of her ears flopping back as she gave him a very good impression of a dismissive snort.

"She's going to be tough to win back," Duke said, but it was a tease.

"She's my protector." Carmella's smile told him she was amused. "He did give you a cookie. You can be nice to him now. If you like," Carmella murmured to the dog.

"I'm too charming to resist forever. And I have a whole box of cookies to share with dogs who love me." He winked at Carmella before paying attention to the fish he was prepping for the grill. "Just sealing these up now." He put some fresh herbs and lemon slices into the foil packets and folded them closed. "I've got potatoes and corn out there now so those will be ready by the time the fish is."

He took the stuff for the grill out and she joined him, ferrying supplies out from the kitchen to the table on his deck.

Late summer in Seattle. The sky, past seven already, would be locked in a purple-and-orange twilight for hours more.

"Your skin is even more beautiful in this light." He paused to kiss her cheek as he returned from turning on some music. "I missed you, Carmella."

"I live next door and we work together. It's not like I was far away."

Duke shook his head. "When you looked at me at lunch today and I saw all that emotion on your face, but none of the warmth you usually give me, it freaked me out. You don't have to be in another state for you to be out of my reach."

He stepped closer, pulling her to his body as the sultry sound of FKA twigs's "Two Weeks" wafted through the air.

She swayed, just slightly, but he responded, wrapping his arms around her as they danced, and he fell that last bit into love with her when she rested her cheek on his chest like she was meant to fit right there.

"I missed you too," she said quietly as the song ended and he needed to get back to the grill.

Emotions in his throat, he was grateful to have something to do with his hands so he didn't leap on her and proclaim how he felt.

"I have a really nice bottle of white wine. I'll run home to grab it." She blushed as she rushed out and he let her, hoping she was feeling as connected and intensely as he was instead of panicking about a bad choice in letting him in her front door earlier that night.

Just that morning she'd been mad at him. No. Not mad. Hurt. Disappointed. And now? Now that he'd come to her and apologized so genuinely, after hearing what drove him to confront her? Now she was all mixed up because her usual *kick him to the curb* button was refusing to work.

Carmella headed for the kitchen, grabbing the bottle of wine she'd tucked away in her pantry. It wasn't chilled, though, and she felt like a doofus.

Her belly still fluttered even with some time and space between them, and Carmella had to pause at her front door to get herself together again. He was a neighbor. A guy she dated and had sex with. A boss—which still made her nervous.

As long as she remembered their differences as well as the things that made them alike, she'd be fine. Because there was no call in getting more than superficially involved with Duke.

From what she could tell, he liked women, a lot of them. He

dated around but never exclusively. She had no reason to believe he was with her either. And no call to demand it.

Even if she wanted it. Even if she maybe, in the smallest part of herself, thought maybe she was different. *They* were different. Which was the sort of thing that got a woman kicked in the feelings and she needed to remind herself of that.

Virgie was a woman with a foolish heart and it had rendered her into a hot, hot mess. It made Carmella cringe to imagine ever having her own child see her the way she routinely saw her mother.

Carmella gave herself a once-over in the mirror hanging near the front door. She had that look. The woman in the mirror smiled, sensual. That woman was one who just had a slow dance with a hot man on a summer night. Her skin was still a little flushed.

He'd said he missed her.

And when he said it, a warm wave of pleasure had slid over her. Duke made her want to sigh wistfully. His compliments were for Carmella. Or at least they felt like they were for her and not a general pickup line.

He spoke like he *knew* her. Even if he didn't know half of what she had packed into the baggage she carried around. It was like he looked at her and saw to her truest self and he didn't want to back off. Or take advantage. He just accepted it.

Even though he'd just had to apologize to her, she trusted him. Even as she knew he'd do something stupid again soon enough.

Then again, she'd trusted Clifton and look where that got her. Divorced at twenty-two and the years since then filled with all manner of people oozing into her life to try to use her connection to him in some way. Usually bill collectors, but she'd dealt with the police several times as well as Clifton himself, who managed to find her whenever he needed something.

She shook her head and then gave her hair a quick brush before pulling it back with a clip. This would be doable as long as it stayed casual. Fun. That's what this thing with Duke was and as long as she never forgot that her heart would remain unbroken.

And as a result, they could still be friends after the sex stuff waned. People seemed to be able to do it well enough and she liked him. They were adults, damn it.

Pep talk delivered, Carmella locked up and headed back to Duke's, feeling better by the time she found him out on the deck, his fairy lights on, some citronella candles burning to keep the mosquitoes at bay.

"Wow. This looks so pretty."

"Thank you. I needed to make sure the surroundings matched my guest." He took the wine off to chill and before too long they were eating a fantastic dinner and she allowed herself to enjoy it.

"This is so good and so fresh. The corn just makes it."

"I had never eaten salmon until I ended up in Seattle after leaving the army." Duke settled back in his chair. "Asa took me to a salmon bake. Have you been to one?"

"When I was a kid, every summer we'd drive out to Kalaloch to camp at the beach." This was such a good memory. "The first full day we were there, we did a big one." She would laugh and play with her cousins. Her aunt and uncle always happy to be able to take her away from her mom's influence when they could. Her biggest responsibility was not getting sand in the watermelon her aunt had sliced up.

Duke grinned. "Exactly. It was a big one at the beach and I tried it and instantly loved it. Sometimes we get together with a big group of friends to fish in Alaska. They pack it in dry ice and send it back here. That's what this is, but Asa and I weren't able to go this year since we had to stick close with all the construction of the new showroom and stuff."

"Still, pretty good friends to share their haul with you."

He nodded. "They are. I'm going to have to invest in some of those outdoor heater things so we can keep on hanging out after work even when it gets cold."

"Except rain. I should probably warn you now that I am not one of those Seattleites who loves to be out and about in a downpour."

"The overhang here will keep us dry. I move the table closer to the house when it's raining. I have an umbrella for the table, but it's not good for heavy rain. Plus, I don't want you unhappy."

He really meant that. Or made a convincing act of it. It brought the flutter back to her belly.

"I won't complain about having a nice dinner made for me."

"That's what I like to hear. What are you doing this weekend?"

He poured the wine, and after she snuck a piece of her salmon to Ginger, they cleared the table, and since he'd cooked, she volunteered to clean up.

And for whatever reason he found it hot to watch her tidy up so why not?

Once they'd finished, they ended up in his living room, snuggled on his couch watching a movie.

His hand was up her shirt and he was explaining just what it was he planned to do with her, when his doorbell started ringing as someone pounded on the door.

Carmella jumped, startled, nearly falling off the couch. Laughing and cursing all at the same time, Duke caught her, sat her upright, and got to his feet.

"I'm going to ignore that."

As she was ready to have sex with the man, it wasn't as if she wanted to argue. But his friends were persistent and kept at it until it was clear he didn't have the option.

Carmella couldn't stop laughing, even though she doubted there'd be any sexytimes that night. "They're not going away."

"I'm going to kill someone," he muttered, heading to the door, opening it hard.

"What took you so long?" Carmella heard Mick say. "We have beer and wings." He walked into the living room, startled into stillness when he caught sight of Carmella on the couch.

"As you can see, I'm busy," Duke said as he came in with three more people. "Carm and I are watching a movie. We had dinner. Carmella, don't eat those or they'll stay forever!"

Carmella shrugged as she dug into one of the wings. "They're already here." If she made a big deal of it, it would only highlight their relationship. She'd grown up around guys like these. They were good-hearted and all, but they'd tease forever if they smelled blood in the water.

"See? *She's* cool with it." Mick sat next to her on the couch and Ginger poked her head around the corner, one ear flopped back as she caught sight of Mick and trotted over. "Hey, gorgeous. Come see me."

Pretty soon the room was full of big men spoiling her dog with love and pets. Duke was annoyed, but he'd given in.

By ten, though, they'd started playing video games and were still drinking beer so she figured it was best to head home. She needed to go to sleep and the last several nights had been hard enough.

"I should go home," she said to Duke quietly.

He tightened his arm around her shoulders. "What? No. Stay here. Stay the night. I'll make them leave."

She didn't spend the night with lovers. She had her own bed. And her own house and that's where she slept. She already explained this to him—sort of—before.

Carmella shook her head. "They're too drunk." She snorted a laugh. "I'll see you tomorrow. *At work.* Thanks for dinner."

Duke glowered at the men in his house but sighed.

"Fine, at least let me walk you home."

At her front door he paused. "So you didn't answer me earlier. What are you doing this weekend?"

She made the choice to give him a little more of her life. "I have to drop stuff at my mom's in the morning but I'll be done by nine. Why?"

"It's supposed to be gorgeous so a bunch of us are going out for a bike ride around the peninsula. Come along." He cocked his head, brushing the pad of his thumb over her bottom lip. "Summer's coming to a close. Not a lot of weekends left to get out for nice long rides left. I want to spend them with you."

She didn't quite know what to say. He touched her in a deep place that was so desolate, so lonely, that she found it hard not to respond. Not to *need* more of it.

"I'd like that."

He smiled, stepping close enough to bridge the gap between them. "Good. I'm sorry about my friends bursting in on us."

"Duke, it's part of who you are. Who they are. It comes with you. I know that. I need to get some sleep anyway. Thanks for dinner."

"I'm glad we worked this through." He kissed her then. Right on her doorstep. Over at his place she heard them oooooh and aaaaah so she knew his friends were watching.

Every one of her cells came to life. This was a public declaration, yes. But for her too. He knew that as he nipped her bottom lip, sucking it into his mouth.

Duke flipped them off and broke the kiss. "They're assholes. Just because they don't have women, they have to cockblock me." He pressed his lips to her ear. "But I bet you're wet right now, knowing they saw me with my mouth and hands on you."

A full body shiver went through her. "You're a cruel, cruel man."

His laugh was a caress. "I can't be the only one feeling this way. I'll see you tomorrow." He gave Ginger a last scritch behind the ear and stepped back, waiting for her to get inside before he went back home.

CHAPTER
Thirteen

Good morning, Carmella." Duke loped into her office and put a package on her desk. "Brought you a little something."

Presents? She tried to remain unhurried as she made her way over to the desk. "I was just about to make a pot of coffee in here. But if you can't wait, Asa skulked out of the break room not too long ago with a mug."

"He *totally* skulks. He denies it. Says he prowls. *Prowls?* Asshole." The entire time he spoke, he grinned.

"Sometimes he stalks. Usually if PJ is around." Then the very darkly handsome man kept his focus on his girlfriend. It was so hot to see that interplay between them, and while being with a man like Asa was way beyond Carmella's skill level, the two clicked perfectly. "Totally sexy."

Duke's grin turned into a glower and he kissed her. *Kissed. Her.* Right there in her office! It was lightning quick, but yes, the crazy man had kissed her at work.

"We talked about this." Carmella stepped around her desk, cutting off his access as she pulled the package toward her.

He raised one shoulder. "We did. But that doesn't mean I agree with anything you said. It's not a secret that we're together and I like that just fine. You should open that."

She gave him a severe look. One just for him and his lashes swept down as he closed his eyes briefly.

"It's my present. I'll open it when I'm ready," she teased.

He nearly made her faint after the smolder he sent her way. "I'm racing tonight. Come out to the track and then back home with me. We need to take up where we left off a million years ago."

She needed to change the subject before he talked her into doing god knew what right there in the office, so she pulled away the tissue paper and gasped when she pulled out a bag of whole bean Kona coffee. Her favorite, and a treat she allowed herself only a few times a year because it was so expensive. "I can't take this!"

He thought this was hilarious, getting even closer, squeezing behind her desk with her, blocking her in.

"Back up," she said, panic and delight warring inside her.

He shook his head. "Nope. See, you make this sound when you drink the coffee at my house. I like that sound. I've got a vested interest in hearing it more. Ergo, I thought to bring you a bag so that happens."

"This is like thirty bucks a pound!"

"That particular bag is forty-eight dollars. It's my money. I like to see you get all flushed with delight like you are right now. I won't say no if you want to offer me some, naturally."

"And you can see me from your office when I make it," she murmured. Man, he must have been a handful as a kid.

His grin widened. "I did think of that, yes. But I'm rarely in my office. I'll have to be sure to get in there more often so I can watch you."

"Or here's something, you can just go about your day and stop trying to cop a feel at work."

"Where's the fun in that?" He kissed her forehead and ducked away.

"Thank you," she said, turning quickly to prevent him from

coming in for another kiss. She headed over to make a pot of coffee, sighing happily when she opened the bag and the scent of the beans spilled out.

He'd even remembered she had a little grinder at work because she loved the ritual of grinding the beans as part of making coffee. That he noticed those details was so unexpectedly charming. Another aspect to his sexiness. He paid attention.

"You were about to say yes to coming out to watch me race tonight."

She loved cars and bikes and racing. But since she and Duke had been dating, that bevy of women friends at the track, several of them former...what? Flames? Sex partners? Just what did you call all this complicated stuff? In any case, it made her crazy. Which made her crazy in and of itself. She wasn't that person! So, then she had to pretend it didn't bother her and that was tiring.

But the thing that had her most unsure about going that night was that there were raggedy edges of that crowd at the track that felt a lot like the losers her mother had living with them over the time Carmella grew up.

Wild boys never grew up. They may be hot as hell and pretty decent in bed, but the ones like her ex left a mess for other people—usually women—to clean up. Being around that again wore on her. Though those guys weren't really part of the crew Twisted Steel hung with, they did have a spot right across from theirs so it was impossible not to see and be around.

She poured the water after measuring the coffee and started the pot, thinking about just what to say to him.

"This seems like one of those times when you're bothered by something and aren't telling me. I thought you liked racing?" Duke asked.

"I do. I'm tired, that's all. I was just thinking about everything I needed to do."

"Now see, this is a problem because I *know* this something you're not saying is about me. I might have to kiss you and rub all over you until you share and people will see."

Carmella nearly guffawed. "You're so spoiled."

"When you're around, I definitely am. Tell me why you're hesitating. Has someone said or done something to upset you?"

This was one of those moments where if she pushed him away, he'd stay away. She could tell. Or maybe it was more like she wanted to share, to open up a little, but it wasn't the right place.

"I really don't want to do this here. Or now. But it's nothing you do. I can say that."

"Fair enough. I do have a rear suspension issue I need to figure out. And a cup of coffee to drink after I hear that sound. I normally would ask you to lunch so we could talk, but I need to work through so I can finish that damned Chevy or die trying before quitting time. Stay home tonight if you want. Leave your kitchen light on if you're awake and I'll come over. Work for you?"

She nodded as the coffee finished up and she didn't even need to fake the nearly orgasmic sound of appreciation she made when she took that first sip.

Maybe she was the one who was spoiled.

Whatever the case, she wasn't going to overthink it. Much.

Duke tried to put whatever it was bothering Carmella out of his mind that morning and afternoon. But as he did his best thinking while he fiddled with a broken machine, it wasn't always easy. Mostly he let his brain go, gave over to that part of him that always just seemed to be able to figure out how to fix things.

But in the back of his mind, he thought about the track from her perspective. He knew she'd come out to racing events for years with her cousin Craig. In the months she'd worked at Twisted Steel, she'd become closer friends with PJ, and everyone at the shop seemed to love her just as much.

So it was nearly certainly something else.

"You have a client meeting at four," Carmella called out as she approached him some hours later.

"Oh shit. I forgot that was today."

"That's why I gave you an hour. Mick will be by soon enough to nudge you and Asa." She kept walking, pausing to speak to Asa.

Duke watched her as she listened to something Asa said. She put her hand on a hip and sent him a look and Asa's shoulders slumped, but he nodded his head.

Duke double-timed it to his office because his cock was so fucking hard he was sure it could be seen from space. God damn how he loved it when she gathered them all up like wayward ducklings and got them back on track.

He sure hoped her kitchen light was on that night when he got home.

Just ten minutes later she tapped on his door, poking her head in. "Asa says he'll handle the stuff about the undercarriage costs."

"He wants this project but this car isn't going to be easy. Or cheap. Oh, can you look at this and tell me what your handwriting says?" Duke pointed to a sticky note covered in impressively neat and legible handwriting.

When she moved around the desk to look, he slid around her to lock the door. He knew her liking to be watched thing had its limits but he wanted her so fiercely he seemed to throb with it.

When the lock clicked, she looked up.

If she had looked even the tiniest bit distressed or not into it in any way, he'd have written it off as a tease and unlocked.

Instead, she licked her lips but stayed where she was.

By the time he reached her—just four steps—that throb seemed to be thunder.

"You're sure?" he asked quietly.

It was only hot if they were both on board.

Carmella swallowed and then nodded.

He was on her in one more half step, sweeping her close so he could whisper in her ear. "We'll have to be quick. A down payment on whatever we do later tonight. And quiet."

His office had windows facing part of the shop floor and her space. But there was a blind spot, one he would sometimes situate himself in so he could get stuff done without being seen by anyone passing by.

That's where he moved her, his body against hers until they hit the corner where he'd placed a comfortable chair.

"So glad you're wearing a dress today." One-handed, he pushed the skirt up and then her panties down. He bit back a curse at how hot and slick she was when he parted her labia and played a finger through her pussy.

She sucked in a breath.

"Hands on the back of the chair," he whispered. Even though they needed to be fast and quiet, that didn't mean he needed to skimp on keeping her satisfied.

Slowly he circled her clit with a fingertip for a few breaths until she relaxed a little. Then he sped his pace, his touch firmer. Her body superheated around him.

Bent over her body, he spoke in her ear. "Hurry now, gorgeous. I need you to come before I fuck you."

Her strangled, whispered response tore at him, sent a pulse of pleasure through him that dragged him right to the doorstep of orgasm.

The scent of her filled his senses, and as she rained honey on his palm when she came, he used a free hand to get his cock out. Just the brush of his skin against his dick sent a shiver through him.

"Now that you're nice and wet," he muttered, rolling a condom on quickly, "we can move to the next step." He thrust into her pussy and she exhaled loudly enough that he put a hand over her mouth. And her cunt got so hot around him he knew she liked that very much.

"Ahh. I see."

He kept his strokes deep and hard. Not fast, but relentless. The entire thing was so ridiculously hot and a little taboo that he was already incredibly turned on.

She squirmed against him, her breath against his palm. Jesus, she was going to kill him.

But first he was going to come. Really fucking hard. It gathered in the soles of his feet and then seemed to rush up his body and out his cock in wave after wave of pleasure so intense the muscles on the backs of his legs jumped.

He buried his face in her neck as he groaned as quietly as possible.

Years he'd had that office and he'd never had sex in it. Not a single time. Clearly he'd been waiting for the perfect woman to have it with because holy shit he was never going to look at that chair without the memory of this moment ever again.

"I'll see you later," she said once she'd gotten herself back in order and headed out to her office.

Her smile, though, damn. She got off on that little interlude as much as he did. Carmella Rossi was perfect for him. She just needed to see that herself.

CHAPTER
Fourteen

Carmella got up early on Saturday to run the pills and some food over to her mom's.

The house was quiet as she let herself in. Given the general state of the place, her mother hadn't come home the night before.

"Too early to be alarmed," Carmella muttered as she put the pills in their usual spot. The others had been taken, but there was no evidence of a problem so she took that for a win.

The dog was also missing, which hopefully meant her mother had it with her, so at least Carmella didn't need to deal with a snarly, enraged houseguest and Ginger pouting for a week.

A check of the fridge when she dropped the food off showed nothing too abnormal. The usual cans of diet soda, some cheese. Virgie had eaten most of the stuff Carmella had left for her earlier in the week. No empties in the recycling.

Refusing to worry about it, she left a note for her mother on the fridge and headed out, stopping by the pharmacy to grab some sunscreen on her way home. A day out riding meant she'd have a sunburn on her cheeks and nose if she wasn't careful.

When she pulled up at her house, Duke was already in his driveway with his motorcycle and several dudes around it and a few other bikes.

PJ was there and she called out Carmella's name, waving. Pleased, Carmella waved back. A few days ago she'd gone to drinks with PJ and her friends and Duke came to pick her up and then they'd gone to Dick's and had burgers and milkshakes, just the two of them.

It had been silly and wonderful.

The night had ended with amazing sex in his front hallway because the bedroom seemed too far at the time.

Never ever in her life had she given over to the sort of unrestrained sensuality that lived in her belly. Except with him. Duke made her feel wild and free, and because she didn't know how not to be freaked out by that, she didn't think about it and went for just feeling it instead.

Before she could say anything, Duke looked up and froze Carmella in place when his gaze landed on her.

Ever since their make-up on Monday, he'd been very intense and there was no denying they were seeing one another.

At work he just sidled up to her when they spoke. At first he might try to keep it cool, but soon enough one corner of his mouth would turn up and he'd compliment her. Or proposition her. Both sometimes. He saved her a seat next to him in the break room, or would shove people out of the way to get to her. He maintained that easygoing thing, but he was being really clear that he *liked her* liked her.

And that didn't even take into account the fact that they'd had sex *in his office* that week too. Honestly, the man stole her wits. Heaven knew what he'd have her agreeing to next. But she probably would enjoy it, so there was that.

He loped over, meeting her halfway.

"Hey there."

"Mr. Bradshaw."

He pulled her into a hug, kissing her quick. "Errands go okay?"

"Yep. I'm going to change and be right back, all right?"

"We'll be here. Still waiting on a few people so take your time. But hurry anyway because I like looking at you."

She rolled her eyes, blushing, and went into the house.

Duke loved to take his bike out for long rides. This trip around the Olympic Peninsula was one he often hit with his friends during the summer and early fall.

He'd never done it with a woman on the back of his bike. And he'd surely never done it with *his* woman on the back of his bike.

Carmella was at home on a motorcycle, which was utterly clear by the way she rode. She didn't hang on too hard, though she was close enough that he felt the warmth of her against his back.

Enough to make it feel like the best Saturday ride he'd ever taken.

"Is it weird for you?" Duke asked Asa as they stood at an overlook, the scent of salt water and pine all mixed up to perfection.

"You're going to need to be more specific than that. I generally disapprove of most things so everything is weird for me."

Duke laughed. "Belonging to someone. Like a few months ago, even though I knew Carmella and was hot for her, I saw other women all the time. Looked. Touched as often as I wanted. And now?"

"Now there are plenty of other women, but none of them matter to you like just one does. And you can try to tell yourself it'll wane. Lessen with time if you just give yourself over to the company you are far more comfortable with." Asa's gaze shifted from Duke to PJ for a moment and then back to the churning, cold water in the distance.

"Yes. Now I feel, I don't know what to call it. Not chained, because that's a negative. But bound? And more than that, none of those other women is Carmella." Duke shrugged. "It's not like I don't see beauty all around me. It's more like nothing else can compare to her. To what she makes me feel. And then I say to myself that I've only been with her a short period of time so how can I know such a thing?"

Mick, who'd been standing on Duke's other side, sighed with so much emotion, both Asa and Duke started, turning to face their friend.

"Something you want to share?" Asa asked.

"Love is fucking love. That's it. You can know something immediately. Sometimes it takes years to know it. Do you love her?" Mick asked.

"Yes."

"You didn't even hesitate," Mick said. "You answered without a second thought. So, I'm going to say this, you love her and that's what you know. There can be myriad ways to go from this point. But you can't unlove her. No matter how she feels. Eventually, if she never reciprocates, your love can wane. Or so I'm told."

"Dude, you're blowing my fucking mind with all this wisdom and you're telling us some shit you have held close for however long. Jesus, I need a beer for this day," Duke said, shoving a hand through his hair.

"To answer your previous question, Duke," Asa interrupted. "It's not weird to belong to someone. It's awesome. It's the best thing I've ever felt and I've felt a lot of great shit. It's one of the few non-weird things in the world, in my opinion. Now you, Mick. Who is he? This guy you love and can't stop loving?"

"It's a she," Mick replied.

Mick was openly bisexual and had been since he was a teenager, so Duke wasn't surprised that a woman was a possibility. But Duke had only ever seen his friend with men for longer than a night or some flirtation.

"And a he. Probably. It's so complicated I don't even know where to start. But I know right now isn't the time. I just ... accept what you feel, Duke. Don't run from it because it seems so big and scary you can't make heads or tails of it sometimes," Mick said to Duke. "Don't you look at Asa and PJ and want that too?"

Duke nodded. He wasn't sure when he'd gone from looking at relationships as something other people did recreationally, to something pretty freaking amazing when it was a real connection like the one their friend had with PJ.

"Look, I'm not going to evangelize on the wonder of being in love with a person who knows you to the bone and loves you anyway. Or of being with someone who works the way you do, wants to build something with you. Huh." Asa stopped speaking and then tipped his chin at Duke. "I guess I just did. The right person is everything."

PJ called out that they were hungry and wanted lunch so the talk needed to end. But when Duke turned around, he saw Carmella, her hair dancing in the wind now that she'd removed the scarf she'd worn under her helmet.

She was his right person. Whether he was her right person or not, he couldn't control. Which freaked him out a little. That's what he had to figure through.

Carmella smiled at him as he approached. "I need to carry PJ with me everywhere I go. The woman gets shit done."

Mick bounded up and handed Carmella something. A bright red crab fridge magnet.

She looked it over, delighted.

"I got it for you at that last gas stop. To commemorate today." Mick winked at her and she blushed.

Duke watched her, greedy for her joy at such a small thing.

"Thank you."

"Do you collect them?" Mick teased.

"Crabs? Or magnets?"

"I know someone who collects thimbles from different places she goes. Some people do mugs. Like that," Mick explained.

"Oh! I hadn't thought of that. How fun." She tucked the

magnet into one of the saddlebags on Duke's bike. He'd chosen the Harley, which had a more comfortable seat for her. It gave him an excuse to have two bikes, which worked out. He'd take the BMW when he went on solo rides.

Suddenly he realized he had a lot of wonderful shit in his future with this woman. As she got close, Duke hugged her and her initial surprise melted away as she returned the embrace.

"Let's get you fed." He handed her the helmet after she put the scarf over her hair once more. When she slid her sunglasses into place, the beauty of her was a punch. "You sure are pretty."

"You're really nice to have around."

He swallowed back that fear and chose the happiness instead.

"I eat a lot more now that I hang out with you guys. I'm not sure I can keep this up without gaining fifty pounds," Carmella said lazily from her place on the blanket.

They'd picked up a ridiculous amount of freshly steamed crab and mussels, along with every side imaginable, and had set up on a nearby stretch of beach to eat their feast.

By that point, she lay sprawled in the sunshine, full and happy.

"Asa can drink two milkshakes a day and still be hard and flat. Not exceptionally fair, but then again, look at him," PJ said. "My theory is all the adrenaline keeps them fit."

"So racing and fisticuffs is slimming?"

Duke laughed from his place next to her. "It's the new diet revolution."

"This explains so much." Carmella kept her eyes closed, but she smiled, knowing he watched her features.

Clifton used to watch her too. But in a calculated way. She hadn't seen that for months, and when she finally did, she'd been married to him and didn't want to just walk away without bothering to try.

Carmella knew Duke was different from her ex on just about

every level, but the way Duke treated her was the biggest difference. He made her feel listened to. Which she supposed was why she'd been so hurt about the argument over the pills. He hadn't listened then. But he'd taken responsibility and apologized for it.

He was really close to perfect.

Another area she didn't want to get near at that point. Not yet. So she shoved it away and let herself have the day with her friends. She didn't have a lot of these in her life.

At least not until Duke had burst into her life the way he had. Which was funny for such a slow-talking dude who rarely seemed to get mad. But he was bigger than life and she got caught up in his gravity every time.

Being with Duke was playing with fire and she did it anyway. Which was probably why it always felt so good.

"I guess I'm failing to understand, but the idea of getting punched for fun seems to miss the entire point of recreation to start with," Carmella said.

"Probably a lucky thing for your potential opponent. In my experience with you, I imagine you'd get in there and tear shit up. It's always the little ones." Duke dropped down to kiss her.

"What? You don't tear shit up when you fight?"

"Do you want to see it for yourself?" Duke asked quietly.

Did she? Did she want to watch Duke beat someone up or get beaten up? Was this any different from the losers she tried to get away from?

"Maybe."

Carmella didn't want to think about it. About how if it wasn't different from those guys, then why did it make her excited? The idea of watching all the nice guy Duke worn away to the badass underneath zinged through her.

And what did that make her then? Like Virgie? Like she was with Clifton at first? It *felt* different, but was she lying to herself the way her mother did to enable her addiction to shitty men with no job and a predilection for prison?

All through this panicked internal monologue, Duke watched her like he knew exactly what she was thinking. And he let her process without pushing. Not speaking to make his case or sweet-talk her off the subject.

"Let's get back on the road, folks," Mick called out from where he stood with some of the other guys from the shop.

Her friends.

Duke stood, giving her a hand up, and when she stood, he kissed her temple. "Ready to ride? This next stretch is a longer one, so if you need to stop, let me know, okay?"

Beyond words for a moment, she just nodded with a smile.

CHAPTER
Fifteen

Come to the track tonight," PJ said as she came into Twisted Steel the following Wednesday.

"Uh..."

PJ just stared at her. "Did something bad happen when you went before? Did someone say or do something? If so, you need to tell me. I can get it to the guys if you don't want to tell them yourself."

Carmella looked out to the shop floor and back toward Asa and Duke's offices to be sure no one was near enough to overhear. "Normally I'd just say nothing was wrong and shoo you away. But *you* don't shoo away."

PJ snickered. "I'll have you know I'm persistent. It's a winner's quality."

"It's something. That's for sure." But Carmella pointed to the coffeemaker. "Want some?"

Five minutes later with coffee and a snack, Carmella knew she'd stalled all she could. "This is totally petty. I know it. But the women there. All the time."

"Petty? Hell no. I understand it as it's the same for me too," PJ said.

"You've been with Asa for over a year and a half, though. And

Asa scowls all the time. He only softens up when he looks at you. Duke? He's sweet and charming like a naughty little boy. He's all slow and sexy."

"You have a point that Duke's genial charm is sexy. And that it makes everyone feel welcome to get close. But he's like that with all of them. Women from two to a hundred and two. It's his base setting. It's like breathing for him. But with you he's real. He's all about Carmella. Everyone knows that."

"Everyone, huh?"

PJ scoffed. "Yes. Everyone. By the way, you'd be surprised at how hot women find that taciturn guy thing. I have to deal with it too. It comes with being with a beautiful man."

"*You* get jealous?" Carmella asked, astounded.

"Well, no. Let me tell you why. Once I was with Asa, I was with him. I never doubted his commitment to me. Things happen sometimes. People break up. But I knew in my heart that he wouldn't disrespect me that way. He's got honor and so does Duke. And also, there's something else, not just the women."

Carmella frowned. "Just weird childhood issues."

"Do you feel unsafe at the track?" PJ's concern made Carmella feel bad.

"I'm not really...I don't know how to casually share stuff," Carmella said.

"You don't have to now if you really don't want to. I promise I won't be upset if you truly don't want to talk about it. I care about you. You're my friend and so I want you to feel like you can tell me stuff. I'd never betray a confidence."

Carmella sighed and chose to share her unease with the group of guys who reminded her so much of the losers her mom allowed into their life.

"I'm so sorry about that. I try to ignore them. They just seemed like loud douchebags. Admittedly, being with Asa and having people know that means I get less trouble than others might deal with."

"I'm not...threatened. Not really. It's just an ugly reminder sometimes," Carmella said. "Duke let me avoid it last week without pushing too hard on my reasons."

"That won't last. They go every week. He knows you went to the track before. He's going to want you there or know why not. He's got the heart of a protector," PJ said.

Carmella knew that too.

She changed the subject. "Have you ever gone to this fight club thing?"

"I'm too queasy for it. Not so much I can't appreciate how hot it is when he comes home and he's raring to go if you know what I mean. I have seen him drag around an asshole like he was garbage and literally toss the guy into the street after he insulted me. Just between us? It was so hot I wanted to jump him right there. If you're with Duke, you're going to see him in a fight at some point. They make trouble like it's their job." PJ grinned.

"Bad boys are great until they aren't anymore."

"Ha. Jerks who pretend to be bad boys are not the same as the kind of bad boy Asa and Duke are. Take a chance on him. I'm biased because I love Duke to death and I think he deserves it. But you're good for him."

"Maybe. It's hard to let go once you've been burned a time or two."

PJ nodded. "I get that. But I hope you come out to the track tonight. Hang out with us. You're like a refreshing estrogen shot after all that testosterone we have around already. And if those jerks give you any trouble, we'll handle it once and for all. It has the added bonus of you being with Duke in public some more. Which means it'll be clear you're together. Most everyone will back off. The rest don't matter anyway."

It did sound like fun. And watching Duke race was really hot. He'd be all worked up afterward too, which would tally in her favor.

"If he asks, I'll come along." That way it would be up to Duke and she wouldn't be assuming anything.

PJ rolled her eyes. "You know you have a standing invitation to go because he's been broadcasting that you two are seeing one another on all channels."

"Do you feel like this is a little like high school? Like I'm going to ask you if he talks about me in fourth period."

"I know. But . . . isn't that part of what makes it all so wonderful? That tingly, oh my god this guy really does it for me, this is new and fantastic and wow the sex! It's supposed to make you a little giggly," PJ said.

Wow the sex was right.

"You probably have a point. I'll probably see you later at the track," Carmella told PJ. "In the meantime, Asa just caught sight of you up here with me and he's headed this way."

PJ turned, just watching her man as he came to her. "He's incredible. You can admit it to me. I won't hold it against you."

Carmella laughed. "Asa is a very fine example of gorgeous man. Absolutely no lie." But she preferred blond with a little gray salted through to black. The rockabilly way Duke wore his hair to Asa's. Duke seemed to flow into a room and fill it with sexy. Asa sort of crackled with his sexuality.

Carmella would take Duke any day. Asa's intensity would exhaust her.

Just an hour later Duke came in with a new client pack and a huge, satisfied smile.

"I don't even need to ask if it was a good meeting. I can see it was."

He headed to the big whiteboard calendar on the wall nearby. "If everything goes as it should, I think we'll be delivering a very fine 'fifty-six Jaguar—drophead coupe—in the new showroom. Maybe even the first week we're open over there. It gives me a chance to rehab the rack and pinion. It's a total mess."

"I can't wait to see it. Mick will get me all the timeline stuff so he and I will handle things on our end," Carmella said, entering the new client information into her system as she spoke to him.

"Thank you. Tonight is race night. You should come along. Cheer for Twisted Steel."

Pleased he asked, she looked up from her screen. "I was hoping you'd ask."

"I should hope I don't need to ask. I always want you to come to the track. I've been trying to give you some space to get used to me and my friends." Duke propped his hip against her desk, his cock pretty much at eye level. "Stop looking at me like that or I'm going to be really fucking uncomfortable when I have to hobble back out to work."

Carmella flicked her gaze up to his face. "You can't just put it there and then say I can't look at it. Jeez. I'm only human."

"You really know what to say today, you know that? Want to catch a ride to the track with me?"

That meant she'd be at the mercy of someone else when it came to leaving. She wasn't there yet.

"I'm actually stopping by my aunt and uncle's house tonight after work. I'll meet you out there, though."

"Deal. I'll keep an eye out for you."

She hadn't lied. She really did promise her uncle that she'd stop by to see him and her aunt that night. It had been about two weeks since she'd seen them last and she missed them. The older they got, the more it became real that at some point she'd lose them. So Carmella tried to keep that in mind whenever she had an opportunity to spend time with them.

After running home to drop Ginger off and change her clothes, Carmella made the quick trip to the house she considered as much her childhood home as any she'd ever shared with her mother.

Carmella parked and followed the noise of Salazars until she found them all in the kitchen and living room, arguing over a baseball game.

At the sight of her, she was hailed to come all the way in and greeted with hugs and kisses.

"You look very pretty tonight." Her aunt looked her over carefully. Carmella should have known she'd notice date makeup and clothing. "Why didn't you bring the dog?"

"I'm going out after I leave here so she's at home. She was at work with me all day so it's not like she's lonely."

"A date going out?" her uncle interrupted.

"I thought you were watching the game?" Carmella teased.

"I can do both. So is this a date?" He'd be a bulldog now. And her aunt already stationed herself at his side so getting out of telling them wasn't an option.

"Yes. I'm going out with Duke Bradshaw. I've been seeing him."

"Your boss?" The tone of her aunt's voice told Carmella she'd have to assuage some concerns.

"It's okay. I mean, yes, he's my boss. And yes, I know it could be complicated. He knows that too. But I have a job offer if this goes bad. I'm not dependent on him for anything."

"He's a really decent guy," Craig added. "He worries for her. Is protective. And if he messes with her, I'll know before Carmella can hide the evidence."

Carmella snorted but her uncle nodded, assured they could hide the body should it be needed.

"I appreciate the backup. But really, things are fine." After she said it, Carmella realized how true it was. She was dating someone she liked. Someone with a real life. Someone who seemed to truly listen when she spoke. A real-life, normal, adult-type relationship.

"Carmella, we didn't step in with that moron you married and it got you hurt. We won't hold our tongues again." Carmella's

uncle felt guilty about how Clifton had been. But it wasn't anything to do with them at all. Clifton was a con man and a petty
thug. Everyone liked him. At first.

It was nice they cared, though.

"And I love you for it." She hugged her aunt and then her
uncle. "But I do mean it. He's not Clifton. Or even in the same
universe. I'm not saying we won't break up. I'm saying he won't
abuse me or steal from me. He doesn't need to do those things.
And truthfully? I don't think it would ever occur to him to do
that to anyone."

"It's about time you figured out how much better life is with a
man like that." Her aunt's look made Carmella hug her.

"Anyway, it's just a date. Nothing serious so let's not obsess on
it until I make a mess out of it."

Her uncle indicated the table. "Hush you. You're just fine. Sit
down a minute. We need to talk."

Carmella's amusement slid away to dread. "Ugh. What? Just
tell me in one quick burst. Like taking a wax strip off."

"I got a call today from your mother." Her uncle was trying to
keep his features bland, but this wouldn't be happening if there
weren't something big to say.

"Is she okay?" Her mom had been absent the last few times
Carmella had come to drop off food and meds. But nothing had
appeared to indicate she'd deteriorated to the point Carmella
needed to worry. She figured there was a new man of the loserish
variety keeping Virgie busy.

Her uncle waved a hand. "Your mother will always be okay.
She knows how to land on her feet. It's you I worry for." He paused
and then went on in a burst of words. "Steven is out of prison and
she claims they're reconciling. I wanted you to hear it from us
first."

Carmella sighed as her stomach dropped. "I should have
known. She wasn't home the last few times I went by to check

on her. I figured she was just sucked up into some new guy. But really she's avoiding me."

Her uncle nodded. "I imagine so, yes. But she knows I'll tell you so I did her dirty work for her. Burns me up when she does that. I got mad, told her she should be the one to give this info to you. If he's around now, him too."

Carmella shook her head. "You can't make her grow up and face reality. Who knows about Steven?"

Her uncle rolled his eyes. "I can say the same to you, Carmella. And that doesn't stop you from trying. Be aware. You know how she is when he's around. Let her make her own mistakes for a change. You don't need to swoop in and clean up the mess."

"And you know there will be a mess when he's done. The two of them are terrible for one another," her aunt said to her husband and Carmella both. "How can she ever learn if you two are always taking care of her mistakes?"

"She's my mother. For all her faults. For all her screwups. What if this time she makes a mistake too big to fix on her own and she ends up dead? Sure, I can tell myself that she brought it on herself. And I'd be right. But I'd also know I didn't help her when I knew she was in trouble."

She took her aunt's and uncle's hands in hers.

"I love her." Carmella shrugged. "She's not malicious. Just weak."

"It's not your job, though!" Craig nearly shouted and Carmella turned to face her cousin as he continued speaking. "Jesus, Carm. What will ever be enough for her? You can't fix her. She's just going to spill her crap into your life again. And those of us who love you will have to watch your heart get broken. Again. If you can't do it for *you*, how about *us*, huh? She's going to suck you dry and nothing will change for her. She used up her life a long time ago and now she's stealing yours."

"Is this an intervention or something like that?" Carmella looked to the three of them.

"No. We know you're going to do what you want to do. And we love you for it even though we're scared for you. Even though you deserve better from her." Craig hugged her and sat back down.

Her uncle nodded, reaching out to pat his son's arm before returning his attention to Carmella. "Will you please, *please* just try to remember to protect yourself? You can't fix him either."

Steven Hay was a fuckup just like Virgie was. In his way he adored Virgie, but in his way he was also a loser with a heavy hand, a problem with excesses of all sorts and a taste for gambling that led to interactions with law enforcement when he turned to crime to pay various people to keep himself afloat.

For a few short stretches of her childhood, he'd been good. Sober. He kept the bills paid as a mechanic, which was how he'd met Virgie originally. He was good with his hands.

He'd lived with them and things had been okay. They'd had real Christmases. Her mother's emotional state had been fairly even. But eventually, he'd find his way to a bar with his buddies and then the gambling would start. He'd spiral, and as he did, Virgie would too.

He'd tried to con Carmella the last time he'd been out of prison. Full of promises that he wanted to be a father to her. Lots of apologies. Predictably he'd failed, which landed him a three-year stretch that apparently ended at two and a half or so.

Carmella really was so lucky to have her aunt and uncle in her life. It was nice to be protected. To know they watched out for her. "I gave him enough chances. I'm not her. I'm done with Steven. Her, I owe. Him I don't. In any case, you warned me. I appreciate that you care about me and don't want me to get hurt. Really, more than you guys can ever understand, your concern and love saves me all the time. I promise to be as careful as I can. I'm not trying to get between them. She'll only close off and stop taking her medication. He'll leave and she'll spend months trying to find her way back to normal."

"You're wasted in an office. You should be a therapist," Craig told her.

"Numbers make sense. Numbers have rules. I like that." She had enough uncertainty in her life. Her job was one place in her life where things made sense.

She stayed awhile longer, enjoying the visit, and after telling Craig she'd probably see him at the track, she headed over.

If Steven was back and her mother told her uncle first, Carmella could only imagine her mother's physical and emotional state. All she could do was hope for the best and be prepared for the worst.

Which was easier said than done, but Carmella would keep trying.

CHAPTER
Sixteen

High off racing, Duke wrenched himself from the driver's seat and into the arms of his team, who shouted their congratulations.

This part was awesome and normally he'd soak it up awhile longer. But all he could think about was Carmella. He scanned the group until he caught the red of her hair.

He held a hand out and she came forward and into his arms for a hug.

"Congratulations. That was some badass driving," Carmella told him as they broke apart.

Asa had already raced a heat so it was time to celebrate and shoot the shit with everyone over at their tent.

"I'm starved. Come on. Let's have a beer and some fish and chips."

"Is that what we're having tonight?" Carmella asked as she allowed him to tuck her against his side for the walk away from the track and pits and into the grassy field that held several tents filled with people and food from all the various teams and shops in the area.

"I thought it sounded really tasty when they suggested it." Duke and Asa hired a few different caterers and food trucks on a rotating basis for these race nights.

"You thought right." Though she smiled, Carmella had lines around her mouth. Lines she hadn't had earlier that day when he saw her last.

"Everything okay?" he asked her quietly before they went in to join their friends.

"Things are...weird. But this"—she waved a hand between them—"is just fine."

"I like that last part. But I don't like the first stuff. You want to get out of here? Talk in private?" he asked.

Carmella shook her head. "No. Let's see our friends. You raced and won. They're going to want to celebrate with you. And you want to celebrate with them. That's what this is about."

He stopped her from going inside, pulling her back to his body. "Will you talk to me later then? Share with me whatever is bothering you?" He hadn't really accepted how much he needed her to do just that until the words spilled from his lips.

She must have heard it in his tone. "Yes. Later tonight or whenever we're alone next and you want to know."

"I always want to know." He kissed her against a mouth that smiled and he considered the kiss and the agreement to share a victory.

Inside the tent their friends waited, already eating, drinking, and talking shit. It filled Duke with a sense of belonging that was the best sort of anchor.

He guided her to where Asa stood with Mick and PJ and some of PJ's friends. He hadn't really expected it when they all moved past him to give Carmella a hug and welcome her.

The surprised pleasure on her face was even better than winning the race. He'd have to make sure to thank PJ privately for the way she'd reached out.

"Okay, back off. I promised fish and chips and a beer to this lady and I keep my promises," he said, putting an arm around her waist.

"Perfect timing then. We're expecting several orders of both to arrive any moment now," PJ said. "Nice racing tonight, by the way."

The talk quickly turned to racing and cars as the food and drinks arrived. Music started up in the background and the night got started in earnest.

Normally Duke would stick around, chat up some women, maybe go home with one. At the very least drink a lot more and hang out a lot longer. But he found himself noting the strain on Carmella's features as things got louder and louder.

"Are you feeling all right?" he asked her.

"No. I'm tired. I'm going to head home. You stay and have a good time."

He just stared at her. "Really? Is that who you think I am? Who you think you are to me? *Oh sure, go home. Hope you feel better. I'll just hang and drink.*"

She crossed her arms over her chest, which cheered him because a bit of her spark showed through.

"I'm trying to be *nice*."

"Well, stop it. We're here together. I drove in with Asa so I could ride home with you. It was going to be all fancy and sneaky but that's not necessary now. Let's say our good-byes and get going. I'm not going to argue with you so you might as well just give in. I'm worth it." He bent to kiss her, resting his forehead against hers afterward. "Let me in a little."

She shuddered against him and then relaxed, sliding her arms around his waist.

"Okay."

They said their good-byes and headed to her truck, where he took her keys. "I'm going to drive and you're going to tell me what's up."

He worried she was going to hold back, even after she'd appeared to acquiesce earlier.

"My dad is out of prison."

That was unexpected.

"He got early release for good behavior."

"Should I be worried about your safety?" Duke tightened his hands on the steering wheel as he navigated through the parking lot and up the road toward the freeway.

"No. He's not interested in me. It's just that he and my mom have this...intense relationship. He does all this damage and walks away but she's going to be fucked up."

"I thought they were divorced. Isn't she remarried?"

Carmella's laugh was bitter. "She married two other dudes, but every time Steven gets out of jail or prison, he comes for her and she drops whatever to be with him. Surprise surprise, turns out most people don't like it when their spouse lets her ex-husband who also happens to be an ex-con take up residence in the living room. Or worse, takes off with him for weeks at a time."

Her mother sounded like a real piece of work.

"So he's out and back in Seattle? Your mother is with him again?"

"She called my uncle to tell him they were together again and could he let me know. It's fine. I'll handle it like I always do. But tonight I guess I just hit a wall. I know you were having fun. I'm sorry you have to leave."

"Oh my god, shut up about that. There are no shortages of opportunities to drive fast machines and drink with my friends afterward. I'm here now because I want to be. I'd rather be with you. And I'm sort of proud that you finally told me all this even though it sucks and I'm sorry you're experiencing it. What are you going to do?"

"I'll keep on monitoring her medication and emotional health the best I can. She'll hide from me awhile because she knows she's making a bad choice and I won't lie to her. Him? Who knows? It depends on what version of a guy fresh out of the joint he's on. Like, is this the 'I found God' version? I've been through that one a time or two. There's angry and resentful guy, he's good at that one. Fake penitent twelve-step guy too. He may even believe what he's saying when he says it. But eventually he'll break her heart and I'll pick up the pieces and put her back together."

"Why is that your job?" What a fucked-up, upside-down dynamic. Something like that could bleed a person dry. He really didn't like that Carmella had to deal with it.

"Because there's no one else to do it. That's how things work sometimes."

Fair enough. And true enough too.

"No one else can help you? Or her? Your uncle is her brother, right?"

Carmella sighed. "She won't listen to him. He tries. I'm the only one she listens to really."

"What the hell, Carm? Why are you trying to mother your own mother? You can't go on like this. She's taking advantage."

She made a sound, an unhappy sound.

"What? Are you mad at *me*?" Duke asked, pissed off at the situation enough for both of them. A parent was supposed to do the taking care of, not the kid. People took advantage when someone had a heart as big as Carmella's.

"You don't know what you're talking about. It is what it is. You can wish it was something else, but wishes don't do anything. Wishes won't change the situation. If I don't help her, who will? Would you let your mother suffer?"

"Well, no. But..." Duke didn't speak the next words he'd been thinking.

Instead, she did. "But she's a nice, upper-middle-class woman who doesn't run off with ex-cons who have bigger problems than her own? Your mom isn't broken and doesn't use pills to soften that? Good for you. Good for her. But these are *my* shoes. I didn't ask for them, but I walk in them nonetheless. You don't know my life so how can you judge it that way?"

He wasn't used to people pushing back. Or if he was being truly fair, he avoided getting into heavy conversations with women he was sleeping with. But she wasn't a woman he fucked. Carmella was so much more and she had a whole lot on her plate. Way more than he'd imagined, and the last thing he wanted to do was hurt her or make her regret sharing with him.

"You're right. I don't know your life. I'm learning and thank you for sharing with me. I'm sorry if I was a jerk. I care about you and got pissed that you had to shoulder this. I didn't mean to make it worse."

She was quiet awhile. "Apology accepted."

"Good. To be honest, my mother is indeed upper middle class. She worked very hard to smooth out anything but that in her accent. You'd never know she started out working in a factory at fifteen. But I would help her, yes. And no, I wouldn't let her suffer." He'd shed blood for his family, biological and otherwise. He should have known Carmella would be the same. "Can I help you? Take some of the weight off your shoulders?"

"Thanks, but no. You have a business to run. You don't need to worry about this stuff. It's happened before. It'll happen again. I keep hoping she'll get past this. Finally break it off with him for real. Or that he really did change this time. But I'm old enough to know that's not going to happen. So I deal in the reality I have."

"I have big shoulders. You can use them any time you need them. Got me? I understand you have this dynamic with your mother. And I accept that you know best in how to handle it. But I'm not too busy for you. Ever."

She sucked in a breath and then exhaled slowly. "Thanks."

The rest of the drive she was quiet, but the tension of earlier had passed, and by the time he parked at her place, she'd perked up a little and he just wanted to hold her until everything was better.

And fix the timing and check the transmission on her truck.

"Come on. Let's get you home and tucked in." He led her up to her doorstep and went in first. Ginger didn't seem alarmed so Duke relaxed a little. Carmella had said her father wasn't interested in her, but if she was a way to get to the mother, or if Carmella was being far kinder than she should be to the man, Duke wanted to be vigilant.

"I'm sorry you had to leave." She stopped herself and he smiled as she put her hands up the way he sometimes did with her. "Just a slip of the tongue. I'm working on it." It was hard not to apologize all the time. But she was indeed working on it.

"I just want to hold you until you fall asleep. Then I'll lock up and head home. I promise."

"Sometimes, Duke? You're so perfect and you say exactly the right thing and I get really freaked out." Carmella hadn't meant to share in that level of detail, but once it was out, she was glad she had.

He led her to the bedroom. "Perfect, huh? Can I remind you of this the next time I fuck up and you're mad at me?" He shrugged a shoulder and winced.

"What's wrong?"

"My back. I screwed it up when I was in the army. Tonight during the race I moved wrong probably. I'll take some pain reliever when I get home."

Carmella pointed to the bed. "Shirt and pants off."

"Uh? Okay."

"I'm going to give you a massage. If you want a happy ending, we'll discuss that after."

He laughed, giving her a hug. "I like you a hell of a lot, Carmella."

He was incorrigible. She kissed him quickly and pointed at the bed again. "I like you too. Now, clothes off, on the bed facedown."

"This is supposed to be about you," Duke said as he pulled his shirt off and all his ink was bared to her.

"Trust me, Duke. I am all on board with what I'm looking at." At his saucy grin she just laughed.

"At least tell me you get naked too." He shucked the rest of his clothes. "I always want a happy ending. I can tell you that up front." He got on the bed.

"You're so full of it. It's lucky for you that you're gorgeous and talented with your hands." She pulled her pants off, but left the shirt and panties as she scrambled atop his body, resting her ass on the backs of his thighs.

Carmella gave in, sliding her palms all over his back and shoulders, just getting a feel for his muscles. There was a knot she found and circled slowly. "This here?"

"Yes." He groaned.

She poured a little almond oil into her palm and slowly began to work her fingers and the heels of her hands into the bunched-up muscles across his back and up his spine.

Carmella let the rhythm of it lull her. Over the minutes, the knot got smaller and his muscles looser. And weirdly enough, she felt closer to him. Like the trust she'd allowed had deepened after the way he'd given over to her touch.

"Where'd you learn that?" he asked lazily into her pillow. "You're so good at it. I don't want to move for an hour."

She kissed his neck as she dropped to lie next to him on the bed. "I was taking an accounting class at North Seattle Community College during my senior year of high school. You know one of those tech credit things? They had a variety of community enrichment-type classes and one of them was massage. So I took it." To have a few more nights a week away from her house as well.

"Cool. A plus. You told me something else about yourself." He turned his face her way.

"I'm not trying to be mysterious. You tell me something now."

He was quiet for a bit before he started speaking. "Like what?"

"You said you loved living near the beach but you enlisted. Why? Why leave that behind to go to war?"

"Truthfully?"

She nodded. "Yes. That's always my answer to that question. The truth might hurt, but lies are worse."

"Good to know. I agree, by the way. I'm not like my siblings. They grew up in a world where they never remember the way our parents had to struggle. They grew up accepting that college was a reality. I came to that too late for it to change me the way it had them. I loved surfing and the beach and all that stuff. But I wasn't at home there. I thought the army would be a way for me to get my shit straight so I could come back and start my professional life. I just...well you can't really know what it's like until you're there."

"The military? War? Or the Middle East?"

"The army was okay. It had rules. I grew up with rules. I was expected to be resourceful to get the job done. I liked that. They appreciated my mechanical skills. Rewarded them even. I didn't mind that, though I hated the loss of my personal freedom. Iraq was hot. Really, really hot. The people, the ones who were caught in the middle? They were amazing despite all the chaos."

He was silent awhile and she thought maybe she'd pushed too far. "You don't have to say anything else if you don't want to." She heard the pain in his voice and realized she'd taken him being in the military more casually than she should have. He was decorated, had seen a lot. She shouldn't go stirring up his bad memories.

He smiled, still on his belly with her beside him. "No, this is good. War sucks. It sucks no matter what or where or why.

But we were out there on the ragged edge. Every week there were firefights. People got injured and killed all the time. It ages you. It makes you wary and suspicious. These nineteen-year-olds get there and within three months they look ten years older. It was hard not to get cynical or bitter. But I learned a lot about myself. I had Asa and Mick and the rest of my crew there. We had one another's backs. It was harder than I ever expected, mainly because I had no idea what to expect."

"Would you have chosen differently if you could do it over again?" Carmella asked.

"I thought things, and did things that I don't know if I can ever forget. And that's probably for the best. I'm who I am right this moment because of the military and because Asa and Mick came into my life and I had a feeling of fraternity that I had been missing before. I realized there was nothing shameful in wanting a profession where my office was under a hood instead of over-looking a cityscape. So, despite the pain, I'd make the same choice again."

"Were you scared?"

"Every day."

Carmella rested her head on his arm. "I'm glad you're here."

"Me too, gorgeous. Now about that happy ending."

Duke hadn't meant to say all that. He rarely spoke about his time in Iraq. He considered himself lucky. He came back to the United States with a lot of secrets and pain, but it was manageable. And for that he was incredibly grateful. Some of his friends never made it back. Others who got home wrestled with demons far greater than getting shot at every day.

He also hadn't meant to be so touched by something as seem-ingly simple as a massage. But everything she wasn't ready to say yet was communicated through her touch.

That, coupled with all the stuff she'd shared, had shredded

every last defense he had. He'd given himself to Carmella Rossi and that was that.

"Damn, you wreck me. You know that?" he asked her.

She wasn't expecting that.

Carmella paused, those big eyes just taking in his face. "I don't want to wreck you. I like you in one piece."

Now that his back felt better, he was able to grab her and pull her beneath him quickly.

"It's a good sort of wreckage."

"I don't know if there's such a thing."

"I'm the one feeling it and I'm saying there is. Contrary." He kissed her, sad that she meant what she had said. Angry that whatever she'd experienced had led her to believe this kind of knock-down-drag-out love was impossible. Or bad. "Your ex-husband, is he the one who made you believe love isn't real?"

Duke realized he wasn't sure he wanted to know once he'd asked.

"My mother has a romantic fool's heart. It's landed her in one fucked-up mess after the next. Clifton only underlined what I learned from her. I thought there would be sex. This is like showing up to a party where there's no food."

"Look at you. There'll be sex." He bent to breathe her in at his favorite spot. Her neck where it met her shoulder.

Pulling the soft cotton of her shirt away, he licked over the skin there. She hummed and the sound wrapped a fist around his cock.

"Oh yes." He bit her nipple through the material of her shirt and bra and her pussy seemed to superheat against his cock. "I pretty much want to sex you up every moment of the day so there's nothing to worry about on that front. I'm greedy for you in every way. I can't help it. Give me more. His name is *Clifton*? I'm having a really hard time imagining you with a dude named Clifton."

She snickered and he felt better. "His name is Clifton. He claims it was after his great-grandfather who was a blues guitarist.

I think it's from his great-grandfather who sold shoes he stole off the back of a truck."

He reared up enough to pull her shirt off. "Keep going. I'm just multitasking."

"You make it hard to concentrate when you do that." Her voice had slowed down a tad and gone down to velvet and smoke.

"Thank god because when you get super turned on, your voice does that thing and it makes me crazy. Crazy for you."

As he'd said all that, he'd gotten rid of her bra and moved to his knees, her thighs open to either side of him as she lay on her back.

So much had happened between them in a short period of time and he gorged on her. On the way her hips felt under his hands as he held her. The power of her inner thigh muscles as he petted her and she arched for more.

Her tits, *fuck*, he had to take them in his hands, loving their weight. This beauty with that heart of a lion, soft and vulnerable but ferocious too. All contradiction.

Perfect.

"You were telling me about Clifton."

"Why, though? Isn't this much better without talk about my ex-husband?"

"It's always fantastic when you're naked and my hands are on you. We'll be done talking about him and then we'll both have a happy ending."

Her eyes went half-mast and her frown tipped up slightly into a feline smile of promise. "You're so good with compliments. Seriously."

He not only loved her, lusted after her, and craved more of her, he *liked* her. He had a lot of acquaintances but the true friends in his life were a small circle. She was there, he realized with a start.

"Well, let me follow up with this. I've had a thing for you for years. I've jerked off dozens of times with your face in my head. Nothing could have prepared me for the reality of you."

She swallowed hard. "Why is it we aren't having sex already?"

He just looked at her until she sighed dramatically.

"There's not a lot to tell. I was young. I wanted out of my mother's house, but without college or marriage, I had no reason to move out. Mainly I know this *after* the divorce. He was a good lesson."

"Which was?"

Duke didn't know why he wanted this so much. But he did and she seemed to get it too. He'd been doing all the chasing and the way she let him in and trusted him with these details made him feel like she wanted to be with him too.

"By the time I started to realize he wasn't the guy I'd thought, I was married. It was a whirlwind thing. You get me? Like this between you and me. It makes me nervous."

"Did you know him at all? When you first started it up with him?"

Duke really hoped she'd say no so he could explain to Carmella why they were different from that angle.

"I met him and two weeks later we were married."

"How old were you?"

"Twenty."

Duke paused. So damned young. He bet this ex of hers used that to manipulate her every chance he got.

"So I don't need to say that what you and I have is based off years' worth of attraction, not two weeks. It went from zero to a hundred once we got our hands on one another, yes. But you're an adult with a lot of life experience, as am I. I want you but I don't need to exploit you in any way to survive."

She reached up to cup his cheek. "I'm trying to keep this casual and you keep saying this stuff. I can't fight you off right now."

He knew she meant emotionally, but he didn't want her to

admit her feelings for him like this either. Carmella needed to come to it on her own and at a pace she chose. He needed to be patient with that and back off when she asked him to.

Duke nodded and she continued speaking.

"Point taken about the differences between my marriage and you and me. I was divorced by twenty-two and I didn't even care that he was gone. I tried as hard as I could. But one person can't hold a relationship together. No amount of trying on my part was going to make things work. And I deserved more. I won't be like her." Meaning her mother. "That's the lesson. And that's the divide between me and my mother because she only sees her worth through men. And she has awful taste in men so naturally the worth she gets from them is nothing. One of those horrible cycles."

He'd never think on this ex as a threat to his relationship with Carmella, but if he ever came across this guy, Duke would have no problem knocking him the fuck out.

"I think that's a very good lesson. If you don't know your worth, how can anyone else? I read that somewhere a long time ago, thought it was pretty true." Duke hooked his fingertips at the sides of her panties and pulled them off.

"I think I might have a few lessons of my own to impart. These are the fun kind, though."

He kept her legs wide so her pussy was open to his touch.

"I'm a lifelong learner," she wheezed out.

"A quality more people should have." He circled a fingertip around her clit and delighted in the way she arched on a strangled gasp.

"No one else in this room now," she demanded. "Just you and me."

"Just you and me," he agreed, shifting to kiss her.

That intensity that overtook him every time he touched her rose to life, drawing him in.

She opened her mouth on a sigh as he kissed her. Shortly after that, a condom got slapped into his palm.

"You should work harder on asking for what you want," he said, nuzzling her neck and shifting her body down so he could lie between her legs.

"I've been told I'm too shy."

Duke laughed, holding her close, content to just snuggle for a moment until the slick heat of her pussy stroked over his cock and there was nothing else he wanted but to sink inside her.

She'd already had that idea so he was fortunate enough to have a solution in his palm, which he rolled onto his cock before teasing it around the opening of her body until he took pity on her and slid in slowly but surely.

"Yes," she whispered.

He kept that pace—slow, hard, and deep—letting the pleasure build between them. He watched her carefully, noting the flush gathering on her shoulders.

He wanted her climax. Wanted to make her feel so good, to know he brought her pleasure. Loved the way it changed her expression as she flung herself into it.

He went back to his knees, pulling her up and on top of his thighs. She gave an *oof* of sound, but held on, not losing the pace. Once he was sure he hadn't hurt her, he grabbed her hips and bounced her on his cock so that they both moaned.

He let go with one hand, burying it between them to find her clit. She was slick and ready for him, inner muscles tightening around his cock with each thrust.

She was so beautiful. All her flaws and broken parts caught the light and made her a diamond. No one was like her.

Her nose was at his, putting them eye to eye. "Don't look away," he said.

She came. He saw it in her eyes before he felt it all around him and it was the last bit he needed to follow her.

CHAPTER
Seventeen

I noticed the other night when I drove your truck that your timing was off a little." Duke dropped a bag on her desk before he stole a kiss.

"We talked about that," Carmella said primly.

"I know. I brought burritos. Have lunch with me and then let me look at your truck afterward."

"Not taking a lunch today. I need to take my mom to the doctor tomorrow so I was going to shift my hour to then."

"You think Asa and I are running a sweatshop here? Jesus. You don't need to skip lunch to take your mother to the doctor. We'd never expect anyone here to do that. Your schedule is flexible and you work your ass off."

"Are you being shirty with me right now?" Carmella asked him.

"I love that word. I'm not shirty. I'm hungry and in the possession of burritos. Come eat them with me. Take the time you need when you need it. Period. You did something the first week and I should have said this then."

She was glad he hadn't or she'd have been mortified.

A burrito couldn't hurt. And she was hungry. The lunch she'd brought could be dinner and she'd get to spend time with Duke.

"All right then. Let's have some lunch."

The room had already begun to fill up, but it wasn't hard to find a place at the end of a long table and settle in.

"You do realize this burrito could feed four people, right?"

"If you actually can't finish it, it's even better cold at two in the morning." He looked up at her. "Then again, ice cream sandwiches at two in the morning are pretty spectacular too."

Blushing, she looked back to her burrito and tried not to think about naked Duke Bradshaw in her kitchen, bathed in moonlight as he ate that ice cream sandwich.

"We're hanging out tonight, right?" he asked her.

"PJ and I are walking Green Lake after work with Ginger but you'll be here until seven anyway."

"Does that bug you?"

She looked up at him. "What?"

"That I work a lot."

"Well, how could you have your own business and keep it successful if you didn't work a lot?"

He grinned like a dork until she started to laugh. "What? Do I have cilantro in my teeth?"

"Nope. You just roll with things." He shrugged. "I like it."

"It's a gift. Inside I'm a seething volcano of rage."

He burst out laughing until everyone turned to look.

"Don't look at me. I found him this way," Carmella said as she watched him laugh.

He waved them all off as he got himself back under control.

"And don't you have a thing with your dudes tonight? Like boy club of some sort? I'll be here tomorrow, you know."

"I know. But I like being with you. You smell good. Way better than Asa or Mick."

"Well, that's super good to hear. Though Mick has this new cologne that I do like, I'm glad you don't want to make out with him over it."

"We're meeting for sushi at eight. I'll pick you up at your house at seven thirty. Okay?"

"Sushi? I'm in." She finished eating and wrapped up the remaining half of her burrito. "I need to get back to work. Thanks for lunch."

He walked back with her. And while they were alone, she stopped him. "I like being with you too. But I don't need to be in every moment of your life. I'm totally cool with you being with your friends and stuff. You're a busy guy."

"I'll see you tonight at seven thirty." To underline that, he kissed her quickly before leaving.

"This place might be cursed, you know," PJ said to Carmella as she and Asa settled in across from Duke and Carmella. Mick and several other of their friends from the shop were at tables nearby or at the bar.

"Cursed?" Carmella asked her.

"The first time I came here with Asa, like on a real date, a fight broke out and I met his ex-wife. Though I didn't know she was his ex-wife for months after that." PJ looked at Asa, who appeared chagrined. "But the sushi is good and they let us come back again, so I guess it's not cursed after all."

Carmella laughed and Duke groaned. "Stop it. You're going to freak her out."

"Sure. I've never seen a bar fight break out before. I might faint if I did," Carmella said, voice very dry.

"Ooh, grab that eel, please." Duke pointed at the belt and she grabbed the little blue plate and passed it his way.

"Duke and I bought a motorcycle and a Camaro tonight. We were driving back from the gym and saw them sitting in an empty lot next to a mechanic's shop. They're not in great shape, but the bones are good. I think we can turn a profit pretty easily as long as no one loses their mind and spends too much," Asa told them all.

"Mick is way better than you are at keeping everyone's eye on the bottom line. And Carmella scares people into behaving." Duke winked.

"They're more afraid of her than they are of Asa. I love that part." PJ waggled her brows.

The joking was lighthearted as they ate and at some point Craig had spilled in with a group of his friends and the entire place had been pretty much everyone he knew.

Duke loved his life. And since Carmella had come into it, things had only gotten better.

Her phone buzzed and she looked down at the screen and frowned.

"Everything okay?"

She sighed. "It's my mother. Excuse me a bit." She left the table, exiting the restaurant but standing just outside. He could see her perfectly.

Craig noticed too and gave Duke a look so Duke headed over, leaning next to Carmella's cousin and keeping his attention on her as she stood outside on her call.

"She said it was her mother," Duke said quietly.

"I thought she looked upset. I should have figured that. Have you met Virgie yet?" Craig asked.

"No. I know she's been upset about her father too. Is she safe? I know she holds back under some mistaken attempt to keep me protected."

"You don't need to worry about him. It's Virgie who always hurts Carmella. She's the problem. And because of that, all you can do is hope it's not too bad and that she'll come to you for help. You can't stop Hurricane Virgie. And Carmella will always be there to clean up after Virgie so the woman doesn't give a fuck about her kid or trying to be a good mother. Steven is your run-of-the-mill loser. A dime a dozen. Virgie is messed up and selfish."

Duke sighed. "Thanks for telling me all this."

"If you use this or anything else to hurt Carmella, I'll fuck you up. She deserves better than she gets," Craig said.

"I'm doing my best to never hurt Carmella."

He moved to her while she was still outside. She looked up from her call and mouthed that she was okay. He nodded and then settled on the bench nearby to finish up his plate of sushi.

Duke had learned patience early on so he hoped Carmella didn't think she could outwait him. The need to protect her and make sure she was okay was a slow burn.

This situation with her family rubbed him the wrong way. He had a difficult time getting over the fact that the very people who should be helping her were taking advantage of her instead. He hated that these people took advantage of her. Hated that she was so upset.

But that's not what she needed. She'd made a choice and he had to respect it. Even if he hated it. So he did what he could to keep his judgment a hundred miles away when he spoke with her about things.

"I can't help that, Mom," he heard her say. "Even if I wanted to, I don't have it. And if I did, I wouldn't give it to you for this."

She was quiet and he wanted to punch someone.

"I'm going now. If he wants that, why isn't he taking you to the doctor tomorrow? Yeah, exactly. So I'll see you at ten. Please don't make me wait for you because I need to get back to work."

With a sigh she put the phone in her pocket and looked up at the sky. "So that was embarrassing."

"Not for you," Duke said, working to keep his voice even. "You have no reason to be embarrassed."

"Anyway. Let's go back inside. Everyone is waiting."

"They're all having a nice time. No need to hurry. It's a nice night. Let's just relax a bit before we go in. I brought you salmon rolls." He held up the plate.

"You did?" She joined him, taking the plate. "Thank you."

"Why are you always so surprised when people are nice to you?"

"I am not."

She apologized all the time and kindnesses weren't as normal for her as they should be. No one should be surprised by someone being grateful. He just wanted her to be happy.

"I could say something witty like, are too. But you heard it in your head before I said it. What's up?"

"She wants a loan. But it's him, asking through her. It's the usual. Nothing new."

"How much?"

"No way are you giving my mother money, Duke." Carmella's voice was sharp enough to slice.

"You're right. I'm not. I wouldn't do that to you. Though if you need it, all you have to do is ask. But that wasn't what I meant. I was just asking for details."

She sighed. "I'm sorry I jumped on you."

"Stop being sorry."

"I'm not sorry then."

He smiled. "Good."

"She wants three thousand dollars. Three thousand dollars! Crazy. If I gave her that money, he'd be betting within an hour. She knows I can't afford it and she asked anyway. God, you wanted me to share and now I bet you're so sorry you asked."

Duke took her hand. "I'm not at all sorry. I want you to tell me what's going on or I wouldn't have asked to start with. Can I do anything?"

"No. You listened. That was nice. I expect I'll be seeing him the next time I go over there to deal with her. I'll relay this to him myself. He needs a job. He's a decent enough mechanic so he can find one. Then he can handle his own bills and pay my mom some rent."

"Do you want me to see if anyone I know is looking for help?"

It was hard for an ex-con, especially one who wanted to keep his life straight and on the right track. There were a lot of shops around the area that tried to hire people fresh out of jail or prison if that person had the motivation and willingness to work hard. Duke was pretty sure Carmella's dad was a piece of shit, but he'd help her if he could.

She turned to him and he saw the tears in her eyes. "No way. I'd never want him to associate with people I work with or for you to get tarred with whatever he's going to do to screw things up. But thank you for asking. For offering. It means a lot. You're a very nice man."

"I'd do anything for you, gorgeous," Duke said, meaning every word.

She didn't say anything else, just put her head on his shoulder for a few minutes until they went back inside with their friends.

CHAPTER
Eighteen

Duke had been watching her office for the last half an hour. His ever-punctual Carmella had not returned from taking her mother to the doctor and he was beginning to worry about her.

Everyone had told him the father wasn't a threat to Carmella's safety, but her mother was unstable too and, as far as Duke was concerned, had shown very little concern for her daughter's well-being.

A person like that was capable of anything if they could write it off somehow as someone else's fault.

"Is everything okay?" Asa asked as Duke took a break and headed to get a soda.

"I have to tell you, man, her mother makes PJ's family look like the freaking Waltons." He didn't want to break her confidence. But he had to talk to someone and he knew Asa would never reveal anything he said, not even to PJ.

They headed out to the small courtyard between the shop floor and what was the old showroom and would be added shop and administrative space once the new showroom was finished and running.

"It's times like these I wish I'd have never quit smoking," Duke said as he cracked the can and took a long sip. "I can't say too much. She's so private and I don't want to betray her trust. I'm just worried about her. Family shit."

Asa nodded. "You've met PJ's family so you know I understand what you're going through." Duke had to agree; PJ's father was one of the worst people he'd ever met. "I know you're used to being the one who gives advice, but listen to me here. I know you. I know you want to go in and knock heads and make people treat her better. But with family, it's tricky. You have to tread carefully. Let her talk to you without trying to fix it. I heard that on television and it's totally true. Don't put her in a place where she either stops telling you, or feels like she has to choose."

Asa was right. It was hard to hear advice when he was the one people came to usually. And maybe it sucked a little bit more because he wanted her to come to him for advice and she didn't.

"I get the feeling Carmella and I had a similar upbringing," Asa said. Duke's friend had come up rough. Though his mother was amazing and protective, they didn't always have a lot. "When she tells you stuff, that's a big deal. She's probably pretty used to keeping secrets."

It hit Duke then, that of course that's what Carmella's mother had done. Forced her daughter to keep her fucking secrets. At Carmella's expense.

"It makes me crazy." He started to pace. "She should be cherished and adored." But Asa was right. It was a big deal that Carm shared with him and he needed to keep remembering that. This was about her, and when he let his anger get in the way, it made it about him.

He was glad they were all getting together that night at the gym. No racing that night. Instead of bare knuckles outside, they were going to do some boxing. He could burn off the violent energy so he could save all his sensual energy for her.

"She should have been back already. I'm going to give her another half an hour and then I'm calling her."

Asa clapped his shoulder. "Good." And walked back inside before Duke could thank him. Typical of his buddy.

He walked around the building rather than go back through to the shop, wanting that bit of privacy to get his shit back together before going back to work.

Carmella sat stone-faced in her car outside her mom's place.

"Can't you ask your uncle for the money? You have this new job, you always look nice. Don't tell me you don't have a little stashed away for a rainy day," Virgie said. "Most kids want their parents to get back together. This would help that happen."

"I *don't* have it. I was unemployed for a few months and had to live off savings. He can find a job, Mom. Save up. I know he's living with you so it's not like he's paying any rent."

"How can he get to work if he doesn't have a car? It's not like he's spending it on a vacation or anything."

Carmella lost that blank mask at those words. "By the time I was nine, I knew the bus schedule. If a nine-year-old can figure out how to use mass transit, I'm sure an adult can do it. There's a bus stop three blocks from your front door. He'll do just fine if that's really what he means to do. I have to get back to work."

"You won't just be happy for me. He said it might be like this. That you'd suspect his motives and that he didn't blame you. But I do. I do because you're hardening your heart against him when he needs you. When I need you."

No matter how much Carmella knew she shouldn't let it, those words hurt like hell.

"You want him to leave again so you can have me all to yourself!" Virgie exclaimed.

Carmella knew her mother said it to lash out, but it made her angry anyway. "I need you to get out of my car right this moment because I'm going to say something I regret if I have to be with you another moment."

"Just say it!" her mother shouted.

"Get out. I'm not one of your friends down at the bar. You can't play me for sympathy. If he wants to turn his life around, he can do it. He doesn't need money I don't have for a car and I don't need to listen to you treat me like shit because you're having a temper tantrum."

Virgie scrambled from the truck and slammed the door, storming off.

"Thanks, Carmella, for taking hours out of your day to run my ungrateful ass to the doctor when my unemployed asshat of a whatever the hell he is sits on his. You're welcome, Mom." Carmella drove off, annoyed as hell but undeniably relieved to be away from Virgie and her stream of lovesick drivel about Steven.

Once she was back at work, no one was angry with her for taking longer than she thought it would take. Duke made sure she ate a snack later that afternoon and kept an eye on her, thinking she wouldn't notice.

But she did and it mattered that someone seemed to give a crap.

At quitting time, she headed out after a quick good-bye and reminder to everyone that timesheets were due the following day if they wanted to be paid. Lottie apparently had been a lot nicer and let them get away with turning things in at the very last minute.

But that made way more work for everyone, so Carmella had trained them all to get the sheets to her or any hours turned in after the deadline wouldn't be paid until the following pay period. Even the worst offender only tested her twice.

Duke walked her out to her truck. "I want to hear how everything went today. You were later coming back than you thought you'd be."

"You're so very pretty, but even that face can't persuade me to go into my day in this parking lot right now."

He hugged her and she let him, needing it. "You know there's no racing tonight. If you want to see me fight, we'll be at the gym I pointed out to you when we got Indian food the other day. Remember?"

Carmella nodded, increasingly curious.

"Seven. We'll be there until nine or so."

That might be exactly what she needed. To see Duke, sweaty and muscly, bouncing around and fighting. It didn't matter how weird it might have sounded. She only knew by that point that the idea made her wet, and after her day, that was pretty much a win.

"All right. It's cool that I come, though? Like you're not violating some code?" Carmella asked.

"It's not like *Fight Club*. We don't advertise on TV or have business cards with the info on them. But we're not doing anything illegal. Everyone is a legal adult. We're all past the point where we think girls have cooties."

That made her smile. "You're so full of it."

"I totally am. I'll make you pancakes at my house afterward. I have a soup bone for Ginger too."

That he thought of her dog made her want to jump him right then and there.

"All right, all right. I'll be there between seven and nine. Stop being so perfect."

He kissed her until she was only capable of hanging on to keep from falling over. Damn, the man was good.

After getting dressed and changing four times, Carmella headed out to the gym. It was eight so maybe he'd already fought. She hoped not, but she hadn't wanted to arrive too early either.

It wasn't like there was an etiquette book for these situations.

She took the side door like he'd suggested. Easy to find as the words SIDE DOOR had been painted on the wall in two-foot-high letters. Inside it smelled like sweat, dirty socks, leather, vinyl, and sneakers.

And in one far corner was a raised fighting ring with two men inside it. Asa was one of them and Duane, one of the mechanics at the shop, was the other.

Carmella made her way over to watch, looking for Duke and not wanting to make a spectacle of herself so she kept quiet.

Even if she hadn't, no one would have heard her over the shouts from the spectators.

PJ's hair was bright blue as she stood next to a few of their friends. "It's handy to be able to find you so easily in a crowd," Carmella said as she approached.

"Totally. I'm glad to see you. Duke fought earlier but he'll be up again soon. For now, watch my honey deliver a beat down. I can't believe I resisted watching this stuff for so long."

Carmella lost herself in the ritualized violence in the ring. In the oddly beautiful grace of it. PJ shouted her encouragement to Asa, but Carmella remained silent. Waiting.

Duke saw her before she noticed him. Her gaze skimmed over the crowd, looking for him. Pride bloomed in his chest as she turned and saw him, smiling. She gave him two thumbs up as he climbed into the ring.

Mick and Asa were in a different class than he was. They were beefy and muscular while Duke was leaner. He was also lighting quick, with a hard head and a high pain tolerance. His opponent was a really good fighter with great instincts who'd give Duke a run for his money. He might even be better than Duke. But that didn't matter because Duke was going to win. He would win as a present to Carmella.

Once the bell rang, all his attention flowed to the fight. Where his hands and feet were. Where his opponent was. He kept his movements fluid and tried to remember to trust his body and training.

Even so, the punches the guy landed would leave some bruises. Duke pushed the pain away and redoubled his focus. His strikes continued to land until the bell rang. Once more and a very lucky punch sent Duke's opponent to the mat.

Once the match was called in his favor, he headed straight to Carmella. He wanted to hug her and kiss every bit of her, but he was bloody and sweaty so he resisted.

"Congratulations!" Her smile sent a shiver through him.

"I'm sweaty, don't hug me. I'll be cleaned up in a few minutes."

She ignored him, throwing herself into his arms. "I'll hug you if I want."

"I'm all stinky, though, and you're gorgeous and smell good."

She looked up, her gaze to his. "I know."

Oh. It was like that. Well, okay then. He could handle that.

"Give me five minutes. I just need to grab my stuff and I'll meet you back at my house. Remember, I'm making pancakes."

"After you make me come," she whispered in his ear.

"As you command, my lady."

Hot damn.

CHAPTER
Nineteen

She headed home after managing to extricate herself from PJ and their friends. It was nice to visit and all, but she had some sex to do with a hot man. He'd been on fire in the ring. Steady, feral, he moved like the predator he was.

The sweatier and more brutal he'd gotten, fists flying, ducking and weaving, the hotter it had made her for the Duke that lived just beneath the cool veneer.

By the time she rolled up, his car was in his driveway and he leaned against the trunk.

Shirtless.

A neck of a beer dangling between two fingers as he waited for her.

Every single dirty bad-boy fuck fantasy anyone ever had was living and breathing just a few feet away.

"Hi," she said because suddenly she was fourteen and tongue-tied as she walked past the cool boys.

"Hey yourself. C'mere and kiss me because my lips are one of the few parts of me that isn't sore."

She used the low wall that made up his drive, which put her face-to-face with him. "Does this hurt?" She indicated the beginnings of a bruise on his cheek.

"Yes. I'll ice it later."

She leaned in and kissed it gently. And then to the cut where his temple and eyebrow met.

He groaned, sliding an arm around her waist to stabilize her balance.

She kissed other parts of his face before taking his free hand from her waist and kissing over his knuckles. These would be sore, she knew. Gloves didn't prevent that.

Duke's life was full of punches and fast machines. Fast people. Sometimes if you didn't slow down, you missed the tenderness.

She didn't have a lot of anything when it came to money or property, but tenderness toward him was easily given.

"We should go inside. I have a few other places you could kiss and make better," he murmured, and she tracked her way back to his mouth.

"I suppose the neighbors might frown on me kissing your cock right here in the driveway," she teased.

"Probably. You want to grab Ginger first?" He tipped his chin toward her house. That's when she noticed something taped to the door.

"After," she replied, distracted. Things stuck on doors were usually junk, but they could be eviction notices and other legal trouble. She didn't want to deal with any of that right then.

"I'm so glad you said that." He led her to his place, where the moment he closed and locked the front door, she found herself backed to the wall, his body pressing tight to hers.

All the breath left her lungs as he was everything she could see and feel.

"What's a nice girl like you doing with her pussy pressed up against my cock? Hm?"

She swallowed hard, licking her lips.

"Your eyes, so big, just waiting for me to do whatever I want. Isn't that right?"

Suddenly feeling a little tipsy, she nodded.

"I'm sweaty and sticky and I smell like cigarettes and violence." His words held more than one meaning, and though she knew she should pretend not to see that, she couldn't.

"I know." Carmella licked up the side of his neck. "And you taste like a man who likes to fuck nice girls."

He snarled, turning to meet her mouth with his own. Kissing her in a gnash of teeth and tongue. He ran his hands all over her, yanking her shirt up and her bra down.

Those hands knew just what to do. Just how hard to tug her nipples, how long to squeeze them to make her even wetter.

He jammed his thigh between hers, pressing it to her until a ripple of pleasure burst through her.

"Nice girls with dirty imaginations."

He brought it out in her. He made her this way. Made it safe to be this way.

He kissed her neck as he pressed his thigh against her clit. "Do you think you can come this way?" Duke asked, his voice a dark invitation.

Could she? Who the fuck knew? It felt good and he'd addled her brains so she nodded like she was sure.

"All right. Ride me then. Take your pleasure and then I'm going to fuck you right here."

Yeah, that worked.

She gasped as he worked some sort of sex magic on her nipples with his mouth.

The neighbor across the street must have come home because suddenly a slow beat blared through the air. Carmella latched on to the rhythm because she'd made a promise that she could come after all. And she wasn't a quitter.

She dug her fingers through his belt loops for purchase as she undulated, closer and closer.

Yes. Yes. Yes.

At some point she realized she was saying it over and over until finally that spark caught and orgasm burst through her gut. Only Duke's hand at the back of her head kept her from the goose egg she'd surely have gained when she arched and whacked the door.

"Don't lose focus now. Pants off so I can get inside you." Duke's voice pulled her back from that blissful post-climax place and she realized he'd pulled his jeans open, had his cock out, and had just finished rolling the condom on.

"Fuck yeah," she managed to say while she nearly fell over getting her jeans and panties down and off.

Duke felt like he'd been hit in the head a lot more than he had. She was so fucking hot. So beautiful and carnal and open to him.

Carnal, yes, the perfect word. He hadn't expected her reaction to his post-fight state, but once he'd taken in her eyes, the way her breath hitched when he teased, well, he was all in.

She was disheveled, the gloss of a recent orgasm on her lips and in her gaze. And when she saw his cock and gave him her *fuck yeah*, it was all he could do not to dive into her pussy and never leave.

Though she was short, she was strong, so it wasn't as hard as it might have been to lift her up and then down onto his dick as she wrapped her legs around his waist.

He was driven to fuck her. Driven to mark her. To possess her and the trust he'd shaken up before.

"Slow down, baby. I want this to last."

She shook her head, leaning the top part of her body away, against the door at her back.

"Now. I want all of you right now."

How could he refuse such a request?

He let her writhe when he slid his cock against that spot inside her. Each time he pressed deep, he stroked it. Soon, her breath was a hiccup of sound, pleasure, and need all bound up, tied to his pace.

With her he didn't have to hide this part of him. The darker, feral man inside who spoke with his fists hadn't even earned a batted eye from her. More, she'd dug it. Begged for more.

What else in life could measure up to someone who accepted the darkest parts of you and wanted more?

He was so, so very close and each little gaspy breath she made pulled him even closer.

"Hands are full of gorgeous woman. Gonna need you to make yourself come in my stead," he managed to say.

Her laugh was equally shaky. But she obeyed and he loved it. Loved the feel of her between them, her fingers on her clit, playing with it. Making herself come because he told her to.

"Hurry," he urged.

She made a sound, a frustrated little grunt, and then the muscles in her forearm corded and her pussy tightened all around him as she began to come.

That was all he needed, pleasure making him blind as he thrust in so deep his vision grayed at the edges for a moment as climax hit.

"I'm beginning to feel like I should pull a chair into the entry or something," he said. "If we can't get any further than the front hall, we might need something comfortable sometimes."

He put her to her feet and she began to gather her clothes, still smiling. "Sometimes a little pain makes the pleasure all the sweeter."

Talk about hidden depths.

"Let's go get your dog. She saw you pull up through the front window so she's going to be mad."

Carmella snorted. "At you."

"What? Why me?"

"Because she loves me. She just has a crush on you. It's cool, you don't need to come with me. I'll grab Ginger while you shower."

"I want to come with you." He opened the door and they spilled out onto the porch.

"Your pants are unzipped, and you don't have on a shirt or shoes."

"You liked that just fine a few minutes ago."

She paused to give him an affectionately annoyed face.

"What? Am I lying?"

Carmella snorted and headed to her front porch, snatching something off the door quickly.

"Is that the lawn aeration people again? They leave so much shit on my door I want to hunt them down and drown them in it all."

"Wow, that's um...okay then." She unlocked and Ginger waited for them. Just like Carmella had said, after a brief sniff of annoyance at her human, she gave in and let Carmella pet her and give her love. Duke got the doggie version of side-eye.

"We weren't ignoring you. We had human stuff to handle," Duke told Ginger. "I have treats for you so maybe you can find it in your heart to forgive my wanting your human all to myself for a few minutes."

"The cookies will do it. She's not that complicated." Carmella straightened. And then stopped, cocking her head, and then she rushed through the house into the kitchen.

Duke didn't know what was up, but he followed her.

The window over the sink had been pried open.

"No." She started to move to her bedroom and he grabbed her arm to stop her. "Someone could be in there!" she exclaimed.

"I know, which is why I'm going first. You stay back and figure out why your dog isn't barking."

She cursed, which meant she hadn't even thought of that, which worried him.

Her bedroom was empty, but it was a mess and he knew immediately someone had been there, looking for something. She'd never leave her house outside of an emergency if it looked this way.

"Holy shit!" She bumped up against his back where he'd blocked her access.

"Wait. We need to call the police."

"I know who did this."

He turned, flipping on the hall light to see her pull something from her pocket. The thing from her front door. Only it clearly wasn't lawn care or Jesus spam.

"Damn it." She crumpled the paper and he held out his hand. She shook her head. "No. It's nothing."

"What the hell is going on? You know who did this?"

"It's my goddamn ex-husband. He left a note saying he *borrowed* some stuff and would get it back to me."

Duke plucked the wad of paper from her hand and read it.

Came by but you were out. Had to borrow a few things from inside. I'll get them all back to you soon. A big business opportunity has just presented itself. We're going to be rolling in it. C

Jealousy warred with offense that this guy would rip her off this way.

"We'll go to his house right now if you won't call the cops. Trust me when I say we'll get your stuff back," Duke told her.

She walked past him into her bedroom and took a look to see what was missing. "I don't know where he's at. That ratfaced goat-fucker broke into my house!"

So surprised, Duke couldn't stop the guffaw at her words. "Can't you call him? If you won't call the cops . . ."

"Oh, I'm calling the cops all right. I just wanted to look at the note to make sure it was him."

Oh. Well, that was good. "How'd he know where you live? You never were here with a guy, not one you saw for more than a few weeks at a time. Okay, so maybe that sounded a little creepy."

"You thought I was going to protect that scumbag? My mother

told him where I lived. Because she's...well, I told you what she is. Anyway. In a moment of weakness, one you saw, I might add, I let him inside the house and then, I was"—she sighed—"horny. Lonely. God, I'm so embarrassed. Anyway, we got down. That's how he knew the layout to my house. He'd never been inside until that day."

At first Duke was weirded out that he'd actually seen her *ex* fucking her, not just some random guy.

"They're all my ex-somethings now," she said as she walked past him into her room, her phone pressed to her ear as she called the cops.

She'd known he was thinking about that.

When she got off the phone, he said, "I know. I get that. I can't regret that time, though. Seeing you in your kitchen. You're so fucking beautiful. I'd never want to erase that memory. Even if he's part of it."

She hugged him.

"Damn, you always do that."

"What?" He hugged her back, putting his rage away until he could deal with her ex in person.

"You say exactly the best thing."

She had no idea how amazing she was. He wanted to wash away all this shit from her past, replace the bad with all the good he could bring her.

But that wasn't how things worked.

He kissed the top of her head. "Let's see what he took. Make a note for the police. Save the thing he left on your door too. Maybe they know where he is."

"They've come here looking for him so I doubt it." She went back into her room and poked around, making a note here and there.

It didn't take long. "He took some jewelry. Nothing expensive. Thank goodness I was wearing my necklace."

"Something special?" he asked as they settled on the porch to wait for the police to arrive.

"My grandma gave it to me. He took my iPod dock. Oh shit." She stood quickly and headed back inside, straight to her bathroom. The medicine cabinet was open, as were a few drawers. "I moved her pills when I heard Steven was out again."

Carmella pulled out a bulk-sized package of tampons and pads and inside that was a lockbox. "He's one of those dudes who thinks it's mandatory to run screaming into the night at the mere thought of menstruation. Steven is too. They'd look around in the usual places for pills and hidden stashes of money, but not if they had to touch a pad. Dumbasses."

"You're brilliant, you know that? Wait, do you think this is connected to your mom asking for a loan?"

"I don't think so. I think it's just a stupid coincidence. He and my father don't know one another, but even if they did, Clifton doesn't work with anyone else. He's a solo practitioner. That's how he says he does his crime alone to make it sound mysterious. He turns up once every year or so, usually to ask for money. But breaking in and stealing from me that way is a new one."

"This guy makes me want to punch him more with each moment," Duke snarled.

The police arrived shortly after that and took her statement along with the note the ex had left.

Once that happened, Duke ran to grab some tools and fixed her window. She looked more exhausted by the minute and he wanted her to get some sleep.

"We haven't eaten and you need to sleep. I'd really rather you slept at my house after I feed you. I don't feel very good about how safe this place is now. Tomorrow when it's light out, I'll give it a look with Mick, who is fantastic with home security stuff. Then we'll make this place shipshape. Bring Ginger's bed and food and some clothes for tomorrow. You're taking the day off, as am I."

She sighed. "Why? You should walk the hell away right now."

"If I wanted to walk away, I would have. I'm not going anywhere."

"I've made some bad choices, Duke. I'm *mortified* right now. My ex-con dad, my recreational-pill-popping mom with chronic mental health issues, my grifter ex-husband who breaks in but I don't have much to steal. It's all so, ugh, tacky."

"You are not tacky. You are beautiful and intelligent. You're great with numbers and ziti. Animals love you. I'm not about to equate you with the personal bullshit of anyone else. Your ex is a piece of shit. But that's not on you. You are not your parents, Carmella."

"I should tell you no," she said so quietly he wondered if he'd imagined it. And then louder, "I'm not taking tomorrow off. I have things to do."

At least she had some of her spark back. He could work with that.

"You can work from my house. I know your boss, he's pretty cool."

She stood in the middle of her bedroom and the ridiculousness of the day hit her with so much force she couldn't stop the tears. Her crying was one of those mixes of helpless rage and embarrassment.

Duke saw it and she hated that. Hated that he saw her at such a low point. But he picked up Ginger's bed and her purse. "I *will* be right back." He called out to the dog and she heard him gather a few things and go out her front door.

Left alone, she went to her knees and let it all go. He gave her the space to fall apart. Gave it because he knew on some level that she needed it.

Being seen like that was...humbling. Carmella used a washcloth to wipe her eyes. Her makeup had to look terrible by that point, so she heaved herself up and began to gather stuff.

Began to organize her thoughts and make a list of everything she had to do. And by the time Duke made a lot of noise coming back inside, she was better.

"Ready?" he asked, standing in her doorway.

She could see it in his face and the way he held himself. He'd made a hard choice to leave her those minutes before.

He'd put her first. *Her* needs.

She nodded, taking his hand and letting him lead her away.

CHAPTER
Twenty

Carmella dragged her butt to work that morning because she needed to do it or go crazy every time she thought about Clifton breaking into her house.

Ginger hadn't been in a panic the night before when Carmella had come into the house because she knew Clifton most likely. Didn't like him really, but he'd been the one to bring Carmella the puppy he'd picked up heaven knew where.

But she sensed Carmella was upset so she'd stuck close, sleeping at the foot of Duke's bed with her head on Carmella's feet.

Carmella had tried to get the dog to sleep in her very nice doggie bed, but Duke wouldn't hear of it. He seemed to know how much they needed each other and he was the one who picked Ginger up and put her on the bed.

Wherever he came from, she didn't deserve him. But it didn't matter because she wasn't giving him back.

Once at work, she had a few cups of coffee and finished the calls she needed to make, and she felt a lot better. Well, enough to call Craig to tell him about the break-in.

She left a voicemail because he was in class. Cowardly, probably. But relating what happened without being interrupted to be told how awful Clifton was was preferable and she didn't have the energy.

By lunchtime, the burst of energy she'd had earlier was beginning to evaporate. And after the phone call she had with her rent-
er's insurance agent, it was all gone.

The deductible she'd have to pay was more than the worth of
the stuff Clifton stole. And money couldn't help the feeling of having her privacy and safety violated. It wasn't like she thought he
perved over her panty drawer. After all, it was utilitarian white cotton for the most part. But he'd been in her house. Looking through
her things. He knew her. At one time he'd professed to love her
and he'd broken into her house to steal a bunch of cheap jewelry
and her household money stash, a grand total of fifty-six bucks.

"You're still here?" Duke came in. "Shut everything down and
go the hell back to my house. Watch movies with me and your
dog. You don't need to be here."

"I had work to do. I can't afford to go falling apart every time
something bad happens."

He knelt next to her chair, taking her hands in his.

"This is inappropriate. We're at work." The words were flat
even to her ears.

"Your boss says this is cool with him. Shut your stuff down and
come home with me. We'll stop and get lunch. Mick and I did
some work at your place so your window is fixed and we put new
locks on your front and back door too." He handed her the keys.
"You'll be much safer now. Here's a set for you and another for
your landlord."

"Thank you. Tell me how much I owe you."

Duke rolled his eyes. "You can make me baked ziti to thank
me. I had the locks anyway. Most of the hardware we needed we
had here or in my garage."

"I don't like owing people."

"Too bad, Carmella. I wanted to do it for you because I care. I
did it. You're safer and things are fine. Say thank you and let's go
get lunch."

"You're very pushy."

"I am. Because I'm worried about you. And because you're so fucking resistant when people try to help you. Which tells me how often it happens and that when it does, it's not always people who are out for your best interests. So I'm pissed off at that. Not at your stubbornly beautiful ass. And I want you to give yourself a break, leave work for the day, and let me satisfy myself that you're okay. Let me spoil you just a little."

She put her hands over her face. She was so accustomed to taking care of her shit, no matter how much of it there was, that having someone help her was foreign in a way that made her uncomfortable as well as happy.

She felt as if she were a very brittle piece of glass. One more bump and she'd shatter into pieces. Carmella didn't want to fight with him. Not when he was trying to be kind. And she didn't want to make a scene at her job either.

"Okay, fine. Thank you." She turned her computer off and let the receptionist know she was leaving.

When she finished, he opened the door and led her out. "I'll follow you home," he said at her car.

"I keep waiting for that thing you're going to do. That thing that makes me say, *I knew it.* You seem too good to be true and it scares me," she whispered.

"Gorgeous." He kissed her knuckles. "I get that you've been let down. But that's not me. It's not who I am or what I do. Give me a chance to show you what it means to be cared about by a real man."

Carmella told herself she was too tired to argue, but really, she didn't want to. Instead, she drove home, and true to his word, he met her there.

"Come on in. Your dog is with me. She misses you, though. Even cookies aren't enough to make her forget you."

She took his hand and they ignored her house and went to his, where she had lunch and they watched movies while she did laundry. It was normal. And relaxing. And by the time late afternoon had come, she knew she had to face her house at some point.

"I'll sleep at your house tonight," he told her as if she'd spoken her fears aloud.

"I have to deal with it. He wouldn't hurt me. Even if he came back."

Duke stared at her for long, silent moments. "I know you came up rough. I don't want to freak you out, but if he knows what's best for him, he'll stay away. Because if I catch him before they toss him in jail, I'm going to beat his ass."

She should have felt guilty that someone threatened violence over her. Clifton was a petty criminal, and Carmella hated that this part of her life had to touch Duke at all.

But there was no denying how it made her feel that he wanted to protect her. Gave her a place that was safe.

It wasn't that Carmella forgot the only person she could count on was herself. It was more that she allowed herself to count on Duke too. Just a little.

"Come spend the night." She stood and he followed, locking up and joining her on her front porch.

The new key was odd. Different. The lock was smooth where her old one was sticky. Ginger ran inside to smell everything and make sure no new dogs had moved in. Duke stepped in next, keeping Carmella behind him until he was sure everything was all right.

No one had ever done that for her before.

"Oh, Mick and I made you a window box. I hope that's okay. I forgot to tell you."

Delighted, Carmella went out the back door to find a pretty white wood window box full of red geraniums.

"This is beautiful." She hugged him. "Thank you." She used the excuse to keep her face buried in his chest as she choked back the lump of emotion in her throat.

"We had the extra wood after fixing your window. That asshole did a number on the sill so we rebuilt it for you. We installed a motion detector light back here too. Don't worry, we made sure it didn't point at anyone's window. But it's better lit back here now and on the side of the house as well."

"Thank you doesn't seem like enough for all this. I feel better knowing you did this."

Duke's smile softened. "Good." He turned them around and steered her back inside. "Let me show you the new lock on the bedroom window. The shower was fine, though I lubed it just a little so it opens and closes better."

"You are so damned handy." She paused at her bedroom doorway. "I need to change the sheets and tidy up in here."

"Let me help." He started toward the far side of her bed. They'd put the mattress back in place the night before after Clifton had tipped it to see if she had anything beneath.

"I'm good. Really." She blurted it and he paused to look her over carefully.

"Right on. I'll play ball with this other pretty lady to tire her out. She guarded us today while we worked so she deserves some fun." He called Ginger's name and she roused herself, casting a glance in Carmella's direction.

"Go on. I'm fine," Carmella said, and after a quick bark, the dog tore after Duke, leaving her alone. What she needed was to get over this break-in. To take back her house and reclaim it.

So she changed the sheets and cleaned her bedroom up, vacuuming and putting her freshly laundered clothes away.

An hour later she went outside to find Craig and Duke sharing a beer and still tossing a ball with the dog.

"Really? A voicemail, Carmella?" Craig asked as he caught sight of her.

"You were in class but I wanted you to know before you found out some other way."

He hugged her and then slugged her arm with big brother strength.

"Ouch! What was that for?"

"Not calling me last night. You are such a brat."

Duke cleared his throat. "That's one free shot as I understand your annoyance and she's your little cousin. But now we're done." He crossed his arms over his chest and looked all bulgy and hot.

There was simply no limit to the ways the man was sexy. How ridiculous was that? If she spent hours doing physical labor in the summer sun, she'd look like a sweaty, sunburned mess. Duke just looked glisteny. A little sweat. A little sunscreen. The setting sun glinting against the strands of gold and white in his hair.

Despite the memory of the break-in, before that? In his hallway like there was nothing else to do but rut and scratch and fuck? That was so honest and raw she was still reeling from it on some level. Together like that, skin to skin, it was the most truthful she'd ever been with anyone else. It was more than sexy, it was overwhelming and fantastic and she yearned for more.

Craig interrupted her filthy thoughts about Duke. "Roger that. I told Mom and Dad what happened and that I was coming over here after my last class. You owe me for that," Craig said, hugging her again, this time without the sock in the arm.

"I've covered your ass so many times in so many ways you'll owe me favors until the end of time," Carmella told Craig. "Anyway, everything is fine now. I didn't want to worry any more people than I already had. It's just Clifton. It's not as if I'm shocked he'd rip me off."

"If I see that weasel around town . . ."

"Get in line," Duke said.

"Okay now everyone spit and hitch up your pants," Carmella said.

"You can make fun all you want. But we don't know what his motivations are here," Craig argued.

"He's smart enough to run some small-time cons, but too lazy to learn the technology to run better ones with lower risk and higher return. So he's caught in a downward spiral with no real prospects of getting better. He's not malicious. He's just pathetic. Yes, I'm mad because he stole from me even after all the times I helped him out in some way. But more than that, I guess I'm just relieved he's out of my life and I feel sorry for him."

"You don't know what the years have done to him. What his circumstances are now. Desperation drives people to do risky stuff," Duke said.

They were right, she knew. And that was sad too.

"I was thinking," Duke said as he settled in next to her in bed later that night. "I haven't taken off more than two days in a row for anything other than work trips in a few years. Want to go out to the coast on the bike? We can stay a few days. What do you say?"

"Yeah. That would be nice. After the grand opening, though." She wriggled her ass back into the cradle of his hips.

"We can do it before. It's not like I'm building it. I'm paying someone to do that part. They prefer it when I'm not around, actually."

"Are you kidding me? They will not take it well if you go on vacation. You're their buffer between Asa. They love you. They're always Duke this and Duke that. I'm pretty sure the big one with the neck tattoo has a man crush like whoa on you. I don't blame him."

"I don't even know where you get half the stuff you say." He kissed the back of her neck.

"I'm gifted. We already talked about that. Remember?" Her voice was sleepy, relaxed. The night before, she'd been a little brittle, but just then she was warm and soft next to him and everything was really okay.

"I remember," he murmured as he closed his eyes and breathed her in.

"We'll go to celebrate the grand opening. Besides, the road will be less crowded in the fall."

On the one hand, he wanted to get her out of town for a while right then. To pick her up, sling her over his shoulder, and run away.

On the other hand, she'd agreed to a trip they couldn't take for another three or four weeks. Which meant she saw them together then. That was a good sign.

"I guess you have a point. It's Bumbershoot this weekend. We're still on for it, right?"

Bumbershoot was the annual end-of-summer live music and arts festival held on the sprawling grounds of Seattle Center. Every type of music imaginable from buskers playing handmade instruments to top-name acts headlining each night.

He and his friends would go all three days and get their fill of music and beer. And this time he would have Carmella along. He smiled in the dark.

"Yes. I can't wait. I also can't believe Twisted Steel actually closes Saturday for it. And you give employee-discounted three-day passes. Thanks for that, by the way."

"Well, it's Labor Day weekend anyway. Not like we're out a lot of money." And people worked twice as hard for you when you treated them well. "We go in with a lot of other shops and buy in bulk to get the discount and some advertising too. It's all good and really the only time I can eat a hot dog in Seattle without everyone making faces at me or trying to put tuna or ranch dressing on them. Who does that? It's like the Wild West out here with that shit."

She started to giggle and soon enough gales of laughter shook her. When she finally settled down, he cleared his throat. "Glad I could amuse you."

"It's just that you're so calm and collected and it's hot dogs with ranch dressing that you get truly worked up over. Your mind is a scary and wondrous place. I promise to never hot dog shame you. Or put tuna on yours."

"You got a deal."

"Can we toast marshmallows? When we go to the coast?" she asked.

"Definitely. Who watches the dog when you go away? Maybe we should drive instead so we can bring her with us."

"You're so sweet. I mean, one minute you can be knocking a guy out and the next you're making me feel better and thinking about my dog. She likes to stay with Craig or my aunt and uncle if I have to be away. But thank you. I feel like I'm bringing you drama and you're bringing me wonderful. It's not really a fair exchange."

He snorted. "Carmella, you bring me a lot. So much happy. This other stuff is stupid. But it's not your fault. I don't blame you that your mother is awful. Or that before me, you had shit taste in men."

"She's not awful, she' s just . . . ugh. She just doesn't know how to love anyone that isn't him. And to be honest, I see the way she loves him and I don't want that either. The obsession that turns greedy and selfish. She lives through him and nothing else matters. But she's not enough for him. And she knows it."

"But if she stays, isn't she saying she accepts being not enough? Like living half an existence?" Duke couldn't imagine accepting that shadow of a life.

"I think she *believes* she's not good enough. So she puts all her energy into trying to be better. For him. He's passive-aggressive. I blame him more than her. I've been told that's unfair."

"Do you think that's unfair?" Duke asked.

"Life is unfair. She's messed up and was before he came into the picture. I'm not kidding myself about who she is. She had a good family. She had roots and she just never grew into them. Her roots are shallow. My grandmother once told me my mother was an African violet. She could only thrive in a very rare set of circumstances. Chances were my mom would never achieve them, so it made her quit at an early age. Like she looked at her life and said, ew, too hard, and just lay down to take a nap.

"But he knows she's all screwed up and he gets off on it. He should stay away, he knows it. But he comes back because no one makes him feel like she does because she's all about whatever he needs. It's toxic but he uses it to get what he wants, and for that, I judge him harsher, yes. She's mentally ill and he's just fine manipulating it. Enough. I just need to stop thinking about that for the rest of the night. It's my horrible underbelly all the time. You tell me something about your life," Carmella said.

In the dark, after she'd just told him all that about her life, he could do nothing but respond in kind. "Like what?"

"What are your parents like?"

"My father is a shouter. He's got a baritone voice, and when he wants to, he really gets the volume up. He's gotten less and less patient over the years. Like the more money he makes, the less tolerance he has for pretty much everything. He started out working in a factory. Making woodstoves. And now he's the CEO of that company. It's one of those stories you'd see on cable television. Scrappy blue-collar family rides into California, where everything is golden. Anyway, the yelling. It used to embarrass me so much because you could hear him outside the house, yelling at everyone. My mother convinced him that if he wanted to rise in management, he had to stop being such a vulgar asshole. She said it nicer, I'm sure. It came in handy in the army. Some of those guys you got the feeling they'd never been yelled at ever in their lives. And they're in basic training and pretty much everyone is yelling all the time and they fall to pieces."

"Do your siblings yell?"

"My siblings don't, no. They're much better bred than my father, you see. My brother is a younger version of the man my dad has been since they moved to California. My sister is very successful, but she married a guy my father keeps employed while my parents pay the mortgage. That way they can disapprove on even more levels because they have a hand in my sister's finances."

She remained quiet but he knew she listened to every word.

"So there are some lovely details. But don't worry, other than them saying they'll come to the grand opening, you'll never see them again. I haven't spent a holiday there in years. I expect I'll go for various graduations of my nieces and nephews and that sort of thing. Otherwise, my home is here." And they all seemed fine with that.

She snuggled into him tighter.

"Wow, so really, pill-popping crazy mother isn't looking that bad next to shouty dad. That CEO thing works in his favor, though."

She'd known he needed a little levity and gave it to him.

"Maybe that's why you're so easygoing. To counter the shouty intensity."

He'd often thought that was part of his personality. His way to cope early on and it'd stuck.

"Whatever it is, I'm glad home is here but I'm sorry you're not close with them. I'm sorry they're missing out on you."

He had nothing else to say so he held on and let himself glide into sleep, knowing he was understood.

CHAPTER
Twenty-one

Duke pulled a hat from his back pocket and put it on her head. "There."

She tipped her face to look up at him, clearly amused. "Was this the one thing I was missing in my festival-going ensemble?"

"I live in fear of you getting burned." She was so pale and the day was already clear and bright. They'd be outside for hours yet.

"I have sunscreen on. Like nuclear blast protection. But I'll keep the hat too. You have the bill all folded up just right."

He bent to kiss her, knocking the hat askew. "I like it on you. And the fact that a hot woman is wearing a cap advertising my shop is gravy." She was adorable. Which he didn't share because he'd come to find short women had a thing about being called adorable. So he'd only think it.

Duke looked her up and down, pausing to take his time checking out the way her T-shirt clung to her tits. Smart woman that she was, she had sneakers on.

"Should I be afraid of what you'll do when we're alone next?" she murmured. "That look of yours usually spells really delicious trouble for me."

He waggled his brows before pushing his sunglasses up his

nose. "I thought it was pretty obvious that I always have delicious trouble waiting for you."

There was no other word for her smile but dazzling. "Thanks for inviting me today."

"Thanks for being my date." He bent to kiss her again because he wanted to and she was his.

"I've lived in Seattle my entire life and I've never been to any of the big festivals on a date. Not Folklife or even Bite of Seattle." She shrugged. "You're my first."

"You're my only. So I guess we're even."

She slid her hand into his.

"Get a room or get a move on!" Mick called out.

Mick had a friend with a house not too far from Seattle Center so they parked at his place and would walk over to Bumbershoot from there. That way when it was time to leave, they wouldn't get caught in the snarl right around the area.

Duke flipped him off and stole another kiss before ambling off with their group.

It was crowded, but not nearly as bad as it would be in a few hours. He liked to go all three days to watch the slow build and then ebb as it all ended.

At one time he also loved the sight of so many hot women. Well, he *still* loved the sight, but none of them held his attention the way the woman at his side did. Still, it would be rude not to smile and nod back. Accept the hug when he saw a friend. Introduce them to Carmella.

He felt like he wanted everyone in the world to see her at his side. Like he'd found the most wonderful, special thing ever.

"Let's head to the beer garden, see what everyone else is up to, and then decide where to go next," Mick said. "Stop walking so fast, Carmella's practically having to run."

Duke looked down and realized they'd been dragging her through the crowd. "Sorry, gorgeous."

"I'm used to it."

They paused on the way to sample a little bit of gamelan from a five-person group in a little grassy knoll and, just around a corner, a ninety-year-old lady playing violin.

"I want to see the big band stuff. It's on a stage near the Armory in an hour," Carmella said as they showed their IDs to get into the fenced-off area where their friends waited.

"Okay. I'm in. Sounds good." Duke looked down at her and got caught up in her smile.

"Mick is going to make a crack if you keep looking at me this way." The right corner of Carmella's mouth tipped up and he wanted to lick it.

"He's just jealous." They headed over to their friends and he found himself enveloped in hugs, handshakes, and hails of his name.

But he kept hold of her hand until she yanked hard and he turned around and realized that she'd been caught up in his wake.

One handed, he moved the two women who'd somehow gotten between him and Carmella and pulled her through the crowd to his side. "You okay? Sorry about that."

She straightened her hat and cast a glare over her shoulder at one of the women he'd moved aside.

"There a problem?" he asked quietly.

"Nothing new." She shrugged and then brightened when she caught sight of PJ and their girlfriends.

It wasn't the time and she'd hate a scene, but there was a problem and he hated not knowing what was bothering her so he could fix it. Even though he wasn't supposed to fix everything and just listen or whatever.

She let go of his hand after he kissed hers and went to join the others after he told her he'd get her something to drink that wasn't beer.

He liked it when the people he cared about were happy. But this was different. She was important on a totally different level. Which was a pretty rad thing when he thought about it.

This being in love thing was pretty fucking awesome.

"You know, I'm just going to put it out there that perhaps you could give the ladies you *aren't* dating some space?" Asa handed Duke a beer once they'd cleared the line.

"I need to get a straw for Carmella's lemonade. Hang on." He grinned his way around a lovely lady behind him and grabbed a straw and some napkins. They moved to the side. "Now what are you talking about? Ladies I'm not dating?"

Asa sighed, looking annoyed. "Dude, do you have any idea how many women rubbed up on you so far today?"

"I try to accept my blessings and be grateful. I didn't do anything out of line, Asa. I wouldn't do that to Carmella even if I wanted to. Which I don't." He frowned as he ran through it all.

"Okay then."

"*Okay then?* What does that mean?" Duke asked, feeling defensive.

"You know, when *you're* not the one giving advice, you're a pissy crybaby. Jesus."

"Fuck off." Duke rolled his eyes at the direct hit.

"Since you're stupid, let me be clear. You have a girlfriend. I know you're not used to it and all. But some women don't dig it when you're with them and they have to beat off dozens of other women hot for their men. This is what PJ tells me, though that's really too bad."

"Has Carmella said something?" He looked over in her direction but she didn't look upset. She looked happily engaged in conversation.

"Do you really think your girlfriend came to me to complain about the wall of pussy that surrounds you at all times? PJ mentioned it to me yesterday. In an offhand way. I didn't think much about it until today when we walked in."

Duke snorted. "Wall of pussy? Don't you think that's an over-statement?"

"Yes. And offensive too, I suppose. Don't tell PJ I said that, though to be fair, that phrase might have come from her. Ignore me if you want."

As they reached their friends, Carmella looked up at him, happy. Clearly she wasn't bothered by the way his women friends said hello so there was nothing to worry about.

As days went, Carmella thought, this one ranked up there. There she was, twenty-seven years old, and she'd never gone to a concert with a group of friends and the man she was seeing.

It was so much fun. Her cheeks hurt from smiling and laughing all day. And right at that moment she lay on the grass, her back to a tree and Duke's head in her lap.

So *this* was why PJ smiled so much. Not just the sex, but the sheer pleasure of having someone along with you. Of your hand in his or the head on a shoulder. She was turning sappy as she approached thirty.

"You sure you don't need more sunscreen?" Duke asked her. "Your nose is pink."

"My nose is always pink if I've been outside for longer than three minutes. It's one of my most appealing physical characteristics."

"You're on a roll today." He grinned up at her.

"It's the day drinking."

He took her hand, kissing her fingertips. "We should start over to Racha soon so we can meet up with everyone."

"Oh yes. I forgot we were having dinner there. This is as cool as finding a five in the pocket of an old coat."

He unfolded himself, all well over six feet, and then helped her up, brushing the grass off her ass really thoroughly. So thoroughly she had to swat him away after a bit.

"I think I'm good," Carmella said, laughing as she removed his hands.

He patted her butt one last time after she let go. "Yes indeed, you are."

They headed out of the Seattle Center and just a few blocks away to meet everyone for dinner. The sidewalks were a crush, people heading to a show at Bumbershoot, or from there to one of the many bars and restaurants within an easy walk.

Add the normal hustle of Lower Queen Anne and Carmella had to yank Duke's hand once already so he would slow down. Finally, he stopped, pulling them off the sidewalk and into a parking lot.

"I'm so sorry, gorgeous." He pulled her hat off and kissed her. "My only defense is that I'm not used to walking hand in hand with anyone."

Charmed, she rolled her eyes. "And the women you were with before me were all tall so they could keep up."

"No call to say such a thing, now, is there?"

"Bring yourself down here, Duke." Carmella tried to look stern but ended up laughing before she could grab his beard.

So she settled for another kiss and ran her fingers through his hair. Which was actually not anything close to settling.

"The truth of the matter is," he said against her lips, "*nothing* I've done before was like you and me."

He was so good at being affectionate. It was easy for him to be open with her. She owed it to him to return that, but it wasn't easy for her. And while it was nice that he felt this way and said these things, really nice actually, it still made her feel inadequate in some sense because it also terrified her.

"Come on then. Let's eat. I'll pay more attention." He gave

her forehead a last kiss and plopped the hat back into place. She most likely had the worst case of hat hair ever and it didn't even matter.

After a really big dinner, they headed back to catch a show. Waxahatchee was one of her recent discoveries, and Carmella loved that straightforward rock and roll fronted by a woman.

Duke was right behind her, the heat of him at her back. He kept people away from her, which was nice and also meant he was getting used to running interference for her.

One of his hands rested on her shoulder. It was possessive, definitely. And at first it had made her wary. But if she was being totally honest, by that point in their relationship, she really liked it. Especially because people got the message that he wasn't available.

Honestly, the thing about that day that hadn't been fun was the stunning number of times a beautiful woman saw Duke, her face lit up, and she had to hug him. Had. To.

It made Carmella grumpy. She hated jealousy. It was useless. But it didn't matter because she felt it anyway. It made her self-conscious too.

It wasn't as if he did anything to invite it. Or that anyone had been overly friendly and insulting to her. He always introduced her right away. Said she was his girlfriend to everyone.

It filled her with pride. Like, *Oh yes, look at him. He's mine.*

Which was dumb. She knew it. But she couldn't stop that smug little warm spot inside when people looked at him.

It was late by the time the show ended, but naturally Mick was ready for more.

"Let's go play some pool," Mick said. "First round's on me."

PJ stood next to Carmella as they watched Asa, Duke, and Mick plan the rest of the evening.

"They make me feel really old and I'm the youngest of every-one," PJ said.

"Where does all their energy come from?" Carmella asked. She knew when they got back home, Duke would want to fuck. Not that she'd argue. She *wanted* to fuck right then.

"Your guess is as good as mine. I have no idea." PJ linked her arm with Carmella's as Mick tossed a coin to choose between this or that bar. "Looks like we're going to play some pool."

Duke turned to her with a grin. "Are you up for some pool or do you want to go home?"

At least he'd asked. A lot of people would have assumed. Though she wondered if he was sick of her yet. They worked together, and now that they were dating, they saw each other pretty much every night and weekend too.

She wasn't sick of him by any stretch.

"Sure. I haven't played since high school, but I'm happy to watch you bend over things."

"What a coincidence. I like to watch you bend over things too," he said quietly into her ear.

You could be seeing it if we went home right now.

Instead, they all headed out to a bar that rode the real dive line, but was still barely on the not quite line. In cases like these, being with men the size of the ones she was worked out pretty well.

She and PJ stood across the room at the jukebox as the guys grabbed a pool table and some beer.

"How is it they can drink all that beer and eat all that food and they're still so freaking gorgeous? Like, Duke has no fat on him. How is that? If I ate and drink the way they did, I'd never want to stop napping." Carmella flipped through the music selection.

"Right? And they do all the things you're not supposed to! Truth be told, fat wouldn't dare live on Asa's body."

Carmella laughed. "Is fat scared of him too?"

"Probably." The two women laughed. PJ slung an arm around Carmella's shoulders. "God, I'm so glad you're around."

Carmella felt much the same way. She wasn't sure what she'd have done without PJ's advice. She had no idea how to manage this relationship thing. Her marriage most definitely counted as a don't. But some dos were nice too and PJ was so open and helpful.

Carmella tried to steer them around a knot of men who were three drinks past acceptably drunk and nearing belligerent. She knew all she had to do was call out and no one would fuck with them because the three men they came in with were big enough to scare anyone. But the men made her nervous.

"Carmella? I thought that was you."

Carmella recognized his voice and she spun on her heel, finger already pointed. "You! You broke into my house."

"Oh shit," PJ whispered.

Clifton—of course he'd been standing with those losers— came out of the shadows with some kind of easygoing smile but it was fake as hell.

"I didn't. I just borrowed."

"Borrowed?" She looked around at the beers on the table he was standing at. "You stole my shit so you could buy beer? Fuck you, Clifton."

"Wow," PJ said in an undertone. "Go, Carm."

"What? You want me to pay you back *now*? All you had to do was ask. But you called the cops on me like a snitch."

Carmella was tipsy, but really mad. To see him there with several hundred dollars' worth of booze on that table and he stole fifty-six dollars from her?

Suddenly *she* wanted to pop him one right in the nose. But since he was bigger and surrounded by greasy-looking guys who looked like they all drove windowless white vans, she figured her best bet was to call the cops instead.

"Come on," she said to PJ and they started to walk away.

"I said I just borrowed it." Clifton moved to grab her arm to stop her, and from the corner of her eye, she saw a flash of blue, which was PJ being picked up and moved behind Asa, who stood next to Duke, who put himself in front of Carmella. Mick kept an eye on the other guys.

Duke moved lighting quick and suddenly Clifton was on the ground, his wrist bent back. He looked over his shoulder to Carmella. "Are you all right? Did he hurt you?"

Carmella shook her head. "He barely touched my arm."

"Do you know this piece of shit?"

"That's my ex-wife the cop caller!" Clifton screeched from his place on the floor.

"*This* is Clifton?" Duke asked. He must have bent Clifton's wrist back even harder because the whimpering cut off with a gasp.

Carmella nodded. "I was young!"

Duke grinned at her a moment and then got serious again.

"Tell him to let me go. You guys, get him off me," Clifton whined to his buddies, a few of whom seemed to take this request under advisement.

"Take it outside!" the bartender yelled out.

"Got it." Duke let Clifton's wrist go and then yanked him to his feet. "There's a parking lot half a block up. Plenty of room for us to have a go."

Asa tipped his chin at one of the guys Clifton was with.

"We could just call the police. They'd come get him." It wasn't that Carmella cared if Clifton got punched in the face. In fact, it might be cathartic to see. But she didn't want Duke in trouble. Or Mick or Asa, who weren't even involved really.

"He won't even spend the night in jail unless he's got warrants. Which he might." Duke looked Clifton over.

"You gonna cry to the police or are you going to let me kick your ass?" Clifton taunted.

Two of the four guys ran through the side door and away and Carmella looked over to PJ, who rolled her eyes.

"You think that'll manipulate me, little man?" Duke asked.

"Out!" the bartender repeated.

PJ took Carmella's arm and they backed up. Mick held an elbow out for each one of them. "Ladies, shall we get some fresh air away from the fray?"

"I didn't want to make a scene in there, but shouldn't we be telling Duke this isn't worth it? If the cops are called and he's brawling, won't he get busted too?" Carmella asked quietly.

Mick just kissed her cheek. "Telling Bradshaw not to throw a punch when he's got that look on his face? Good luck with that, red."

Duke and Asa came out next, followed by Clifton, one of his dumbass friends, and the bartender, who called out, "See you later, Asa. You guys have five before I call the cops," as he went back into the bar.

Clifton's friend was talking to him, egging him on, and Asa rolled his head on his neck. PJ sighed and murmured, *"So hot."*

Once they were on the sidewalk near the action but out of direct harm, Mick spoke again. "Look, darlin', eighty percent of the time Duke is the most chill motherfucker who walks this earth. But you put him in or on a machine? Put him in a ring or a fight? Well, he lives *hard* and full-out in that next fifteen percent."

"And that last five percent?" Carmella asked him.

"When you push him too far. When you threaten something or someone he is bound to protect? He is a motherfucker you don't want coming at you. Because all that mellow surfer *right on* stuff is gone."

Shouldn't she be outraged he was going to fistfight her ex? Who, granted, said and did some stupid shit, but he wasn't worth Duke getting arrested over.

"She didn't even have anything worth stealing! Not even her

crazy mom's pills I could sell." Clifton took a wad of money from his pocket and threw it.

It hit Duke in the face.

Everything went very quiet until Mick spoke. "Well. Now this is going to happen for real. You two stay back here. I'm going to make sure everything goes by the rules."

Duke could have made a witty retort.

But for long moments he said and did nothing. Carmella moved farther up the sidewalk to the edge of the lot so she could see Duke's face. PJ joined her and they linked arms and watched like weirdo perverts.

Duke had been across the bar, unable not to watch as Carmella and PJ swayed over to the jukebox. Even as they'd ordered pitchers and gotten the balls at a free table racked up, he'd watched her.

The dudes in the far corner had his attention when they'd first arrived, but he didn't figure any of them for a threat they couldn't handle.

But when Carmella had been walking near them, he'd definitely been paying attention, and by the time she spun on the guy, he was making his way over.

And then the fucker had actually *touched* Carmella. And then he'd used that taunt about her mother and was so nonchalant about the way he'd violated her home and stolen from her.

Truly this man needed a fist in his face in the worst way.

Mick watched their backs as he and Asa faced Clifton and his no forehead–looking ape of a friend.

Duke simply took the ratfaced goatfucker, as Carmella so poetically called him, in. Tallied up his strengths and weaknesses, and once he was sure he could hold off dropping the dude until he'd gotten to punch him three times, he began to move.

"I get it. She is really good in the sack," Clifton taunted.

Before he could even fully accomplish his sneer, Duke had

given over to that feral part of him, that part who would protect what was his, what was fragile and special, and landed a kidney punch on each side and then a jab, quick and hard, to the nose.

A snap, a howl, and Clifton dropped like the sack of shit he was.

His friend grabbed the back of his shirt and dragged a half-walking ratface away.

"I catch you anywhere near Carmella, you utter her name, use, or abuse her in any way, and I will break your nose again. And your arms too. You get me?" Duke asked their retreating forms.

Any defiance either man had shown was gone by that point as they shouted their agreement and kept retreating.

He looked at Asa, who looked his fists over. "Thanks."

"You do always know how to have a good time." Asa tipped his chin at Mick, who laughed at both of them as he headed over.

"I think maybe we can call it a night. Take your women home and let them kiss your bruised fists," Mick said.

Carmella and PJ approached. Now that the rage had settled back, he worried how she felt watching him that way.

But her eyes held that light it had the night at the gym when he'd been boxing. It really did work out when a man's kinks lined up so well with his partner.

"You're going to want to ice these." Carmella took his hands gently in hers.

"Yeah. Come on. I'll let you drive me home."

She paused. "Should we take you to the emergency room?"

"He didn't even land a single punch. His face made my fists sore, though."

Her eyes widened. "Will this affect your work?"

He slung an arm around her, pulling her close as they headed back to where they'd parked the cars earlier that day.

"Sometimes when I fight, it might mess me up the next day or two. But I don't work until Tuesday so I'll be fine."

"So why are you letting me drive your car?"

He was a little protective of his machines, that was true. It amused him that she was so easygoing about it.

"Because I'm drunk on adrenaline, which will crash in a bit. And I've been drinking and you haven't in a few hours."

"Can I do doughnuts in it at the high school parking lot?"

He snorted. "I take it you're not upset over the fight?"

"Well, it's pretty embarrassing to have your ex-husband be such a douchenozzle in front of your friends. And the crack about my mom and her pills wasn't my favorite." Carmella's voice didn't waver. That was good. "But it was really fucking hot when you punched him out."

He'd had a rock-hard dick ever since she took his hands after the fight so her words just then made him groan.

They said their good-byes at the cars, with everyone agreeing to meet up for breakfast before starting day two.

She had to pull his seat up pretty close, but he wisely held his tongue.

"Stop staring at me. I'm not going to wreck your car. I'm a good driver."

"Everyone thinks they're a good driver. It's stunning how many people do. You are, though, so get that frown off your face. Such a stubborn frown. Makes me want to kiss it away."

"Mellow Duke is back, I see."

"Mellow Duke?"

"The guy who lopes along with a sexy grin. The guy who makes everyone smile."

"You said I was sexy."

"And drunk." She laughed.

She really was a good driver, Duke decided.

"Not entirely sober, but I do know what I'm hearing."

"You're totally sexy. And when you're all *grrr, arrrrr, punchy punchy, grrr*, it's also sexy. Though I'm not sure if I'm supposed to be uncomfortable with that or not," Carmella said.

"I get hard when you wipe a counter down. Who am I to judge what gets you hot? As long as it's me, I have no beef." He gave over to laughter at her.

The rest of the drive was pretty quick, which was good because he wanted to fuck her. Wanted to strip her down and remind himself she was fine and his.

CHAPTER
Twenty-Two

Thanks for defending my honor tonight." She pulled up in his driveway and keyed the car off.

"It made my year that I got to finally punch that guy out. I don't trust him as far as I can throw him, though. Now that I know what he looks like, I can watch out for him better. The bartender is a friend of Asa's. He might know something."

Duke got out and joined her on the driver's side. "Should we go get Ginger and bring her to my house for the night?"

"Craig texted me earlier to ask if he could keep her until tomorrow. He can't have a dog right now. He's too busy usually. But he loves animals so he sometimes steals my dog to get a canine fix. Plus, he takes her to the dog park—so he can meet women—but Ginger loves it at his house. I'll swing by his place tomorrow on the way home and grab her."

He dug that little dog and couldn't deny a twinge of jealousy that Craig had her right then.

"I miss her too," Carmella said quietly.

What Duke liked most was that she didn't joke about it. She was serious and it was cool that he was too.

"Right now, though, you're sweaty and roughed up and unbelievably hot. I'd like to utilize this as it's all my favorite."

He bent and picked her up. "I vow that we'll make it to my bed this time."

"If you say so." She kissed his neck as he got his door unlocked and them both inside. He kicked it shut, locked it, and headed straight to his bed, where he tossed her, pulling his clothes off as she did the same.

"I'm going to wash my hands as they're covered in ratfaced goatfucker sweat and blood. Don't go anywhere."

He came back out with wet hair. "I dunked my head under. I hope I didn't spoil that tousled sexy thing you liked so much."

"Get down here and let me show you just how much you didn't spoil it."

She pushed him to his back and kissed him. Slowly at first. And fell under, her mouth on his.

Carmella kissed across his face, over his nose, digging her fingers into his hair as she moved down his neck and collarbone. She licked over his ink, tasting the salt of his skin. Loving the way he shivered and arched into her kisses.

She drew the tip of her tongue around his right nipple until it beaded and he made a ragged sound.

It did something to her to be able to evoke such a response from him. It drove her, pushed her, made her want more.

"I want to be what you see when you close your eyes," she said without meaning to give voice to her thoughts.

"You are." Voice ragged, he caressed her shoulders.

She nibbled across his belly, down the ridges of his muscles and then the trail of downy hair that led straight to his cock.

Sighing happily, she licked from balls to the tip and then once and twice more. His fingers kneaded the comforter as he groaned.

Carmella grabbed the base of his cock and angled him to swallow as much as she could. He got even harder each time she sucked and then pulled back. This big, gorgeous, powerful man who she'd just watch pummel someone else could easily turn that on her and he never had. Not even a shadow.

Even when he'd thought the worst of her, he'd never threatened her like that. For someone like Carmella, that meant everything. Watching her mother fall in with one loser after the next had hardened her heart to any hope of a relationship of equals.

And then there'd been Clifton and she figured the only way to survive was to never let herself be vulnerable with anyone again and she'd never turn out like Virgie.

Everything was different now. He changed everything. Whether she wanted it changed or not.

She licked around the crown and just below where she knew he liked it best. He grunted and said her name, letting go of the bedding and grabbing her instead.

"I don't know why you always stop me," she said, laughing as he flipped her to her back.

"I don't always stop you. But I have been doing little but think-ing about shoving my cock in you since about eleven this morn-ing. Someday soon we need to talk about the discontinuation of this condom business," he muttered as he suited up.

"Hush up and fuck me already."

"On your belly."

She quickly got into position, not even caring about how eagerly she shoved her ass toward him when he pushed her knee up the mattress to open her up more fully.

He played around her entrance as she attempted to shove her-self back on his cock. But he held her in place with his thighs. Being wedged just how he wanted her drove her mad. She wanted more from him.

He played her desire, made her tremble, gasp, groan with satis-faction when he finally thrust into her pussy fully.

"Goddamn. What a fucking fool that piece of shit was to let you go. Good thing I'm not a fool."

He kissed her back between her shoulder blades as he angled down over her body. She put a hand between her belly and the bed, finding her clit ready.

"Yes, gorgeous. That's fucking it."

She worked her clit in time with his thrusts, knowing that as she got closer to climax, he'd feel the changes inside her. Feel her heat up, tighten around him. That friction was so delicious all she really had to do was let him push her body up her finger, grinding and creating a wave of pleasure each time he fucked into her.

"Mine," he whispered against her skin.

"Yours," she agreed into the pillow. Not knowing if he heard it or not, not sure if she hoped he had.

He made her lose her head. Did something to the filters she'd kept in place so long to protect herself. Devastated every single defense until all that was left was the heart of her, exposed to him. She only hoped he didn't use that against her.

She came then, in a deep, nearly painful rolling climax that left her muscles jumping at the end. Carmella loved the way he snarled a curse, the way he tried to resist but he couldn't because she made him feel so good he had to come.

He sped his thrusts until he pressed in that last time and stayed for long moments until he finally flopped to the side, gasping for breath.

"It doesn't matter if my fists hurt. I can't feel anything below my neck anyway," he mumbled and she kissed whatever part of him that was nearest, which turned out to be his forearm.

"You fought over me. Should I be embarrassed?"

He snorted. "Why? That guy was in desperate need of a beat down. What a disrespectful asshole. Sometimes the only lesson a loser like him gets is underlined with a fist. He's the one who should be embarrassed. I'm just happy it was me who got to do it."

He got out of bed to get rid of the condom and do a quick check of the locks. Naked as a jaybird.

Maybe getting his ass kicked would scare Clifton off for good. But Carmella was a realist. Chances were, he'd sniff around to see if Duke was still in the picture, but he'd try to use her again if he thought he could benefit.

"Uh-oh," he said, returning to her side in bed. She snuggled down, pulling a sheet over them both. "I don't want you feeling guilty over this, Carmella."

"Well, I don't. And *that* makes me feel guilty. I mean, you've seen all this from me. The mother, the father, the ex." Carmella rolled to bury her face in the pillow, feeling the heat of her blush against the case.

"Do you think I'd hold you responsible for any of that? You have no choice who you're born to. And you're certainly not accountable for whatever other people do. I'm not him."

She moved to her side to face him because she heard the emotion in his tone. "I know you aren't. I'm sorry if I made you feel that way."

"Stop apologizing!" he said, frustrated.

Which sort of pissed her off. "Hey, I can apologize when I do something that needs an apology for. I'm fucked up but I'm not four years old."

He raised one brow at her. "I don't want you treating me like these leeches who screw you over. I'm not down with that. You don't have to say you're sorry for having feelings. Even if I don't think those feelings are appropriate. Now I'm sorry for making you feel that way. But I don't want you treating me like them."

"What have I done to make you feel that?"

"Why do you care? That's not a flip question, I'm serious. Why does it matter to you if my feelings got hurt?" he asked.

"I care about you." She linked her fingers with his.

"You look like you're fighting not to run out of the room."

"I am." Her smile wasn't amused, though. "I'm not open like this. It's uncomfortable sometimes." She sat up, crisscross applesauce-style, and he sighed, putting a sheet over her before sitting across from her and doing the same.

"If I see you all pretty and sexy, it's hard enough to concentrate, but with all my favorite, secret spots on display, I can't focus at all." He took her hand back. "Now, you were saying?"

"Like this thing right now. The way you respond just how I need you to. It's . . . I don't know what to do with it."

He cocked his head as he thought.

Of course, now it was Carmella all caught up in his beauty. She'd just had her mouth all over him. That man had been inside her and not just in the physical sense. He went out of his way to make her life easier. Better.

"I think you should accept it as your due. Sometimes when we click like that—when you do the exact thing I needed, even if I didn't know I needed it until right then—I take it as a reminder that I am one lucky dude. It's cool for you to let go of that fear that I'll shred you the way they do. You deserve to be adored. To be treated like a queen. Got me? Because you *are* a queen. Strong. Fierce. Beautiful. You are a fucking survivor, Carmella. Like a phoenix."

Tears filled her gaze until she wiped them away with the back of her hand.

"See? I don't want you crying when I tell you what you are to me. I want you to say, fuck yeah I am!"

"Fuck yeah I am."

He nodded. "Not bad. Keep working in it."

"They're not sad tears. You say these things to me and they're different because you're different. I'm crying because I know that. And that's terrifying and wonderful. And I really just don't know how to do this so I'm messing up."

He leaned in to kiss over each eyelid. "Now you're making me all choked up. You're a gift."

Carmella sighed, deciding to let hope win over fear. "When I grew up, I was ashamed pretty much all the time. My mom was, well, she wasn't like anyone else's mom, that's for sure. I had my aunt and uncle and my grandmother, and I'm so glad because they were a stable thing in an unstable world. But I kept a lot of secrets because if the school or my family knew how bad my mom got sometimes, they'd have taken me away. And she wouldn't have had anyone."

"I'm out of fucks to give for your mother. Kids shouldn't raise parents."

"Of course they shouldn't. But for heaven's sake, Duke, when you were in Iraq, weren't you faced at least a few times with the least horrible of a bunch of horrible choices? You've never done something for love that you wish you didn't have to? Never?"

He closed his eyes as pain crossed over his face. It was gone when he opened them to look at her once more. "Fair enough. But I still hate it on your behalf."

"Do you want to tell me about it? Whatever you were thinking just now?" she asked.

"We're talking about something else right now. You were saying that you kept your mom's secrets."

Since he'd let her avoid the subject more than once, she let him do the same. For the time being. He had a preference toward being the one people came to for help instead of asking for it himself. It was one of the things she loved about him. He was a man she'd grown to count on.

"I don't know how to be good at this relationship thing. Pretty much since day one I've broken my rules for you. And . . . sometimes I'm worried you're going to look at what I come with and realize it's not worth it—the fights in parking lots and interactions with all types of law enforcement. I'm shitty at being someone's anything."

He shook his head. "You're not my anything. You're my every-thing. Honey, *I'm* fights in parking lots. Just so we're clear on this. I'm barely respectable."

"Bullshit. You're incredibly honorable."

He grinned. "Thank you. But that's not the same as respect-able. But you look at me and you see the honorable. That's why I love you."

Carmella's heart stuttered as she tried not to burst into tears or react in a way that would freak him out.

"I didn't mean to say that yet. Cat's out of the bag. I didn't say it so you would feel compelled to respond. I said it because I want you to understand the Carmella I see is the one I'm look-ing at right now. I will slay your fucking dragons. I will have your back when you need to be the one slaying. I'm all in. You dig?"

It was the *you dig* at the end that did it. She nodded. "I've been pressing my nose against the window just to look at you on the other side a long time."

"That's a winner of a compliment."

She smiled at him for a moment.

"I don't need your shame. All I want is everything but your shame and guilt. I want it all when you want to give it."

Carmella blew out a breath. "No big deal, then."

"You can wrangle a shop full of meatheads on a daily basis. You got this."

"Ha. That's a work in progress. And Duke? You don't get to tell me when I can be sorry."

"You're one hundred percent right."

"Okay. I'm suddenly exhausted. I need to get up early tomor-row," Carmella said around a yawn. "Being someone's girlfriend is really tiring."

He snickered. "I like to keep you on your toes. But why get up so early? We don't have to be at breakfast until ten thirty. If we shower together, which is the green way to do it, we don't have to wake up until nine thirty. Don't tell me you're going to work."

"I need to drop off medication and some groceries at my mom's house. I'll run over there first thing and get back in time for that shower and then breakfast."

"We'll go on the way to breakfast."

"No, really. It's cool. I'll handle it."

"Carmella, didn't I just say I didn't want your shame? I won't even go in if you don't want me to. I would like to meet them both at some point, though. Maybe if they know you've got people around you who aren't going to let you get taken advantage of, they'll ease back."

"That sounds like an *awesome* Sunday morning. I'll devote a whole scrapbook to it."

Laughing, he pulled her into a hug and she turned in his arms, scooting back into his body.

"I just get worried for you. And I know how much you do for your mother, so naturally I'm curious and want to meet her. I want them both to know I'm around. And if I meet them, I can make my own judgments. I want to try to understand."

"Stop being so perfect."

"You're so fucking adorable when you're grumpy."

"Good night, Duke."

"Are we getting up at eight? If we stop off on the way to break-fast, how long do you usually spend there?"

"This is messing with my calm," she mumbled.

"It's my gift. Answer me and then we can go to sleep."

"Fine. We can go on the way. I'll bring her out to meet you if she's in an okay state of mind. I haven't seen him yet, so if he's there, I'll play it by ear. We don't have to get up until nine. Now hush and let me sleep or I really will get grumpy."

CHAPTER
Twenty-Three

Duke parked at the curb, turning the car off. Carmella turned to him. "I'll be back shortly."

"I'm here whenever and however you need me." He kissed her when she leaned his way and then got out.

He watched her walk up the steps, and before she could use a key, the door opened. Duke tensed, his hand on the door as Carmella jumped, but it appeared to be from surprise.

But she didn't go in and she took a step backward. That's what had him getting out of the car. She turned to look in his direction and that's when a man came out onto the porch.

"Everything all right?" Duke called out.

"What's it to you?" the man replied.

Duke's ground-eating stride had him up to the porch in a few breaths.

Carmella closed her eyes and rage fired Duke's blood. Again these fuckers made her feel bad.

"I'm Duke Bradshaw. Carmella's boyfriend." He held out his hand, keeping eye contact and seeing the monster of addiction in the shadows in his gaze. There was a nervous sort of animosity coming from him that made Duke wary.

"I'm Carmella's daddy, Steven." He looked Duke over, sizing

him up. Duke let him, wanting the old man to know what he was up against should he try to harm Carmella.

"This is Steven Hay. I was just going to leave once I came in to drop Mom's stuff off." Carmella's hand gesture when she introduced them gave Steven the chance to weasel out of a handshake and shove his hands in his pockets.

"As I said, you can give it all to me and I'll be sure she gets it. We sure appreciate the food you bring over. You're a great cook. Better than your mom even." Steven's smile was calculating as he turned it to Duke. "I didn't know Carmella had a man friend. She doesn't tell us much. I suppose that's how it is when they grow up and move away."

Carmella made a half-strangled sound.

"Where is she?" Carmella moved to the side to go in, but Steven put a hand up to bar her entrance.

"She's resting. You and she have been fighting and she's tired. She doesn't want to see you."

"I'll go ahead and verify that for myself. Anyway, I don't have to be her friend to drop this off. Move your arm." Carmella was like one of those terriers who hunted stuff. She was all fluffed up and ready to rumble. She hated this man in a way she didn't extend to her mother or that ex-husband of hers.

"She doesn't want to see you," Steven repeated. "This is her house, Carmella. Respect that."

"Actually, it's my house. She nearly lost it two years ago. We made an agreement. I pay the mortgage. She gets to live here rent-free. You're not part of that equation. I was hoping you'd pay her rent, but obviously that's not going to happen. But I can, and I will come in my own house and I'll do it now. You can move your arm or you can do it when the police take you back to jail." She shrugged.

"I'm going to have to insist you move out of the way, Mr. Hay," Duke said.

He dropped his arm and Carmella rushed inside. Clearly she was worried about her mother, so Duke left Steven in their wake and followed quickly.

"It's not what you think!" Steven yelled as he slammed the door and followed them in.

Carmella stood outside a bedroom door and knocked. A dog barked on the other side. "Mom, I know you're here. Come out."

"I don't want to see you. We'll talk next week. Leave the pills and the food and go."

Sighing, Carmella looked over her shoulder to Duke. "Scrapbook memory time." She pulled a pin from her hair and unbent it, using that to poke through the hole in the doorknob.

The lock popped and Carmella marched inside and then skidded to a halt. And when she reached out to open the blinds and light flooded into the room, Duke understood why she'd halted.

"Duke"—Carmella's voice shook but she held it together—"can you please take the dog? She's nasty, but probably hungry. There's some ham in the bag I brought. Give her some, okay? Water too."

Duke found a clean-ish towel and he picked the snarly little creature up. Pity filled him as he could see how hungry it was once he gave it some ham. He didn't take his attention off the bedroom doorway, or from Steven Hay, who stood not too far away, wringing his hands.

"It's not what you think," Steven said.

"That so? What is it then?"

"I was inside a few years. I just got a little carried away. We drank too much. You know how it is."

"What I think is that you beat up that woman in there. And now you're sticking around because you're trying to figure out how to manage Carmella into shutting up so you don't have to go back inside."

Virgie yelled out as Carmella reached the doorway. "You're

making him stressed out. We just needed to chill a little. I fell, that's all."

Carmella ignored her mother, heading over to Steven. "She's on medication that shouldn't be mixed with whatever you gave her. I'm guessing barbiturates. She likes those best. Tell me now," Carmella ordered.

"She said it would be fine. She knows her health, Carmella. You can't be so overprotective."

"*Did she ingest barbiturates?* You tell me right now or I'll see if someone over at the courthouse can help you be more cooperative."

Duke knew Carmella well enough by that point to know she was on the verge of losing her shit. The more precise and controlled she got in her threats, the closer she got to breaking.

He stood closer to Carmella to enforce the question. Steven nodded and rattled off the street name for whatever shit they'd taken.

Carmella shook her head. "Usually it takes you a lot longer to get to this part of your spiral back to prison. You have twenty minutes to gather your things and be out of this house. You are to have no further contact with her, do you understand me?"

Steven paled. "Now wait a minute. I'm your daddy. I don't have any place to go. I have to have an address. It's a condition of my release. Have a heart. I'm trying, Carmella. It's hard for a man on the outside after being in so long. We were stressed because I spend so long on the bus trying to find a job. It's hard without a car. I tried to protect her. You know how she can be."

"She's *high* and *covered in bruises*. You tried to hide her from me. She tells me she wants to sell the house for your future together."

"You have no right to keep this house from me." Virgie stumbled out in little more than a long T-shirt, and when she saw Duke, she halted, patting her hair down. There was a bruise on her calf that looked a hell of a lot like a shoe print. Several other bruises stood out in vivid purple on her legs.

Around her wrist were fingerprint bruises and not the digging in during sex kind.

She smiled self-consciously at Duke. Pity filled him. And then rage when he saw the marks around her throat.

"Company? No one said. I look a fright." Virgie headed his way. "I'm Virginia Hay but everyone calls me Virgie. I'm Carmella's mother, though I hear we look like sisters."

Her words were slow.

"Say your good-byes to Steven. He won't be living here anymore."

"Stop being so selfish! For once in your life, do something for someone else, Carmella," Virgie snapped and then looked back to Duke with a smile. "You didn't even introduce this gentleman to your mother. Where are your manners?"

"Ma'am, how about you go to the doctor now? Let us take you so they can make sure you're all right?" Duke wanted to set this place on fire and drag Carmella away from it forever. But he knew she still felt responsible for this monster and so he'd go along with that direction.

For the moment.

Virgie laughed gaily. "Oh, I'm all right. We had some champagne and I fell."

"No one believes that. Steven, you're not packing," Carmella said.

"I won't allow you to kick him out of my house," Virgie said.

"You don't have to. This is *my* house."

Steven moved to intercept Virgie but Carmella blocked him. As hurt as Duke was on her behalf, he had to admit she was pretty freaking stunning right then. She turned on her heel and got in her father's face.

"I said get out. You only have ten minutes now. Tick tock."

Virgie reached for Carmella and Duke stepped in, picking her up and moving her over to the kitchen.

"I'll call the police if you don't leave," Virgie screeched.

Carmella went to hand her mother the phone, but it had been ripped from the wall.

"I don't know how that happened." Virgie's words had begun to slur again. The only pity he had was for Carmella.

"Fine. I have a cell. I'll call the police for you. Or do you want to do it yourself?" She held her phone in her mother's direction.

"No. I'll go," Steven said. "If her heart is this hard, she's never going to change, Virgie."

"I'll go with you then," Virgie proclaimed.

"And do what?" Carmella asked. "You're not taking your medication but you're on something. Did you sell your pills or trade them for something else? What is it?"

"You're always accusing me of things. You only like it when you have me all to yourself so you drive them all away. Every man." Virgie looked to Duke. "I was alone, struggling to raise a kid. Who'd begrudge me some company to get through?" She attempted to point at Carmella but her depth perception was off. "This one here. And when her daddy is home from being away, she doesn't like that either. You be careful of her. She stole this house."

"Don't engage with her," Carmella said to Duke.

"You'll hear from my attorney!" Virgie shook her fist and then looked at it awhile.

"Steven, you now have seven minutes. When you run out of time, I will throw everything left in here out the window." Carmella kept her expression blank as she faced him, hands folded across her chest.

"Come on, Virgie. You and I will get out of here," Steven said and Duke *knew* he'd done it to manipulate Carmella's concern for her mother. Eventually he'd worm his way into staying.

Duke wanted to say something but Carmella spoke first.

"Mom, you can't go."

Duke watched the emotions on Carmella's face. The exhaustion of dealing with this scene. The years of this behavior and abuse from her parents. Neither of them deserved her.

Virgie straightened slowly. "I will go to be with him. You can't stop me."

"You can't, Carm." Duke pulled her off to the side. "She's an adult. What are you going to do? Tie her to a bed? Doesn't she always come back in a day or two when she does this?"

"She *doesn't* do this," Carmella hissed. "I only bought the house two years ago. I've never had the power to kick him out. He doesn't have any place to stay, but he's got some family he can go to. Or whatever. I really don't care. He beat my mother up."

Steven Hay was not the problem. Everyone had said that, and Duke could see now that they'd been right. Virgie was the real issue. Carmella had managed this woman pretty much her whole life, but this wasn't something she could keep up.

"You can't make anyone leave a bad relationship. You can't make her better any more than you already do. You can let him stay here, or you can let them both leave. She's not going to go for being separated from him. Not in the state she's in now. He's made it a choice she has to make." And her mother was a rotten, selfish person who'd choose a man over her child without a second thought.

She wrung her hands and he took them in his own. The anguish on her face also sounded in her voice. "I can't let him stay here! He's already doing this? What's he going to be like in two weeks? I'm going to come over here and there'll be strangers on the couch. Dodgy characters. The neighbors will call the cops. I had to make some serious peace with them when I took over the mortgage."

Duke had no idea she'd done all that.

"Do you see how she is?" Virgie taunted. "She hated fun even as a kid. Why aren't you keeping her satisfied and happy, Duke? Is it that she's secretly a lesbian?"

"That again?" Carmella said.

Duke had no idea what that was about, but he was entirely

finished with these people. "I see a woman who works her butt off so she can pretty much be your personal assistant. She pays your living expenses at huge detriment to herself. She brings you food and your medication. She takes care of you. I see a woman I'd be proud to claim as my daughter were I in your shoes, Ms. Hay."

Virgie smiled. "*Mrs.* We got married again a few days ago."

"Jesus on a skateboard," Carmella muttered. "*He beat you up.* That's not normal. That's not okay."

"It's not your business what happens between us. Do I get in your business? This is why you can't keep a man."

"I'm calling an end to this," Duke told Carmella. He would talk with her about the real options once they left. "We're getting nowhere, they're being abusive, and it's only upsetting you more."

Carmella sighed. "I want to speak to my mother alone."

Rather than ask, Duke nodded, carrying Steven out of the room with him as he did.

"I know what you're thinking," Steven said as Carmella went into the bedroom with her mother and closed the door.

"You must be pretty disgusted with yourself then."

"You can't just stroll into my life and act like you know anything. Carmella has always been difficult. Granted, it was hard for her growing up. But she needs to get over it."

Duke scoffed. "Does she? If my father touched my mother the way you just did hers, he'd be in the hospital right now."

"Ironic that you taunt me with violence to condemn violence." Steven avoided responsibility with the ease of a longtime master liar.

"Look, I've been around enough losers in my life to know every single way you can take this conversation. Let's see, we've got your: It was a moment of weakness. You were stressed. She pushed you there. She hits you too. She gets off on it. You'll never do it again. Or maybe you're one of those who thinks hitting a woman makes him manly. Whatever it is, it won't be you taking responsibility.

You don't need a punch in the face because I think it'll disabuse you of the notion that hitting someone you should love and protect is okay, you need a punch in the nose because you're a woman-hitting piece of shit. I don't like that Carmella takes all this crap from her mother and I don't like you even less."

Duke wanted to call his parents right then to tell them he loved them. For all their faults, for all the yelling his dad did, there was never physical violence in their home.

Steven went for contrition now. "I am sorry we got off on the wrong foot. I'd like to be a family. I do love my wife and daughter, you know. I'll be out and with her mother. If you're with Carmella, we'll be family too. I'll prove you wrong. You'll see."

Duke shrugged. "Your kind of love sucks. I care about Carmella's well-being. That's it. That's why I'm here. If you love people, you don't beat them up. Not really a complicated rule."

Carmella came out a few minutes later, but didn't look at Steven. "Let's go," she told Duke.

He kept his body between Carmella and Steven on the way out. Once they were in the car, he drove around the corner and parked.

"What's up?"

Duke pulled his phone out. "I'm texting Asa that we're taking a pass on today."

"No! This is something you do with your friends every year."

"It's breakfast, we can do that another day. As for Bumbershoot? There's another day tomorrow. And more next year. *I want to be with you.* Away from a crowd and noise. Away from you having to pretend to be okay when you're not. How about you and me grab my bike and take a ride up to Snoqualmie Pass? We'll get some lunch and hang out. And you can tell me whatever you want to do. Or ask me advice, or just talk. Or none of those things."

He could see indecision on her face.

"I promise. I'm not disappointed to miss today."

She nodded.

That Carmella didn't turn to something chemical to deal with the astounding amount of shit she had to shovel sometimes was a marvel to Duke. So that day he'd take her away from the city. On the back of his bike she wouldn't have to talk. Wouldn't have to be responsible for his reaction to her expression or feel any pressure to explain until she was ready.

She needed that and he knew good and well Asa would do it for PJ in his shoes. You did that for people you loved.

She looked at the phone in her hand the whole way back to his place and then finally texted someone once he got to their street.

"Craig knows a guy on the Seattle PD. I can't *not* say something. I just can't. She said she'd deny it if the cops came. Told me all the stuff she usually does. She loves him. It's passionate. If she's okay with it, why can't I be? I still want to scream every time I hear it."

She sighed and they stayed in his driveway because he didn't want to interrupt these moments when she finally shared and let him take some of the weight.

"So, I told her I would not call the cops. But I didn't say I wouldn't tell Craig, who'd tell his buddy. They can still prosecute, even if she won't cooperate, but it's hard and she's pretty experienced with the system. I've been down this road with her before. I'm backed into a corner and I don't know what to do. Every one of my options is terrible. He's hurting her but she won't leave. She won't listen to me. If I kick him out, she'll follow him and they'll both be homeless. And the thing is, Duke? I know he's telling her all this. He's manipulating her and I can't stop it."

"You're doing the best you can. Which is all you can do. There is a really messed-up dynamic going on there. But you cannot make her change her life. You know that. It hurts to see her that way and you have done all you can given the set of circumstances you're faced with."

"I hate that she thinks she's not worth more than this."

Duke reached across the console to hug her. "I know, baby."

CHAPTER
Twenty-four

It had been about two months since Duke had checked in with his parents, and after all the crazy shit with Carmella's, he was reminded to count his blessings.

After the weekend, the work week had gotten back to full swing as the new showroom space was nearing completion.

Carmella had gone out for a walk around the lake with PJ, leaving him alone in his office, so he put his feet up and dialed his parents' house.

His mother answered.

"Hey, Mom. I just wanted to call. It's been a while. How are you guys?"

"Hello, sweetie. Things are going well. You just missed your father. He went up to Ventura to see your brother."

"Everything okay?"

"Well, you know how your brother is."

"Smart? Educated? Destined for a stroke by thirty-five because he eats stress for dinner?"

His mother's laugh was strained.

"What's going on, really?" Duke pushed. He didn't like the way his mother hedged around the topic.

"He and his fiancée broke up recently. He's taking it hard.

Your father is just going to see if some company won't cheer him up."

Duke tried not to think about how his dad had never picked up to come see him during any of Duke's most trying times. It wasn't important by that point.

"I didn't know he and Shelly had split. I'm sorry to hear it. I'll call him later today. Do you need me to come down?"

She laughed again. "It's fine, I'm sure. But you should call Danny. He'd love to hear from you. He looks up to you."

Duke snorted. "Sure he does. You're still coming up at the end of the month for the grand opening, right?"

"We wouldn't miss it. Thank you for handling our hotel reservations."

"Carmella did that. She's . . . well, she's my girlfriend. The real deal. You can meet her when you come up."

"Really? That's wonderful. Tell me all about her."

The last time he'd talked to his mother about a woman was when he was in high school. But it was okay because as he started to describe Carmella to her, he realized none of the women in between then and now were noteworthy the way Carmella was.

"So she's your employee? You know you're leaving yourself open to all sorts of trouble if this goes badly."

He'd hoped she'd have said something positive first. But he supposed it was a mom thing to say, to guard his business.

"You'll meet her in a few weeks so you can judge for yourself. She's not like that. She's not like anyone I've ever known before."

"I'm just so thrilled to hear you've finally met someone. I was beginning to wonder about you and Asa."

He nearly choked on the soda he'd been drinking. "Asa's in love with the woman he lives with. They'll be married in a year or two."

"Good. He needs to get started on a family. So do you. Your sister already has two. Where are my grandchildren from my oldest?"

He dangled some shiny stuff her way, promising to take them on a tour of the area when they visited, and hung up.

He was glad they'd caught up, but the discussion they'd had about his brother still nagged at him. Duke couldn't just get in the car and go check on Danny, though he was glad their father was.

Breakups were hard. Danny's fiancée had seemed very nice the time he'd met her when he was down visiting for his nephew's baptism. She was like Danny. Career minded. Intelligent. Ambitious. Duke figured they'd stick it out and he hoped the breakup wasn't an ugly one on either side.

Duke called and left a voicemail for his brother asking how things were and inviting him up for the grand opening once more. He'd invited his siblings already, but maybe if he underlined how much it would be nice to see Danny, his brother would come.

Seeing Carmella's difficulties made him realize his family issues weren't nearly as bad as he'd once thought. A dad with little patience and a loud voice wasn't the same as the guy who beat your mother up. Even if he felt like he didn't fit the same way everyone else did, he loved them.

"I think that's a monumentally bad idea," Carmella said to the foreman the next day. "If you go that way, you have to tell Asa to his face. There's no way I'm delivering that news to him."

They were running late on getting some electrical stuff dealt with. City and county people had come out, everything was signed off on their end, but the foreman had just told her they needed to send some of their crew to another site, which would set them back another four days.

"Aw, come on. It's still within the deadline."

Carmella shook her head. "Whatever. I'm not delivering this information to him. Which means he'll come looking for you, or send Duke or Mick."

The guy winced. Duke usually handled the contractors. He and

Mick did nearly all the public face of Twisted Steel stuff because Asa was better left alone to do his work. He wasn't really a people person.

Which was an understatement, naturally. But as the date for the grand opening approached, all three guys behind Twisted Steel were growing impatient, Asa most of all.

"Exactly," Carmella said of the foreman's wince. "So, if you don't want to tell him yourself, I suggest you keep your crew here and finish what you're supposed to on time. Then you can tell Asa happy news."

Grumbling, the guy stomped off and Carmella got up to get more coffee.

Duke poked his head in, smiling as she got to the door. "Hello, gorgeous. Wow, I love looking at you." He just took his time staring at her as she blushed.

"We talked about this," she said for the dozenth time.

"And we talked about how we talked about it. I remember. You said words. I listened to them."

Like a naughty little boy.

But it worked. "By the way, the foreman was just hinting that they might split guys off from their crew to work another site. I told him he needed to inform Asa in person if that was the case."

Duke sighed. "They better be done. We have catering, equipment rental, party planning, all that stuff set for the end of this month. So much fucking money. Jesus." He ran his hands through his hair and it messed up for about thirty seconds before it flopped back into that wave at the front. Perfectly.

"I don't even know what dark magic you've done to get your hair so perfect."

He brightened. "Yeah?" Duke bent to catch his reflection in the glass of the open door.

"You look like a *GQ* magazine version of a fifties pompadour. Not that poofy. Just exactly right. Even the gray you're getting highlights the shape of your hair. It's amazing."

He smiled. "That's my favorite compliment today. Thank you. Want to grab a cup of coffee with me?"

"Doughnuts in the break room?"

Duke nodded. "The manager at the Top Pot is a client. He sent them over as a thank-you."

"Much better than flowers."

"Just one of the many reasons we're together. Any word from Craig today?"

The cops had stopped by her mom's house a few days before, but Virgie denied Steven was responsible for her injuries and claimed she'd gotten them falling down some stairs. Steven played the super helpful guy just out of prison trying to keep his life on the straight and narrow, though from what Craig said, his friend saw right through it.

"Yeah. He called earlier. They just don't have enough to push here. But the guy said he'd keep an eye on the situation. They're busy, I know. But I appreciate it. My uncle says he's done with her totally. I can't blame him."

"But that leaves you holding even more weight."

Yep. Carmella shrugged.

They headed in to get doughnuts and take a few minutes to share a cup of coffee.

"I'll be here late tonight. We're putting in overtime on that fastback now that the parts arrived," Duke told her.

"PJ showed me the paint. I love that color so much."

"I'm a big fan of that stock orange myself. The upholstery should be coming in tomorrow. I'd like to push it out by Monday."

Mick came to sit next to Carmella and she patted his hand. "Hey, you."

"What's up today, Red?"

"I'm eating a doughnut, so that's a win. Looking at handsome men. Also a win."

"I like your attitude."

"I'm a ray of sunshine." She stood. "I need to get back to work. I'll see you both later."

"I'll escort you." Duke pushed his chair back.

"Nah. Finish your coffee and your break."

Duke watched her leave with a happy sigh.

"I'd make a crack about that look on your face. But even I'm not jaded enough to not see the beauty in what you have with her," Mick said as he grabbed another doughnut.

"She seemed to float into my life, and once she touched down, the roots grew very deep very fast. I wasn't expecting love. Knocked me on my ass," Duke said.

"Is it scary? I mean, are you freaked about a long-term relationship when you were just dating three women at a time six months ago?"

"It was two, not three. At first it was startling more than scary. By the time I realized how deep I was with Carm, it was too late. There was no way to stop loving her. Love is pretty awesome, though, Mick. I highly recommend it."

Mick spun his coffee mug slowly, clearly working through something.

"You still haven't told me what you meant that day we went out on the ride. About loving someone. Or two someones."

"Like I said, it's complicated. Way too complicated to go into here. The very short version is that I ran away from something. I hurt people to do it. I fucked up."

"Can it be fixed? Do you want to?"

Mick tipped his chair back. "We'd need hours, lots of liquor, and privacy for me to get into this whole thing. For now I have to ride herd on about two dozen people."

"All right. I *do* want to hear, though. So let's get together with Asa and pick a time. We'll go camping or you can all come to my place. I want to know," Duke told him.

Mick nodded and left the room.

CHAPTER
Twenty-five

The rain kept Carmella in bed that next Saturday morning. Duke had worked late the night before—as the whole shop had been doing to finish a project—so she'd been on her own.

She'd gone to her aunt and uncle's for dinner and then out to a movie with PJ and Craig and had turned off her kitchen light at one, so he hadn't been home by that point.

She stretched and grabbed her phone to text Duke. Ten minutes later she and Ginger opened the front door to find him standing there in sleep pants and a T-shirt.

He took her hand, twirling her into a circle and then into his arms for a hug. He smelled good and was so warm she dragged him to her bed.

"You really did just wake up. And you texted me first thing?"

"Did I wake you?" Carmella asked, nuzzling his throat.

"No. I had to be up anyway. I need to get to the shop in a bit. But you contacted me right when you woke up."

Carmella nodded, not sure why he was repeating it. And then he smiled, pulling her up his body to kiss her and then hug her tight.

"Keep it up, Bradshaw. This is why I text you first thing."

"I love that you reached out for me without hesitation. I miss it when you're not next to me when I sleep. I got used to that really fast. I don't miss your dog's farts, though, and I stepped on one of her gooey chew things on my way over. Gross."

Carmella started to laugh. "Don't. She'll hear you. She has a complex about it."

"I guess I'm just glad it's her and not you who makes that smell on a regular basis."

"Me too."

"Now. As I have limited time and I did not have the pleasure of you next to me last night, I think we need to rectify my absence."

He said this as he pulled her shirt off.

Then Ginger made a racket barking in the kitchen, startling them both. Duke was up and moving to the door before she could even manage to free herself of the bedding.

"You stay here," he ordered and moved down her short hallway.

"So help me god, if anyone I know is here trying to rip me off, I am going outside, topless, to rip their fucking heads off," she muttered as she slowly looked around the corner he'd told her to stay behind.

He prowled—oh yes, prowled—through her house, looking out windows, and then turned to her with an amused face. "She went out the doggie door. I think she's chasing squirrels."

Carmella joined him in the kitchen to peer out the window. Ginger trotted between two trees, giving her conversational bark.

"She just wants to play with them."

"Some guard dog." Duke started and then his gaze went hooded when he noticed she stood there topless and in her under-pants. "Well now. *Hello.*"

"I was wondering when you'd notice I made a booty call. Booty text. Whatever. I requested your sexual services. Maintenance, you see. I'm used to a certain level of satisfaction now. It's all your fault."

"I'll have you know, I give excellent customer satisfaction."

He picked her up and carried her to the table, depositing her ass on top.

"I'm very aware. Five stars of five."

He sat, scooting his chair close, resting his chin on her knee.

Duke rendered her shaky, breathless, and wanton. She watched, rapt, as he turned his head, kissing one of the dimples at the inside of her knee.

She drew in a ragged breath at the rasp of his beard against that sensitive skin. Then the flick of his tongue made her shiver.

"It's a good thing I know this table is clean enough to eat off, hm?"

"Extra clean now because I know you watched me cleaning up in here night before last." Carmella lifted her butt so he could pull her panties off.

"You're so good to me." He moved his chair closer as he pulled her to the edge of the table.

He spread her labia and looked his fill. It might have been embarrassing or odd but he always had this expression of wonder and delight when he took her in. Made her feel beautiful and sexy.

He took a lick. Just a quick one.

And then another.

She went back to her elbows, watching down the line of her body as he feasted on her.

He ate her hungrily at first and then he'd ease back, letting her go return to simmer. Closer and closer to climax each time.

Duke rendered her incoherent as she made sounds she thought were words begging him to make her come.

He hummed against her pussy and then sucked her clit into his mouth hard and fast. He did that over and over again, filling her with so much pleasure she nearly hurt when climax seemed to explode from her belly and into her legs.

"Goddamn, I love it when you come that hard." He kissed her belly as he stood. "Don't move."

He jogged from the room. Like she could move even if she wanted to?

True to his word, less than half a minute later he was back, condom on and making himself at home between her thighs. Again.

He teased her with the head of his cock. Circling through her pussy, dipping inside just a little and pulling out to do the same thing over again.

"You're so fucking wet," he croaked as he tapped her clit with the head of his cock.

"Be a shame to waste it. Put your dick in me!"

Laughing, he obeyed. She wrapped her calves around his hips and hooked her heels around his thighs.

"No escape for me, huh?"

She shook her head.

"Thank god." He grabbed her hips for purchase and began to fuck her, sending her boobs to bounce with each thrust all the way home.

"I think this is the perfection of breasts. That moment when they bounce so prettily that way. I considered letting go of your hips to grab them, and then when I go balls deep, they do that. And I think it would be blasphemy to stop them from moving."

Caught between a laugh and a gasp, Carmella writhed when he ground himself against her.

There were no more words after that. She couldn't take her gaze from his face. He was so expressive, especially during sex. Tenderness in his eyes rendered her utterly helpless against the rush of her own in response. Then determination as he got closer. A sort of feral satisfaction when he leaned forward, taking her hands, stretching them above her head as he came, kissing her hard.

She closed her eyes for a moment, trying to catch her breath. And when she opened them, he was straightening to stand. Smiling.

"Now then. Coffee and breakfast?"

"Don't make me bacon until you're wearing pants," she called out as she headed to find some clothes of her own. Fucking in the kitchen and maybe being seen was one thing, but sitting bare-assed at breakfast wasn't her idea of fun.

Duke tucked a new bag of coffee in the drawer for her in her office. She'd frown at him, but he didn't care. It was a little treat, and if anyone needed more treats in their life, it was Carmella.

The Wonder Woman mug he'd given her a few weeks before sat on her desk and it made him smile.

The office was thoroughly hers by that point. Two and a half months in, and she'd created a well-oiled, hyper-efficient atmosphere that was also human.

Duke wasn't the only one who brought her things. In the drawer she kept the coffee in, there were also honey sticks from Duane. His family had bees, and once he'd found out Carmella liked honey in her coffee, he brought them for her.

And the most wonderful thing: the magnet collection.

That crab magnet Mick had given her when they'd gone on a ride around the peninsula had been the first in what was an ever-growing cast that took up the side of the large metal filing cabinet in the office.

Once the guys had heard about Mick's crab, they began to bring her back little trophies whenever they went anywhere. Every single time someone gave her a new one, she was so tickled and thrilled it filled him with joy just to see it.

Naturally, as it was Carmella's collection, it was very organized, but it reminded him every time he came in, to choose to be happy and find delight in the small things.

"What are you up to?" Asa called out as he came in through the shop.

"Just putting something in Carmella's office." Duke came out and met Asa partway.

"Mick said we're on track to deliver that fastback later today. The client is coming at three," Asa told him.

"Excellent." They stood in front of the shop board. "Carmella told me last week that we're up twenty-seven percent from this time last year."

And once the space in the existing building was freed up, they'd start a remodel with new administrative offices, expanded inventory capacity, and some extra shop space.

Spending all that money made Duke nervous, even as he knew it was the right choice. He and Asa were going to meet with Mick shortly to offer him a buy-in to the business. Having him in charge was great. They all worked well together. But Asa and Duke had more power because it was the two of them who owned it.

"Lots of change going on these last few years," Asa said.

"There were times in Iraq when I seriously wondered if I'd see another birthday, you know? And now here we all are, safe and healthy. And this thing everyone thought only losers did has given me a fantastic life." Duke was fucking proud of what he'd built in Twisted Steel. Proud that he'd done it even when his family thought it was a waste of potential.

The sound of the number pad being used on the door made both men turn. Carmella came in, talking with PJ.

Both women smiled at the sight of the two men. "Fancy seeing you here," PJ said to them. "I'll be starting the detail work on the Ford this morning."

Duke broke away to approach Carmella. He bumped fists with PJ on his way past.

"Good morning. Don't bolt on me, I promise I won't kiss you. Yet." He winked. "And yes, we did talk about it."

"Don't poke at me. I haven't had coffee yet."

"Come on up to your office. I'll make you a pot."

She gave him a suspicious look. "People are already here. None of your hanky-panky."

Even when she was Monday morning cranky, she was adorable.

"Cross my heart, I only have making you coffee on my to-do list right now."

As he ground and measured out coffee, he watched her set her world in order. She had a little ritual to start every day, and as she finished each step, she brightened, as if bringing that order lightened her heart.

But she was still cranky until that first cup of coffee so he wasn't surprised when she left to use the machine in the break room, which was already done brewing.

After she'd finished half that cup, the scent of the fresh pot filled her office and she looked up at him with a smile. "You are really nice to me. Thank you."

"My pleasure. You're very nice to me so it's only fair. How come you didn't get coffee at home? I'm sorry I got home later again last night. But we finished and the guy will come to take delivery this afternoon."

She made a note in her calendar quickly. "Excellent. I was in a rush this morning. I woke up late and then I took pills over to my mom's."

"You said you'd only go when I came with you from now on." He frowned her way.

"You've been working eighteen-hour days. I'm not going to get in the way of the scraps of sleep you were getting to have you escort me over there. It's still the same."

Meaning her mother didn't speak to her. Once the police had come over, Carmella's mother had refused to speak to her. Duke felt like maybe Carmella should let her mother manage her own shit then, but Carmella wouldn't go for that.

She had, however, stopped taking over meals. When Duke found out Carmella also paid for those groceries for her mother as well as paying the mortgage and utilities, he'd been so angry. Her mother had income from a settlement after being injured several years before while working as a waitress and Carmella's grand-parents had left her money that was paid monthly. And yet, Carmella had to scrimp.

She'd hated feeding Steven and her mother was being horrible and so there'd been a compromise where she took over pills and some basics like bread and milk, but nothing more.

Duke figured the minute her mother started speaking to her again, she'd start making her meals once more. But even this small step away from Virgie was one Duke applauded.

"Well, I'm sorry I wasn't there for you when you needed me."

She hugged him and it made him so happy he kissed her right there in her office just to see that prim look she always did when he took liberties. It was such a hot little game between them. He'd never actually kiss her at work if she truly didn't want him to. But she'd also never initiated that sort of affection at work either.

"I'll allow your forward ways just this once," she said as she poured herself a fresh cup. "So good. Thank you. You're always there when I need you. I have stuff to do and so do you." She flapped a hand to signal she was done letting him push about her mother.

He'd been so caught up in finishing this job that he hadn't been around much. After spending so much time with her before, he'd gotten used to her, spoiled by that.

"I haven't seen enough of you for days and days. How about we go on a real date? Din Tai Fung for dinner?"

Her eyes lit with pleasure. "Yes, please. That sounds awesome. Are you sure you wouldn't rather just go home and sleep for fif-teen hours and go out to dinner tomorrow night?"

"I'll be done by five, so we'll go home and change and drive over. We can pick up cupcakes at Trophy while we're in Bellevue if you like. And then we'll come home. We have some major reuniting to do. There's plenty of time to sleep after that."

Mick came through, rolling up the bay doors on the north side of the building, interrupting his train of thought and reminding him he had a meeting in a few minutes.

"Asa, Mick, and I will be in a meeting for a bit," he told her. "I'll see you later on. Maybe we can do lunch if this finishes up in time."

Mick saw Duke and tipped his chin. "Be right with you. I just need to check something with Duane."

He detoured through Carmella's office again, refilled his coffee mug, stole a kiss, got an adorable glare, and headed to Asa's office, where Mick joined them both.

"What's up?" Mick asked.

"Last year when you left the army for good and came home, you said you wanted in at Twisted Steel as a partner," Duke said. "We brought you on as the shop manager not only because you're good at it, but because we wanted to see if you really meant all the stuff you'd said about wanting to buy in."

"You wanted me to prove myself after I left the way I left the last time." Mick nodded. "I get it."

"We had to get the business appraised when we decided on all the renovation." Asa handed Mick a piece of paper. "The real question is how much you want in. The top number is what a full third is worth. We have information available about what our profit share is like as partners, what our overhead is. You know a lot of it having run the ship all this time. But we've got more detail if you want to look it over."

"This is great news. I've been saving money for this." Mick's smile made Duke even more glad he and Asa had decided to finally bring their friend in.

"Have an attorney look over all the paperwork. Don't make a decision until you do that. There's all this tax stuff I didn't have any idea about and it was a total pain. Make sure you understand everything. If you have questions, we can hook you up with our attorney."

"We can announce this at the grand opening party, right? I'll take it to an attorney, so stop frowning, Asa." Mick flipped through the papers.

"Yeah. If you decide to do this for sure, we'll announce then. Another reason to celebrate," Duke said.

"Excellent." Mick looked from the papers back up to them. "Thank you. I won't let you down."

"Dude." Duke shook his head. "You made a quick, rash choice back then. That's your business. Naturally we'd like you to tell us what's up, but we get it if you aren't ready. But we're your brothers, right? Whatever happened, it's not about letting anyone down. Stop going back to that stupid choice and look forward. That's all Asa and I want for you."

"Now let's go back to work. I have a metric faction of work to do before we do the delivery later today," Asa said.

"Indeed. I have a date I can't be late for tonight so I need to get to it as well."

CHAPTER
Twenty-six

Carmella had taken one look at Duke up to his elbows in engine and knew he wasn't going to be going to lunch with her.

She paused at the Chevy he was working on. "Hey, you. I'm going to lunch now, but I can see you're too busy. Would you like me to bring you back something?"

"That would be great. Thanks, gorgeous."

She headed out, needing some fresh air and to satisfy her craving for teriyaki. Once she was at her favorite little strip mall place a mile or so up the road, she saw one of the mechanics at Salazar inside at a table.

When he saw her, he boomed out her name and bounded over, giving her a big hug.

She joined him and they caught up. He'd worked for her uncle's shop for seven years and they'd sort of grown up together. Things were going well for him at his new job, and he and his girlfriend were expecting a baby early the following year.

They talked about Twisted Steel and she told him about Duke, and it was his turn to be happy for her.

She headed back to work with a smile on her face.

Duke wasn't working on the Chevy so she headed to the break room but he wasn't in there either.

She didn't want his food to get cold so she swung by his office. She heard his voice as she approached.

Inside he was having lunch with a woman Carmella had never seen. She had her hand on Duke's leg as they spoke and they were eating teriyaki. What the fuck?

Duke looked up at her and then down at the bag she had in her hand.

"Some lunch, as promised." Wow, she was *mad*. Carmella was surprised at how mad she was.

It wasn't even the leg. It was the *traitor teriyaki* when she'd told him she was bringing lunch back. The absurdity of it nearly set one of those crazy woman giggles free. But she thought it extra hard.

She put the bag down on the table in front of him.

"Thanks. Don't worry, I'm hungry enough to eat that too," he said and she thought extra hard that he was a dick.

She smiled, totally fake, and headed out.

"Wait, Carmella. Let me introduce you to Lori," Duke called out.

While her back was turned, she allowed herself the snarl she wouldn't give herself permission for in front of tall, blond, and stunning with her hand on Duke's leg.

She pulled it together and smiled again as she turned to find him standing very close. He put a hand on her arm. "Lori, this is Carmella. Carm, this is my friend Lori."

Carmella shook the blonde's hand and tried to ignore the way the other woman looked her over.

"He's been talking about you nonstop," Lori said.

Huh. He'd never mentioned Lori to her. Instead she said, "I hope it was all good." Subtly, she tried to move from his grasp. "I need to get back to work. I just wanted to drop off your lunch. It was nice to meet you, Lori." She stepped backward with a wave, breaking free and heading to her office.

* * *

Duke knew she was mad. Like really mad. It wasn't that she'd been rude, quite the opposite. The face she showed Lori had been friendly enough.

But she'd seen that hand on his knee and how the hell could he have forgotten that she was bringing him back lunch? He'd been hungry and wanted to deal with Lori and get her out of there.

"I should get back to work too. Just tell your brother to come by and fill out an application by Friday." Her brother needed a job, he wasn't a bad kid, and they needed a general hand around the shop and were currently looking for someone for that very thing.

"So, that's her, huh? I've heard you've gone all domestic."

"It was going to happen sooner or later." He kept standing near the door.

"Huh. I just saw her with Porkchop over at the place I got the food at. They looked pretty cozy."

"What does that mean?" Duke demanded.

"Nothing. I'm just saying I saw her having a cozy lunch with a hot guy. Not here with you. I guess she had lunch first and then brought it back. No big. I'm sure you were busy." Lori stood. "I'll tell Gabe to come by tomorrow to bring this back." She held the application aloft. "Thanks."

She made sure to brush her entire body against his as she walked through, and of course, once she'd gone past Carmella's office to leave, Duke saw that from where Carmella stood with PJ, she'd seen the way Lori had walked past him too.

With a sigh, he headed over to deal with this situation.

PJ gave him a raised brow when he joined them. Carmella ignored him totally as she tallied something up on her calculator, writing down numbers on an invoice and totaling it all out before handing it to PJ.

"That's the current total for everything I've got so far this month. Look at it and make sure I haven't missed anything and I'll turn it around for you to have by this Friday," Carmella told her.

"Appreciate it. You busy tonight?" PJ asked her.

"She has a dumpling date with her boyfriend," Duke said.

PJ just gave him a look.

"I'll call you later," Carmella told her.

PJ left and Duke shut the door after her.

"Let's just deal with this now," Duke told Carmella. "Don't say this is work. I don't want this hanging over us all day."

"Go on."

"Did you see a friend today?"

She looked confused and then, then she looked *really* pissed off. "Really? This is what you think we need to deal with? I had lunch with my friend of seven years, Tracy."

"Was Tracy there with Porkchop? Because I hear that's who you were sitting with there."

"Tracy wasn't there with Porkchop. He *is* Porkchop. Do you think his mother named him that? His given name is Tracy. I've known him my entire adult life because he worked at Salazar when I did. He told me today that he and his girlfriend of four years are expecting a baby. They're getting married after that. I told him about you. We had a lovely visit and I came back here with the lunch I said I'd bring you."

Duke blew out a breath.

"Everywhere we go, I have to deal with women you know. Women, like Lori there, you banged awhile. Your flirting is like background noise. Even when I hate it, I accept it because that's part of who you are. But I come back here to find a woman in your office with her hands on you, eating food when I'd just brought it back. Because I told you I would. And then you come in here and actually have the nerve to Sherlock Holmes me into confessing my secret affair in broad daylight in a teriyaki restaurant? That's your take on what's going on here? *I'm* the problem?"

He remembered what Asa had said while they were at Bumbershoot about keeping some space around himself when it came to other women. She'd been pissed that day and he'd known there was something up but then it had been the fight with her ex and all that mess and he'd allowed himself to blow that off.

And now he was paying the price because holy shit was he wrong and about to have to grovel like he never groveled before.

He hated being wrong. Hated being that guy who needed advice instead of seeing the issues himself.

"I pride myself on being good about people. Knowing how to read them. And I totally fail with you."

She blinked, surprised.

"Isn't it like part of the superhero lore? A blind spot?" she said at last.

A laugh bubbled up from his gut. "You keep surprising me. Over and over."

"It's why you keep coming back."

"I'm an asshole."

She shrugged. "Yeah. Pretty much."

"I'm sorry I came at you that way with the Porkchop thing."

"She's the one who saw me with him, huh? You aren't new at women, Duke. But wow, that was a newbie move, letting yourself get played by blondie."

"Why did I think you'd be mad at me?" He chuckled.

"Oh, I *am* mad at you, Duke. And you are an asshole. I'm not cool with that touchy-feely stuff. And if I say I'm bringing you back food, eating some other woman's food is going to piss me off."

Duke was as surprised by her anger as she appeared to be. "You know how you said the other day that you didn't know how to do this? Neither do I. I was trying to get her out of here before you got back. I was hungry. It seemed best to just combine the two and let her tell me why she'd come over. Which was to see if we had a job for her kid brother. Then you came in."

"And you were eating traitor teriyaki."

He fought back a smile with all his might. He knew without a doubt that she would *not* find it charming.

"To get her gone."

"Yeah, you said that. Which means you were hiding it from me? Or you didn't want me to see or know. Why?"

He paused. He hadn't hidden it because he had any plans at all to do anything with Lori. Or anyone other than Carmella. But he had a girlfriend now so he'd known having a woman's hand on your leg wasn't okay.

"I would have taken her hand off. But you came in before I could. Nothing other than talking happened."

"Not the point. I don't think it did, by the way. If I did, we'd be done. Remember that trust thing? Cheating would be the end for me. I think I can deal with normal relationship fights. That's what this is unless you want to fuck it up and say something stupid."

"Can I smile yet? I mean, you're really fucking cute right now and I just want to snuggle up all over you while begging your forgiveness."

"No snuggling at work!"

"Maybe I thought I could handle it. Like let her talk to me and flirt a little and then she'd go and everything would be cool. Maybe I was pissy that I had to think about it at all."

"Or maybe you like it when people need you. Which I can accept. And you can be proud of."

"I don't need people to need me."

She shrugged. "Okay. Just a thought. Anyway, you were apologizing so please continue."

"Is it weird that it makes me hot when you get like this?"

"Get on with it, Duke Bradshaw!"

"Okay! I'm sorry. I understand why you're angry. I'll work a lot harder to tone down the flirting and there'll be no more traitor teriyaki going forward."

"I think your being flip is not even cute. So, I'm going to send you on your way because you have work to do and a delivery to make later and I'm not in any kind of mood for this." She made a shooing motion.

"I'm not being flip."

She went past him to the door and pointed. "Go. I have work to do too."

"We still on for tonight?" he asked on the way out.

"Probably."

He skulked off, dejected, but relieved she seemed not to be in a kick Duke to the curb state of mind.

"What did you do?" Mick asked when Duke stomped over to his tools.

"Nothing. Just dumb guy stuff. I should have listened to Asa."

"He gives better advice these days. I think you're both getting old and starting to make sense." Mick snickered. "Lots of apologies are in your future."

"I made a dent in that already. I hate when she's mad at me. Or sad. It's those big blue eyes." But she had clarified that it was normal dumb stuff and not burn shit down stuff. There was that.

"I'm guessing next time you won't be taking hot blondes into your office."

Duke snarled, but he couldn't argue. It had been a stupid move and he should have thought about it more.

"I need to get back to it. I'm taking her to dinner after work and I want to get a lot more done before quitting time."

CHAPTER
Twenty-seven

He showed up at her door five minutes early carrying a brown paper bag. "I brought you bulbs to plant for spring. I was going to buy you flowers, and then I realized you'd just think they were a waste. Bulbs last and are still flowers so I went that way. How'd I do?"

He passed them her way.

She gave him a smile because how could she not?

"Nicely done. Come in a moment. I'm just finishing up getting ready."

She left him in her living room as she normally would have done so she could run back to put on some lipstick and grab her shoes.

The bulbs were truly lovely. Not only because he came with a present she'd like, but that he thought about the why. He'd remembered things about her far more important than her favorite color.

She ditched the robe she'd been wearing over her clothes while she did her hair and makeup. And thought about what he liked too. She'd worn one of the vintage dresses her grandmother had kept at the back of her closet and given to Carmella when she passed.

The one she'd chosen was blue. The linen had gone softer with time, as had the color. But she loved it still. A Peter Pan collar, three-quarter sleeves, with a skirt that had a little bounce but not too much as her grandmother would have worn this one to work while her grandfather had been in Europe during World War II.

Duke liked her in blue, and he seemed to prefer her vintage stuff and that sort of overall look.

She pulled out a tube of lipstick. Red. Also a tip from her gran, a fellow redhead. The right shade of red lipstick made Carmella feel like a fierce, beautiful woman. It was like armor.

And Duke favored it.

She headed out, shoes in hand, to find him having a chat with Ginger, who sat in front of him, resting her chin on his knee. The adoration in Ginger's eyes was enough to let the last bit of annoyance she'd had drain away. The way he treated Carmella's dog always made her soft for him.

Another woman he flirted with. Good gracious.

"If she had opposable thumbs, I might have to worry about her killing me in my sleep to get to have you all to herself," Carmella said.

They both looked to her.

"You both have the same dumb grin." Probably the one she wore too.

"So many beautiful women live here I can't help myself." He gave Ginger one last scratch before he stood. "If the plan was to look the absolute most beautiful I've ever seen you look to punish me because I was a dick, you win."

"I did consider that. But I wasn't really that mad at you anymore by the time you arrived and the bulbs did the rest."

He kissed her, just to the left of her mouth. "Don't want to smudge the lipstick." When he straightened, he looked her over slowly. "I do love this dress. And the hair and makeup. Absolutely perfect. So beautiful and sexy."

"Thank you." He was better than a tube of lipstick. "And thank you again for the bulbs. Very thoughtful."

"I'm sorry again about today. Let's go stuff our faces with dim sum. That's part one of my forgiveness plan." He held his elbow out for her to take as she slid into her shoes and they left.

Carmella settled in, watching him as he drove. That night he chose the '67 Mercury Cougar. Most likely because he knew she loved it. The traffic was heavy so he wore a look of fierce concentration. He rarely got impatient, so his intensity was of a different sort.

"I called home last week."

"Is everything all right? You told them about the hotel information, right?" She'd wanted so much for his family to come and be truly happy for Duke's success. He deserved their support. So she'd gone out of her way to set them up at the Inn at the Market and to take care of a bunch of other small details that she hoped kept them happy and ready to heap some praise on their son.

"I told my mom about you."

Oh. She hadn't been expecting that.

"What did she say?"

"She said she was glad I found someone because she was beginning to wonder about me and Asa."

That would be so hot. Like uber hotter than fire hot to see the two of them going at one another.

"As much as my mind is totally happy to go there with you and Asa, I'm glad you like me better when it comes to where to put your penis."

He burst out laughing. "I hate when you're mad at me. I don't laugh nearly as much."

"It was like four and a half hours of your life, Duke. You're spoiled, that's your problem."

"One of many. But I sure do like it when you're doing the spoiling. I did tell them about the hotel reservations. She was very appreciative of the itinerary you'd set up for them. That's how I brought up that you and I were together."

"Oh, lovely. You can't tell me she didn't look sideways at the fact that I'm your employee."

"She's a mom, it's her job. But she honestly sounded pleased and said she wanted to meet you. I think you'll like her well enough to see her once a year or so. And how can they not like you?"

"Lots of people manage that just fine."

"Lots of people are dumb. We established that. Anyway, when they arrive, will you come and have dinner with us? My sister and her family are coming up Friday afternoon after her kids are out of school. The grand opening is at eight. But I thought a dinner with me, you, and my parents when they get in Thursday night would be good."

She'd never in the entire time she'd dated, even when she'd been married, had dinner with the guy's family. She knew people did. Craig used to go to his ex-girlfriend's house to have dinner with her family regularly.

She wanted them to see her as worthy of their son. Even though they needed to see him as worthy first and foremost.

"Do you think it'll be too much? Like maybe you guys should be together alone to catch up and then we can all do brunch on Saturday with your sister's family, your brother, and your parents." That would be way more crowded and less prone to awkward moments of silence.

"Too much for who? My parents? No way. My dad is a meat-and-potatoes guy and the Met is an old-school steakhouse. My parents would like it. It's in downtown so not too far from here and near their hotel. I just wanted to make sure you like it too before I made reservations."

Carmella said, "I love steak. I can handle the reservations if you like."

"Nope. I can do it." He was quiet awhile as they crossed I-90 heading to Bellevue.

"There's something else," she said to him. "You don't have to share it until you're ready. Or even with me. But keeping secrets is hard on your heart."

"You should know, huh?" It wasn't a mean or cutting thing to say. He hadn't meant it like that.

"Something like that. I only know I like you too much to want you carrying around something you should share."

"You tell me something."

"Like tit for tat? Because I have to tell you, I've sort of vomited up enough gross details of my life for you lately. My boobs can compensate for only so much truth about my life."

He snorted. "Nothing about you is gross. Especially not your boobs. It doesn't have to be something bad, or sad. What makes you happy?"

"You do," she admitted. "Ginger. Music. Coffee."

"How'd you find that dog?"

"Clifton brought her home. He'd been gone for three days so he thought he could deflect with a cute animal. I'm quite sure he stole her from someone, but he denied it, saying there were kids out front of a grocery store with a box of puppies. She was so tiny and sweet. When she wagged her tail, her whole body would skid back and forth. I looked around for two weeks because I couldn't really love her until I was sure I'd done whatever I could to reunite her with an owner. But obviously I didn't and I loved her and she became my little protector. The best thing about my time with Clifton." She laughed.

"Of course you tried to find out if she had a home."

"She was so adorable. You have no idea. But she wasn't a stray. Her coat was glossy. She had a fat little puppy belly. I wanted to pretend she was all mine to love, but I just thought about some little girl with a lost doggie and I had to try. Maybe he did get her at the grocery store. But she's been mine ever since."

"It does gladden my heart every time I see her little face and that floppy ear."

"She adores you. And not just for the bones. She used to look out the front window at you when you and your friends were in your driveway. She's a hussy like her human, I guess."

"She's like my dog too, by proxy. Cool. I haven't had a dog before. Just another thing you brought me. You make me happy, Carmella. You make me feel lighter and yet heavier at the same time. I love you."

The first few times he'd told her he loved her, she'd had to fight back panic. She wanted so badly to believe it. To believe a man like Duke could love a woman like her. But the fear and dread that it would wear off, or that it was a shallow love and he just didn't know it, swamped her.

He didn't shout it out every time he saw her or anything. But he'd seemed to find it easier to say and she'd found it easier to hear and maybe even accept.

"Hearing that makes me really happy. So you can add that to the things that make me happy list. Along with men who bring me bulbs instead of flowers."

Duke loved her in that dress. Loved that she'd worn it to delight him. Torture him too, if he hadn't met her basic standard of behavior. And then she'd shared that story about Ginger and he'd realized that was another blessing of having her in his life.

They'd had so much dinner he could barely move. But they were in synch enough for him to realize that even when she'd been mad, their connection hadn't really waned.

Something clicked into place as he climbed into bed that night, pulling her close, the dog snoring nearby in her bed. This was *right*. This would withstand a lifetime of stupid fights like the one they'd had earlier.

What he felt for her wasn't transitory. It was real and solid and the piddly shit wasn't going to rip it apart. She hadn't told him she loved him back yet. But in everything she did and said, he heard it. And it was enough until she could say it out loud.

When she'd told him that day that he could and should be proud of the way he was with people, he realized she knew him— really knew him—better than people he'd known for years.

And like those few, close people he cared about what she thought. Wanted her to respect him. To see him as strong and forthright.

She made him want to be better.

He smiled against the back of her neck and let himself fall.

He heard the front door close and lock as he realized she wasn't in bed with him.

Duke stumbled to the front door, noting the dim, early morning light as he yanked on a pair of boxers before he ventured outside.

At the call of her name she turned and Ginger bounded back his way. At the sight of him on the porch in his shorts, Carmella rushed over, whispering at him to go inside.

"You're going to give someone a heart attack looking so good and nearly naked on your front steps," Carmella said as she came in.

"You didn't wake me up. Where are you going?" He got close enough to catch her in his arms and back her against the nearest wall.

"Work," she said, her voice gone breathy.

"You didn't wake me up. I have to go in too. We could have showered together and then driven in at the same time. Lessened our carbon footprint and all that."

She put her hands on his face to yank him down to where she was to kiss him. "It's six. You don't have to be up for another hour. I set your alarm for you."

"Before you, no one took care of me like this. Thought of me the way you do. I'm getting used to it, but sometimes I forget."

She blushed and he kissed her cheeks.

"Let's play hooky today. Go to breakfast and hang out reading, napping, and having sex for the rest of the day," he said.

She closed her eyes a moment. "Stop being a bad influence. As much as I'd love to do just that, you have too much to do. A client consult at one and another at three. You have multiple deliveries to make by the end of the month. The parts for the Chevelle should be arriving today so you can get that moving. And I do payroll today, which is why I'm going in early. If I can get things started before everyone shows up, the checks are signed and ready for everyone at three."

He groaned, remembering just how full his plate was. "Fine. But I'm not planning on being at work past seven. You want to see the real bare-knuckles stuff?"

He realized she might not be comfortable and he nearly told her she didn't have to if she wasn't okay with it.

But when he noted her pupils were suddenly huge and her cheeks flushed, he got it. "Ah. If it makes you hot that I mix it up with people who're there to mix it up, I'm all for you watching me mix it up."

"Okay."

He kissed her quickly, remembering he'd just woken up and hadn't brushed his teeth. "I'll see you at work soon."

He watched her until she and Ginger drove away.

A few hours later she came to him as he stood in the middle the engine he and Mick had just disassembled. Sometimes it helped if he could spread it all out around him on a tarp and get a different way to view the problem.

He was distracted by the puzzle to be solved, but not so much he failed to appreciate the way she looked in nothing fancier than jeans and a pretty blue blouse.

And then he noted the expression on her face. "Carmella?"

"Duke, your mother is on the phone. She says it's urgent."

Nodding, he stepped over the parts, hurrying to the phone on the wall nearby.

"Hello?" He walked around the corner into a back hallway to get some quiet.

"Duke, it's Danny. He's in the hospital."

"What happened? Is he all right?" Duke's heart sped.

"He got into a car accident. He's in emergency surgery right now."

"I'm on my way. I'll catch a flight as soon as I can."

"Wait until we know what's happening. There's no use you rushing down here at this point. I just wanted to call you to fill you in," his mother said. "Your sister is staying home until we get more information too."

"She's got two kids, a husband, and a job that's far less flexible than mine. Of course there's a reason for me to rush down there. My brother is in the hospital. You and Dad will need the help."

"I know you're busy with your work, Duke."

"They're just cars and there's no reason I'd put them before my family."

"I'll have your father call you when Danny gets out of surgery."

He spoke with her a little longer, and then once they hung up, he headed back out to where Mick and Carmella were talking.

"Everything all right?" Carmella asked.

"My brother got into a car accident. He's in surgery now."

"What airport do you want to fly into? I'll make your flight reservations for you." Carmella hadn't asked what he was going to do. Unlike his mother, she'd known there was nothing else Duke wanted to do.

Still, he wasn't sure they wanted him there. His mother had put him off to the point where he had second thoughts about rushing anywhere until he'd heard from his dad.

"Probably LAX. I'm waiting to hear back from my father before I decide for sure. Thank you."

"Okay. I'll transfer your calls to my office so you don't miss anything. Unless you want to go home now."

He wanted to hug her but Mick was standing nearby so he resisted. That's when she hugged him instead.

With a sigh, he gave over to how good it felt. Let himself take comfort in the gesture meant to do just that.

"I'm here to help with whatever you need," she told him before she went back to her office.

"Me too," Mick said as Duke came back to that pile of parts.

"Appreciated. Let's work awhile. I need to get as much as I can done if I do need to run down there."

"We'll hold it down up here. You know that. Do what you need to do," Mick said.

Trouble was, he didn't know what he needed to do. He knew what he wanted to do. But that wasn't the same.

Carmella kept an eye on him as the morning progressed. He'd immersed himself in that engine and everyone had pretty much left him alone. Asa or Mick would pass by here and there, but no one bothered him for very long.

Their first client consult of the day was coming up so Carmella grabbed all the paperwork and slid it into a file folder before she took it over to Asa's office.

She held it up once he'd waved her inside. "This is the paperwork for your upcoming consult."

"I'll look it over. Thanks." He took her in with serious eyes. "Have his parents called yet?"

She shook her head. "Not yet. I have the phone in my pocket, though, so it'll ring right to me if I'm not in my office." She was worried about Duke. About the way his features had gone so carefully blank when he'd said he wasn't sure if he was going to fly down immediately.

"Just keep doing what you're doing. The stuff between him and his family is complicated. Like most families, I guess."

"I don't know what I'm doing. So I'm glad my aimless wandering is working out."

Asa's snort made her smile.

"You're not in his face, which he'd hate. But you're there. That's what he needs. I don't normally give advice, that's usually Duke's gig. But without telling tales, for as long as I've known Duke, he's gotten the backup he's needed from us. From his friends. We're going to get him through whatever happens with his brother. He's maybe a little off balance right now because love fucks you up." He gave her a quick grin that had her responding in kind. "And because he's used to being needed and maybe they don't see that in him so much. Because, and this is my biased opinion, they don't see him at all. They don't understand him."

And Duke craved that. She knew him. He wanted people to see the best in him. Wanted people to see him as a man worthy of respect. And he was. Always there for the people he cared about. Including her.

Carmella nodded at Asa. He'd told her to be there for Duke because his family would most likely fail him. And that Duke had trouble being the one who needed help instead of the one who gave it. Which she already knew, but it was nice that she wasn't the only one who saw to the heart of Duke Bradshaw.

"Thanks, Asa."

He tipped his chin. "Can you remind him about ten minutes early? Mick will probably tell him, but you're nicer to look at."

And she wanted the chance to check in with him again anyway.

"Got it." She headed out.

*　　　*　　　*

"Again my day gets better when I look up and see all my gorgeous right in front of me," Duke said, meaning it. He looked at the clock on the wall. "Did my family call?"

"Not yet. Your meeting is at one. So if you clean up now, you can eat the lunch I have waiting for you in the break room before you go in. You haven't eaten all day and you know how you get when your blood sugar drops."

He grinned. "I do." But she did too. How lucky he was. And it was exactly what he'd needed. "Will you take your lunch with me?"

"Of course. I like looking at you." Her smile was prim and just for him.

"You must be worried about me," he murmured as he passed by her on the way to clean up.

That made her laugh. "Why do you say that?"

"Openly flirting? We're at work, Carmella. I know we've talked about that at least five dozen times."

"I know. But just because you say words, Duke, doesn't mean I agree with them," she repeated back his usual response.

Though there were already six or seven people in the break room eating and talking, he saw her immediately and headed her way.

"I got you a cranberry juice. I made a turkey and Swiss and a roast beef and cheddar. I figured we could switch halves."

He grabbed her gaze. "You made these this morning? While I was sleeping?"

She blushed, and despite his worry about his brother, the agitation and anxiety that had been clawing at him seemed to fall away. "You have all those groceries in your fridge, I figured you should use them."

"Thank you for taking such good care of me." He ate, listening more than he spoke, and Carmella filled the quiet, instinctively knowing he needed that.

By the time he needed to go to the client consult, he was recharged and far more focused.

"I'll interrupt if anyone calls," Carmella told him as she headed back to her office.

Caught up in the sight of her walking away, Duke leaned against Asa's doorway for a few moments more.

"Let's head to the showroom now that you're done staring at Carmella's ass," Asa called as he headed the opposite direction.

Duke caught up with his friend. "I'll never be done staring at Carm's ass. It's fucking perfect. It'll be perfect when she's ninety."

"I told her love made you sideways."

Duke snorted. "I saw it happen to you. I've seen it happen to other people. I figured it was like, only amplified. Super-like. But it's . . ." He broke off, trying to find a way to express it. "It's different than anything I've ever felt. She's everything. I'm all about it."

Asa tipped his chin in agreement. "Settles down all that stormy shit inside me."

Yes. Exactly.

CHAPTER
Twenty-eight

He came out of the meeting with a new client and the possibility of a collaboration to enter a build contest at a major show the following year.

But no call from his parents.

They had another appointment to follow, but he had enough time to call his mom before then and ended up leaving a voicemail. Then he tried his sister and got the same.

"No calls?" he asked Carmella when he stopped by her office.

"Not yet. I've had the phone with me at all times so I haven't missed anything. Have you tried calling them? Maybe they got caught up in dealing with stuff and haven't had the chance to call yet. You know how it can be sometimes."

"I figured that might be it. I tried my parents and my sister and got voicemail on everyone."

"The waiting room at my mom's doctor's office makes you turn off cell phones. Some hospitals do."

He let go of some of the fear. "I should have come to you earlier. Okay, that all makes sense. We're getting ready to go back into the next meeting. I just wanted to check."

It wasn't until he'd come out of the next meeting and called his mother again that someone finally answered.

"What's going on?" he asked the moment she picked up.

"We've been dealing with the medical staff and the police for hours," his mother said.

"Police? About the accident?" Jesus, had it been Danny's fault?

"They're saying it might have been a suicide attempt. Which is nonsense, of course. It was a traffic accident for goodness' sake."

"Mom, is Danny out of surgery? Is he all right?" First things first.

"He got out about three hours ago. He's in recovery."

Duke blew out a breath. "And he'll be all right?"

"They think so. He'll be in ICU for at least the next few days."

"Now, what's this about the cops and this being a suicide?"

"Ever since he got out of rehab the last time, he's had a rough go of it."

"Rehab? Danny was in rehab? The last time? It was more than once?" Why didn't anyone tell him anything?

"He didn't want it to be broadcast. He was embarrassed. His job is very stressful and he used alcohol to cope. They said he also had trouble with that crystal meth, but Danny said it was just liquor."

Meth might explain why his brother could keep up with the insane demands of his life. And then couldn't anymore, apparently.

"I'm coming down tonight. I'll grab a hotel near the hospital when I get in. I'll text you my hotel information when I arrive if it's too late."

"Why on earth would you do that? Duke, you can't do anything. He can't see anyone even if he was conscious, which he isn't. Come down for Thanksgiving and bring your friend."

"You're going to need help with all that. With getting Danny help. Was he intoxicated when he got into the accident?"

"He ran off the road on the coast. Right off an embankment. If he'd been just a mile further, he'd have gone off a cliff and into the ocean. Your father is sure it's just that the roads were slick.

Sand blows over them sometimes. Your brother did not try to kill himself and he'd never drive drunk."

Looked like maybe Danny wasn't the only one in denial.

"Thank god he's going to be all right. But he's going to have to deal with a lot of stuff when he starts to recover. I can help with all that."

"We have people for that sort of thing, Duke. Professionals. Stay in Seattle. Right now there's nothing you can do. It's just going to upset him more if you come. He'll be ashamed to have you see him like that."

"Mom, what the heck is happening down there? Why would Danny be ashamed for me to see him? The addiction stuff? He's trying to get help. I love him."

"I'm going to have your father call you in a little while. Don't make reservations you can't cancel until then. I need to go. I love you."

He looked at his phone, utterly thrown for a loop.

"Everything all right?" Mick asked as he approached.

"I don't know. My brother is out of surgery but he'll be in ICU for the next few days."

Asa joined them. "Mick and I have it handled. You're good, but you're not the only mechanic we have. If Carmella can't take you to the airport, I will."

"I'm not going just yet."

"What? Why not?" Mick asked.

"They don't want me down there just now."

Both his friends got very quiet as they tried to figure out what to say.

"Right? I'm confused about it myself. She said my dad would call." But she'd said that earlier. Danny had been out of surgery for hours and no one even texted him just a few lines? His sister wasn't even there and she couldn't have taken a moment to let him know what was going on?

"Go home, Duke. It's already four thirty. Get some rest. If you do go down there, you'll need the sleep now." Mick squeezed his shoulder.

"I need to go for a ride."

He grabbed his Windbreaker and helmet, stopping by Carmella's office. "I'm going for a ride. I'll have my phone with me if anyone calls here looking for me."

She stood, walking to him. "No word yet?"

"I just got off the phone with my mother. I need to get the hell out of here. My brother is out of surgery. That's pretty much it at this point." He kissed her cheek as he moved past her. "No fights for me tonight. Sorry about that."

Her gaze took him in carefully. Missing nothing. But she didn't push him for more. "Go. Ride awhile. I'll leave the kitchen light on until I go to sleep."

Glad he had a bike at work, he headed out, grateful the rain had leveled off and the late afternoon was dry. The roar and throaty growl of his engine drowned out all but the thoughts in his head as he drove north.

Carmella took her mother's stuff to her that evening after work rather than get up earlier the next morning to do it.

She unlocked, not caring whether or not her parents liked it, though she did knock and call out. Boxes were stacked against the walls and half the place had been packed up.

"Hello?"

Virgie came out. "Why are you here?"

Carmella held up the bag. "What's going on?"

Virgie snatched the bag from Carmella's hand. "We're moving to Eastern Washington. We leave the day after tomorrow. Your father has a job offer in Spokane. He got permission to move there for it. I'm going with him. You don't own the things in this house, so I'm taking those."

"You're going to move across the state? When were you planning to tell me?"

"It's not your business, Carmella. You can't run my life anymore. I'm tired of you making all my choices. I'll take care of my own pills. My own medical needs."

"Do you have a doctor there? A place to live?"

"This isn't your business. You won't accept your father? We won't accept you. I don't need you to do all this for me. It just holds me back."

"Excuse me? I hold you back? Can't you see he's filling your head with lies?" Carmella asked her mother.

"I have to wait around for you to feed me. For you to bring my medication. I'm a grown-up and you treat me like a child. Let me make my own choices! My own mistakes."

Carmella was at a low point, her filters threadbare. "And when he starts gambling again? Or decides a kick and a punch is how he needs to deal with stress?"

"If you can't be happy for me, I don't want you around. In fact, I want you to sell this house and give me my fair share."

Carmella laughed bitterly. "What fair share? I used up my entire savings to pull this house out of foreclosure. If I sell it, we'll be lucky to cover closing costs. There's no secret pot of gold at the end of the rainbow, Mom. There's me, saving your ass over and over. Because *I* think you're worth it. You think about that for a while, why don't you?"

"Give me control over my medication. I demand it."

Carmella heaved a sigh. "Mom . . ."

"I'm a grown-up. Respect me enough to let me make my own mistakes. I need to transfer my prescriptions to my new house. You can't come all the way to Spokane every three days to deliver it. I don't want you to. I want you to let us live our lives."

"He hits you. How can you expect me to let that happen?"

"Because I'm asking you to. And because you don't get a say

in my life. You don't understand anything. You don't know how to love anyone. You can be alone, all right. But I don't *want* to be alone. All I've ever wanted was Steven. That's it. I won't let him go now that I've got him."

Carmella walked out, not knowing what to do, but knowing she sure wasn't going to figure it out there.

Duke hadn't returned home yet when she got back. Carmella grabbed Ginger and her leash and they headed off for a walk around the lake.

She'd gotten home, done her laundry, made dinner, and had settled in bed reading when she heard the sound of his car pulling up next door.

Carmella wanted to rush over to see how everything was, but she didn't know if she had the right just yet. Or even more important, she wasn't sure that's what he needed.

Hell, she didn't even know what *she* needed. So she'd wait, hoping Duke saw her light and made his way over.

Duke had driven around for hours until his father had finally called. Then he'd driven around for a few more hours, dropped his bike off, and grabbed his car to come home.

And as he sat there in his driveway, all he wanted was to see her kitchen light on.

She opened her front door just a few minutes later. Ginger gave him a friendly bark, hopped around until he'd given her some attention as he came in.

"Hi there. Want some tea? I just had a cup so the water is still hot."

He went into her arms and she hugged him, snuggling into his body and being there.

"Tea is good."

"Come on then." She took his hand and led him to the kitchen. "Want some toast or a peanut butter sandwich?"

He settled at her kitchen table and the dog flopped over his feet.

"I have strawberry jelly even."

"Made me an offer I can't refuse."

"Sure. Everyone can be jealous at my PBJ skills."

He let the rest of his agitation go as she moved about her kitchen efficiently, dropping off a cup of tea and then a sandwich she'd even cut into triangles.

"Do you want to talk about it?" she asked as she joined him.

"Yes. No. I don't know."

"Whatever you decide."

She didn't push.

"How was your night?" he asked.

"I'm not sure if I want to talk about it either." She snorted.

"What's going on, gorgeous?"

"My mom dropped a bomb tonight. She's moving to Spokane with Steven. This week. She told me to sell the house and give her a fair share." This time her snort was derisive. "Maybe it is my fault for doing everything for her. But Jesus, how can she pretend like there would be anything left? She had the house paid off and then took out a second mortgage and nearly lost it. I spent my entire savings—that I was going to use on my own house—to save her and she just took it as her due. And now she thinks I did it to steal from her. I'm furious that she'd say such a thing. But so sad she'd actually think it."

"I'm sorry I wasn't around when this all came down." He'd been out licking his wounds and she'd needed him.

"Sometimes you need to handle your own stuff before you can deal with anyone else's."

"That's true, Carm. So why don't you try it?'

"Do you know the cost if she fails?"

The anguish in her tone tore at him.

"She's an adult woman. You can't get her committed. She won't leave him. What can you do? Huh? If you keep pushing, it's not like she'll change her mind. You'll just push her away even further. At least at this point when she fucks up, she knows she's got you."

"She's got no one. My uncle is done with her. I'm terrified."

He got up and moved to her, pulling her into his arms.

"I'm sorry. I know you've got a lot on your mind," she said, face buried in his chest.

"I don't accept your apology. Whatever she does isn't yours to feel sorry about. You're a *good* thing on my mind. They're saying my brother tried to kill himself." Once he got it out, he felt better.

She pulled away so she could see into his face. "Oh my god."

They sat back down and he stuck close to her this time. "My dad finally called me a few hours ago. Danny isn't conscious yet but they say it's not unusual for his level of injury."

"Suicide? Has he been dealing with depression or any other type of illness? I didn't get the sense that this was even a thought with your siblings."

He scrubbed his hands over his face and then drank some tea. "I've been trying to make sense of it for the last few hours. I found out stuff today and I still don't know what to do with it all."

She got up, grabbed a bottle of tequila from above the fridge, and brought it back with a shot glass.

"I have a counteroffer," he said.

"Does it involve your penis?"

Love washed through him, taking away the heaviness in his head. His heart would take longer, but she was there. She was his and she made things better.

"It always eventually involves my penis when we're talking about anything to do with you. I was going to suggest I finish this sandwich and then we take this to the bedroom. I can tell you out here, but I'd rather have you in my arms."

"I accept those terms. Finish up your sandwich."

She said the last as he shoved the last of the PBJ she'd made him into his face. He waggled his brows at her as he finished chewing and then cleared his dishes. Ginger trotted along behind them, settling into her bed as Carmella climbed into hers.

He stripped down to his boxers and got in beside her, sighing as she snuggled against him.

"My brother's been to rehab three times. All three times for alcohol and the last two were for meth as well. His health is a wreck because of his high-stress job, made even more stressful because he's been high all the time. His girlfriend dumped him because she got sick of his shit and because he got someone else pregnant and she's now seven months along. Danny has been paying her condo rent and medical care." He sighed and sat up enough to swallow the shot she'd poured for him.

"I knew *none* of this. I only heard that he'd broken off his engagement when I spoke to my mother last week. She moved out so at least he has a place to live, but he's going to lose his job. My dad says they're trying to work out a deal that Danny goes to rehab and then gets to keep the job. But I feel like maybe the job is part of why he's so fucked? But what do I know? Because I don't know my brother and I had no idea he was in so much trouble. This has been going on for six years on and off. How the hell did I never even notice?"

"I'm so sorry. I hurt for you. For him and your family."

That last bit clicked into place for him. The thing he'd driven around and never quite grasped. Until right then.

"You are and you do. Thank you. For being genuine. And for trusting me. They don't."

"They don't trust you?"

He shook his head. "If they trusted me, I'd have known this stuff. They would have told me. One of them at least. But I moved away a long time ago and they didn't miss me that much. They love me, of course. But they don't know me and they don't miss my presence. And I have to own the fact that I never made the effort either. In all the times I've seen them in the last six years, I never noticed anything wrong. I thought my kid brother had his shit straight and was a huge success. But he was hurting and I didn't see."

She shifted so they were looking at each other. The last few times they'd shared, it had been dark, or they'd been facing away from each other. This time she looked him straight in the eyes.

Carmella didn't need to say anything. He understood. She wanted him to know she accepted him. That he could say anything to her and it would be safe.

"They have a different family than the one I had. I talked about that a little before."

"So you feel like you don't belong." Not a question.

He nodded. "They're my family. My parents love me and want me to be happy. I wasn't abused. They worked hard to give me and my brother and sister a better future. And they did."

"You don't have to qualify your feelings with all this positive stuff. It's just me. Feel whatever you need to feel."

He sighed, pausing to kiss her. "I wish you could be this wise with yourself."

Carmella said, "Me too. It's easier to give advice than to take it. I think you know this."

Bull's-eye. "Anyway, I drove around tonight and I thought long and hard about everything. And there was something just out of my reach. I have parents and siblings. They're a family I'm part of. But I don't belong there. I wanted to help my brother. I wanted to be there for my parents. I offered multiple times and they're just not interested. Not because they're mad at me. But because they don't need me."

"They don't see you and understand how much it means for you to help the people you love. That the way you step in and take care of your family is that you make things easier for them in whatever way you can. They don't know you like I do. Like Asa and Mick do. It doesn't mean they don't love you. It means they don't know you."

"Like you do, yes. That was it. The epiphany. I've had this stick up my butt about them not coming to me. And how why didn't they because I give great advice. But they're not rejecting me or my advice. They just don't think to need it. It's not about me. Not like that. Not how I was seeing it," Duke said.

"Wow, that's pretty freaking smart."

"I love you, Carmella. Because you know me. You understand me. You don't need me to live, but you want me around. That distinction wasn't one I even really got until tonight. Just a few minutes ago. I came back here to you to seek your advice. To bounce ideas off you, and because you always make me feel better when I'm around you."

"What time do you fly out?" she asked because hadn't he just said she understood him?

"I'm probably going to wait until the end of the week. Only two people get to see him in ICU for five to ten minutes. My parents are there, but my dad said Danny's ex showed up and they're thinking of letting her have one of their spots." And Duke wanted to be with Carmella as her mother left town.

"Do you think the ex is a good thing? Like maybe she left because she thought if she gave him an ultimatum, he'd get it together? Or did she use with him and it would be bad?"

Duke kissed her again quickly. "I hadn't thought of it that way. Truth is I don't know. I just don't know enough about the situation to say with any certainty and I don't want to make things worse."

"That must have been hard." She wasn't teasing. She knew what it meant to him that he could give the people he cared about good counsel.

"I don't like it. It makes me feel useless. I can't fix this the way I can an engine. I don't have the skills I need for this problem."

She hugged him tight and then lay facing him, resting her chin in her hand. "And you feel like what? You're bad because you don't?"

"If I did, it would be fixed."

"Maybe if they'd opened up to you more, gotten to know you, they would have shared and you'd have seen and you'd have the skills. Maybe if you'd called that morning, Danny would have left later and wouldn't have gotten into an accident. Or if your mother had a cold and went to sleep the night you were conceived instead of making you. Or. Or. Or. You don't have superpowers, no matter how much I joke. You *are* intuitive and smart about people. But how can you be with them if you're not part of their lives? If you don't know them any better than they know you?" Carmella asked.

"They're a great family."

"You just don't feel like they left enough room on the couch for you."

He paused with a snort. "Again, I wish you listened to your own advice. It's really good advice and you need it. What are you going to do about your mother?"

"There's nothing I *can* do. I can't make her leave him as you pointed out. I can't stop her from going to Spokane. She's forty-three years old. She managed to survive all this time."

"You'll be here when she needs you. She'll remember that when she has to," Duke said.

Carmella breathed him in at the crook of his neck. "I can see why you like to sniff me here. This is a nice place for all your sexy smell to collect." She nipped the skin there. "I don't want her to go. I'll worry about her. If something happens, I'm going to blame myself."

"I know. And you'll be wrong. I'll tell you so. I expect your uncle and aunt will too. Sometimes the best option is still a shitty option. I'm sorry. I wish I had better advice to give."

"Aren't we a pair?"

He flipped her to her back, looming over her. "We are. Who else gets me the way you do? Who else truly knows me and never turns away?"

"Would you like me to come with you when you go down to see your brother?"

"I would. But then I'd be worried about you and if they were being nice enough and I wouldn't be focused on Danny and getting down to the bottom of this problem."

Which was what he needed. Though she wanted to be there to soften what would likely be a tough visit, she knew she couldn't do this for him any more than she could live for her mother. Thank goodness he only had a penchant for driving too fast and fistfighting.

"You know I can entertain myself. But I get it. I'm here if you need me. I can be on the next plane down there."

CHAPTER
Twenty-nine

Carmella smiled at the bouquet of roses on her dresser. Next to the vase sat a brown paper sack that, once opened up, appeared to hold more bulbs.

"He's really slick, that guy." PJ came in. "I'm assuming those are from Bradshaw?"

No card had been necessary. She'd known they were from him. "Yes."

He was coming home that day. With his parents, and they were all going to dinner in an hour.

Duke had left nearly two weeks before. The morning after her mother and Steven had driven away from Seattle in a rickety truck she wasn't sure would make it over the pass, but that wasn't her problem anymore.

She worried, though, and couldn't deny how relieved she was when Virgie had called to say they'd arrived in Spokane. She'd even said she loved Carmella before she hung up.

PJ was there to help her pick out what to wear as she had zero meet-the-parents experience.

"I think that black dress with the embellished collar. It's feminine and fits you so well. You can bend over and your boobs won't pop out. Black hides it if you get a little food flecks here and there. And it makes your hair look even more red."

Carmella changed into the black dress and PJ helped her zip it up.

"I'll do your makeup. I promise it'll be pretty."

Carmella put on her robe while PJ did her makeup and hair.

When she was done, she got pretty close to what she hoped a woman who deserved Duke looked like.

"You look gorgeous. Asa said he and Mick talked to Duke day before yesterday and all he did was moan about how much he missed you."

Carmella smiled. "Good. Because I've missed him too. I'd rather that than have him realize he really just isn't that into me after being gone for two weeks."

PJ got on the floor with Ginger. "As if. Take it from me, Duke Bradshaw is totally in love with you. You. Not the idea of you. Or only while you're around. This is the real deal for him."

"How do you know? I mean, he's got everything on the ball and I don't. I'm a glorified secretary renting a house and he owns a business and has, like, eleven cars."

"Where the hell would the world be without secretaries, Carmella? And anyway, you're not a glorified anything. You're amazing. And smart and really organized. He loves you."

Carmella hoped so because she'd begun to really believe it. And to believe she loved him too. Which was scary!

Carmella hugged PJ, who'd stood and was giving her the once-over.

"Perfect. You look classy."

"Classy works. I should get going. I said I'd meet them all downtown. He took them to their hotel and was getting them checked in."

"Why don't I drive you and drop you off and you can catch a ride back with him?"

Twenty minutes later she walked through the front doors of Metropolitan Grill and was being shown to the bar, where they were all waiting for a table.

She saw Duke before he'd noticed she was there. He sat at a high-top table with the people who had to be his parents. His father was an older version of Duke, only softer in the middle and clean shaven. His mother was a woman Carmella bet had her nails done at least once a week, had her hair done every six weeks without fail, and would never be caught dead at the grocery store without full makeup.

He was so beautiful and certainly she wasn't the only one who noticed. Women all over the place checked him out but he didn't notice them at all.

As she approached, his gaze flicked up from the beer in his hand to Carmella and there was no other way to put it than that he lit up when he saw her.

Relief nearly made her legs go out from under her. He still looked at her like she was the only woman in the room. It was going to be okay.

He stood and in three of his gigantic strides he was hugging her.

"Gorgeous, damn you're a sight for sore eyes and a lonely heart. I missed you so much."

She hugged him back, glad she'd worn her highest heels so she wasn't so much shorter than him.

"I missed you too."

He rested his forehead against hers for a last moment and then straightened. "Ready?"

"As I'll ever be."

He turned and walked with her over to the table where his parents were. He introduced her; they shook her hand and said they were pleased to meet her.

Over dinner they made small talk. Asked about Carmella's dog and how the shop was doing in Duke's absence.

They seemed to be looking forward to the grand opening the following night, though they were headed back first thing Saturday to be with Danny.

They were cordial and Carmella noted the way Duke and his father looked back and forth to one another as they filled her in on the situation with Danny. She hoped they had done some major work over the time they'd had together. Duke deserved it.

The strain showed around his eyes, though. As the evening wore on, the toll of the time he'd been gone grew more and more plain on his face.

Finally, when she began to wonder if his parents would ever see how tired their son was, or if Duke would just admit it and they could leave, Carmella was done waiting.

"Duke, why don't we finish up so your mom and dad can get some rest," she said before looking at his mother. "You must be so tired. The last two weeks have been so hard on you all."

He signaled the server and turned back to the table. "They're getting the car from the valet."

Carmella and his mother headed to the ladies' room and had inevitable mirror chitchat.

"Duke talked about you a lot." Here and there, a lot like Duke, her accent would come back. Just a word or two. She tried harder, Carmella bet, to get rid of it. Duke didn't seem to care. It only made him sexier anyway.

Carmella had to leave a good review for the stuff she put on her hair earlier because it was doing a decent job of keeping her hair from tripling in size in the wet weather.

She turned to face Carmella because the woman didn't need to smooth down flyaways, even on a rainy day. Her hair was perfect.

"I was uneasy when he told me you worked for Twisted Steel. A romantic entanglement with an employee is something that could go disastrously wrong for him and his business. He doesn't think we're proud of him. But we are. And he talked about you in the same way he talks about Twisted Steel. Both make him happy and appear to be pretty central to his life. He hasn't talked to me about a girl since he was in high school. She was a redhead too."

Carmella relaxed, laughing. "I'll have to thank her for tossing him back so I could have him instead. He makes me happy too. Your son is pretty much everything I always dreamed of but figured I'd never find."

"Like what? Tell me something you love about him."

"He's got an unswerving sense of loyalty. You can see it when he's around Asa and Mick. They have this connection, a deep sense of brotherhood. These burly dudes with facial piercings and ink from neck to toe are so funny together. Like naughty little boys. Quarreling. Breaking things. But they're thick as thieves. Would—and did—risk their lives for each other. He does that with people he considers family. I am astonished and humbled that your son loves me and considers me part of that family. You did a good job with him."

"Do you think so?"

"He's the way he is now and I don't think that's a coincidence. He learned it somewhere."

"Thank you for saying that." His mother headed toward the door. "I invited Duke—and you, of course—to Thanksgiving at our house. I would love it if you could come down. Having him around has made me realize how much I miss him when we don't see him more than once a year, if that. His sister would love to meet you. And the kids love their uncle Duke."

"Thank you. I hope we can make it. I don't know what the shop does as it's my first year there."

Carmella blushed as they headed to the front of the restaurant, where Duke and his father waited.

The car pulled up and she gave Duke a look.

"Don't worry, I didn't buy another car. This is a rental."

He took them back to their hotel and then drove to his place.

"I need to get inside my house. Go get our dog so she can sleep with us tonight."

Carmella laughed. "She's going to lose her mind when she sees you. She's mad at me because I think she's suspicious I did away with you somehow."

"Come on. I'll go with you because I admit I'd really like to see her too." Duke unlocked her door, calling Ginger's name. She barked and hopped around as he knelt and let her lick his face.

"You're soft for my dog."

"I always have been." He straightened. "Get yourself whatever you need for the night and let's go to my house. Because I'm hard for you."

"I've missed your sexual innuendo."

"Just one of the services I provide."

He looked really tired, so once they got to his place, she urged him to take a shower.

"I'll give you a massage when you finish and you can tell me all about it," she told him.

"That's the best offer I've had all day."

CHAPTER
Thirty

When Duke got out of the shower and headed into the bedroom, he had to force himself not to rush.

And there she was. Candles were lit and he had to grin at the sight of her in actual lingerie.

"You like?"

Black against the pale of her skin. Freckles dancing here and there. Creamy white lace framed the cups of the bra and made little ruffle things on the ass.

"I really, really do. Wow."

"I told you that I could pull out the stops for sex dressing from time to time."

"You sure did."

"I also thought the outfit sort of had a maid thing going."

"My mother has a cleaning lady. I was there around her, and I have to tell you, my thing about you cleaning? It's got nothing to do with anyone *else* wiping down counters or scrubbing a floor. It's a one hundred percent Carmella fixation."

"I'm not complaining. On your belly. I'll give you a massage while you talk to me."

He shucked the sleep pants and shorts.

"I've missed you so much." Carmella stepped close and slid her hands all over his torso. "Missed the way you smell. The way you keep me warm at night. It's been cold here this week. Missed your voice."

He cupped her cheeks. "I missed you too, gorgeous. Damn I love you. Love you, love you, love you."

She threw her arms around him and tipped back. "I love you too."

He nearly choked. The crap with her mother being so fresh, he really hadn't expected it this soon, if at all.

"You do?"

"I do. I guess I have a romantic fool's heart too."

He kissed her, easing her back to the bed. "There's nothing foolish about you."

"Whatever. Regardless, the situation is this. I realized earlier tonight as PJ was here helping me get ready that I believed you loved me. And that I loved you. And when you looked at me tonight when I came into the bar, I was the only woman in the room for you. There was nothing left to do by that point but love you and stop pretending I didn't."

"You are the only woman in the world as far as I'm concerned." He insinuated himself between her thighs. "I don't really want a massage," he said, kissing her in between the words.

"You don't? You should. You looked so tired tonight at the end of dinner. I wanted to put you in a wagon and pull you home."

"I can see you doing just that and daring anyone to stop you." He undid her bra and slid it from her body.

"See? Five minutes, tops. Why spend the money on that kind of stuff every day when cotton underpants are way cheaper and more comfortable?"

He tried not to smile but gave up. "I have no complaints about your white cotton panties. All I want is what's in 'em anyway. But I do like this little number. The panties do something for me." He ground himself against her pussy.

She shuddered a breath. "That's worth it right there. Bravo."

"Just getting started." He slid the panties aside to get access to her pussy. Already slick and ready for him. "The problem with finally falling in love after years of being single is that I got used to you. In my bed pretty much every night, or me in yours. Your smell on my hands and on my sheets. The way you feel as I slowly push my cock into you. You ripple all around me and it's so hot it makes me insane. In the morning first thing when you're relaxed and easy. In the middle of the night because I woke up and couldn't *not* be fucking you."

He slid the pad of his thumb over her clit in circles. She gasped and it tore at his control.

"I got used to your smile when I come into your office or show up at your door. No one told me I needed to eat something besides onion rings, or made sure my DVR is scheduled for all the weird car stuff most people don't know anything about. Being away from that made me realize a thousandfold how much I have in you. Hot and sticky sweet. Strong."

Her nipples beaded hard and dark and he stretched up to flick one. Her pussy superheated around his fingers.

"You are everything. Give it to me, gorgeous. Let's get started with a climax to take the edge off." He twisted his wrist, sliding two fingers deep. She arched her back and then rolled her hips, riding his hand.

This was so beautiful—she was so beautiful—he'd begun to wonder if he was imagining it. Thought perhaps he'd embellished it in his head while he'd been sad and lonely twelve hundred miles from home.

Not much had been farther from the truth.

This was coming home. Being away from her had only cemented that.

"Take it from me."

Carmella circled her hips, pressing her clit against his thumb, meeting his fingers. Her skin had gone pink and the valley between her breasts glistened with sweat.

She moaned and came apart around his fingers.

His cock hadn't been this hard and smeared in precome since he was sixteen. But then he'd had to settle for an awkward hand job that ended about a minute after it started.

Now he was confronted by a gorgeous woman all curves and heart.

She reached down to wriggle free from her panties, tossing them to the side before rolling up to her knees. "On your stomach."

"Carm, baby. I—"

"Don't Carm-baby me. Have I ever let you down?" She shot him a saucy grin.

He turned over and she straddled his thighs like she had before and then the drizzle of the almond oil against his skin had him closing his eyes.

She began to knead his muscles. "I'm sure you spent the last two weeks taking care of everyone else so let me take care of you. There will definitely be a happy ending, just so you know that going in."

"Counting on it. But I'm always glad to hear it." He smiled into the pillow.

"Do you want to tell me about it?" She dug in a little deeper and he groaned.

"Later. After. I just need you right now. You tell me things." His voice was muffled by the pillow but she understood him.

Because she loved Duke and had spent two weeks without him, realizing it more every single day, she needed to tell him.

"I never believed in real love until you. I let myself believe a huckster was the best I could do. And because of that, I let myself get jaded. I told myself that because Virgie was a fail in the love department and my previous try had been a disaster, it wasn't possible. I had a life before you. Responsibilities. But I also had fun. Admittedly way less. But anyway."

"I want to turn over for this. I want to see you when you're talking."

"You want me to massage your chest?"

He flipped her over, tossing her to the side to grab a condom from the table nearby.

"No. I want to fuck you."

"I want to suck your cock and then fuck you. After the massage. I had an itinerary."

"Uh. I'm sorry?"

She started laughing. "I'm saying I never let myself believe anyone like you could exist for me. And there you were. You're nothing like the men I grew up around. You're strong and you keep your word. You take care of me. I can't quite believe that you love me. I've been in shock since you told me the first time because how does a girl like me get you?"

"A girl like you gets me because I'm really fucking lucky."

She scooted down, kissing over his hips and breathing against his cock. She rubbed her cheek against it and then licked against the crown.

"I missed your taste."

She had.

Carmella swirled her tongue around the head, digging the tip into the slit and then into the spot just below. He was close, already sticky with come. Excitement flared in her belly that she'd been the one to do this to him.

She kept it slow, not setting a rhythm that would send him over the edge. He wanted to be inside her and she'd be just fine with that. But a warm-up wasn't going to spoil anything.

She knew he watched her, which was hotter than any stranger. Carmella gave him a show, licking him slow, keeping her fist around him loosely. The vein throbbed with the beat of his heart.

Carmella risked a meandering lick around his balls until the fingers he'd dug into her hair tightened.

"Going to be hitting that point of no return very soon," he ground out. "I want in you."

She gave him a parting kiss, and once he'd gotten the condom on, she straddled his body and then backed up slowly, taking him inside bit by agonizing bit until she sat up straight and tucked her feet back up, and under her butt.

"I was going to have you use my cock against your clit to make yourself come. I've been jerking off to that fantasy for a while now. But I don't think I can stand it right now. I'd come in two seconds."

She gave an experimental bounce and his resulting groan made her do it again.

"I saw this in a porno. The woman sitting this way, I mean. She is way more acrobatic than me. But the bounce is nice and I don't feel like I'm going to crush anything necessary."

His laugh was edged in discomfort. "Saw it in a porno?"

"Yes. Did you think I never watched porn? Jeez. I mean, well, I don't. Not for very long. But it gets the job done."

He grabbed her hips and held her in place. "Don't move."

Carmella writhed at the pleasure/pain of his fingertips digging into her muscles.

He cursed under his breath and urged her up into a bounce. A bounce he met with a thrust. It wasn't as artful as a movie, but it was a million times hotter to have Duke's hands on her, his cock deep inside over and over. He'd moved one of the hands at her hips to her pussy as he squeezed her clit.

She'd lived in the same place growing up. She went there at the end of every day, but it had never been her home. Her little duplex was the same. A house, not a home.

But in his arms? Well, that was home. Beautiful, wonderful, and it made her feel like she could do anything. Be anything with him on her side.

Climax the second time around was intense. The edge of it was nearly too much. Nearly pain. She forced herself not to cringe away, knowing if she did, it would only reward her with the bloom of pleasure that hit her moments later as she came on a hoarse shout.

He continued to meet her bounces with his thrusts until he did a little growl and fucked her hard enough she saw little white stars at the corner of her vision.

And then he froze, his growl cut off as he came.

"Don't move," he said, voice rough.

He needn't have said anything. She couldn't have moved outside a real emergency. In fact, when he came back, he had to pull her into place against him.

Her voice worked, though. "I love you because you see me. And because you make me feel like I can do anything but that if I fuck up it's okay too."

"That's a really good one." He kissed her. "I'm not sure if I'm ever going to tire of hearing you say that."

"My brother needs some major help," Duke said finally. "He needs a type of program that can deal with the type of problems he has. I think I convinced my parents to support that plan. His doctors and the ones at the hospital in Los Angeles all agree that it's the best option. My parents are going to get counseling too. Danny's ex is pretty cool. She'll help if he makes a commitment to get treatment. He'll lose everything if he doesn't."

"Did you work on anything with your parents?"

"Most of the time I was just around. I did a lot of listening, gathering up all the information I could get so I could under-stand what was going on. Once I did, and once I was convinced what they were recommending was the best for him, my parents and I were able to talk a lot more. It was difficult and it's not solved by any means. I don't know that I'll ever be as close as the other four are. But it's okay for me to be whatever kind of close we are."

"Are you truly?" He heard the challenge in her question. Most people would have let what he'd said about being okay pass. Not this one.

He paused, thinking because it was a smart question and one he'd skirted. "I *want* that sort of relationship Asa has with his mom. I was wrapped up in this idea that I should want to pick up the phone to share things with them. And them with me, especially the big stuff like rehab. But the longer I was there, the more I realized even if I lived next door, it wouldn't be like that."

"It's not you." Carmella put her hand on his chest, above his heart.

"Doesn't matter," Duke said. "I wasn't sure even on the plane back up here if this situation with my family was something I could be all right with until you. When you walked into that restaurant tonight, I *knew* you. I looked into your eyes and I saw to your heart and all the worry and upset dropped away. I thought, *Carmella's here, everything will be okay now.*"

And what a revelation that had been. To see her and feel suddenly so very safe and all right. She calmed down all that agitation he'd had in his belly for weeks.

"How are things with Virgie? I'm sorry I haven't been here to help you through it." The guilt of that hung heavy in his gut. He'd been torn the entire time he was in LA because he'd known she had to process all the stuff with her mother moving.

"I haven't spoken to her in a week or so. I'd be lying to say I hadn't considered just driving over there to see it for myself. I got to Issaquah once. But I stopped and got doughnuts and came back home."

"She doesn't deserve how much you care about her." Virgie and

Steven Hay made him livid. "You're so fucking good and kind and they just shit all over you."

"Just because I love you doesn't mean I want to hear this. It is what it is."

He kissed the top of her head. "I hate it, Carm. You're over here worrying and she doesn't even check in?"

"Now it's my turn to say you should listen to your own very good advice." She shifted so they lay side by side, hands linked. Ginger hopped up on the bed and looked carefully over the mound of blankets to see if she was going to get busted.

Carmella wore a smile as Duke patted the mattress for Ginger to lie down.

"I know you want to fix things for me because you love me. But you know as well as I do that some things can't be fixed. I hope she'll have a happy ending. But I feel like her story will end in tears."

He heard the emotion in her tone. "I'm sorry. The last thing I want is to upset you."

She snorted. "Now you're going to apologize all the time? Neither of us knows how to be with someone like this. So we'll feel our way along. Fight. Because you're pushy in a chipper and yet steadfast way and that's super annoying."

He laughed. "I missed this most of all."

"Me telling you how annoying you can be? That's probably true as most people are too busy fawning over you."

"You don't fawn over me?" he teased.

"I ogle you. I don't have to fawn, though, because you're mine. But you're vexing sometimes and I'm going to say something when you are. I'll blow it off mainly, I've come to discover."

"I do have a superhuman ability to piss you off."

"You *like* to rile me up."

"We all know I'm a danger junkie. You're so fucking magnificent when you're mad I can't help it."

Carmella sighed. "Tomorrow is a big day, Mr. Bradshaw. Grand opening. Wait until you see the new showroom. It's gorgeous. You left before they did the last bit of paint and finish work."

"Everyone has been sending pictures but I'm pretty excited to see it myself tomorrow. I love you. I'm going to say that a lot more now since you've finally admitted you love me too."

"No complaints here. I love you too."

Adam Gulati can have any woman
he wants—but there is only one he
craves. Mick Roberts has lived all over
the world—but there is one pleasure he
still seeks. Jessalyn Franklin loves
two powerful men—but fear has
kept her from both.

One night will bring these three people
together, open the door to a forbidden world,
and change everything...

Please see the next page
for a preview of

COMING BACK.

CHAPTER
One

Jessi gave herself one last look in the in the rearview mirror. This would be the first time she'd seen Mick since moving back to Seattle just the month before.

The last time she'd seen him, he'd broken her heart.

She'd come back to Seattle after living in another state and trying to love someone else didn't take. She admitted to herself at long last that Franklin women loved too damned hard, but it was what it was and despite that broken heart, it still flowed with love and it didn't matter that she shouldn't love who she did. Or whether or not that love was returned.

So, she bought a sexy new outfit, had her hair and makeup done at the salon near her studio, and as soon as she finished her internal pep talk, she'd get out and saunter right through the Twisted Steel doors.

"You can do this. You are awesome and you have nice tits and pretty eyes and you know all the words to 'Bohemian Rhapsody.' You are the perfect woman," she told herself after touching up her lipstick.

Red. She wasn't normally a red lipstick, smoky eye, perfectly coiffed chick in a sexy dress. But this new stage of her life needed a little drama and magic. Mick needed to get an eyeful of what he was missing so she could get the man to come to his senses.

All right then. Jessi grabbed the pretty little bag that went with the fantastic shoes and dress and got out. As she hit the alarm on her key fob and turned to face the main doors of the new Twisted Steel showroom, she saw a shiny black Mercedes.

Shit. Shit. Shit.

Jessi had to walk past the Mercedes anyway to get to the party, and when she got close enough, she could see it was indeed an AMG GT. Super pricy. Very fast. Powerful everything. And only one man she knew would have one with that license plate.

Of course Adam would be there too. She turned around to walk away, trying to get her breath. Could she do this with both of them at the same time? Maybe she should try again another day. Take each one alone.

Three beautiful women walked past. *They* were going inside, so why not her? Jessi firmed her resolve and followed them through the open bay doors where the party lay just beyond.

Inside it was all ink and chrome. Cars and motorcycles gleamed as men and women rocking a whole lot of tattoo work and piercings milled around them. Every imaginable idea of party wear was on display, from suits and ties to leather and denim.

This world wasn't one she was very familiar with. She'd known Mick since they were kids, and while he was good with his hands and had loved cars, this was a whole different level. This was a *culture*, and she suddenly felt like a total outsider.

He was different now, obviously. Maybe he was done with her forever. Maybe he'd moved on. She wasn't used to being out of her element and it left her on shaky ground.

A server paused, offering a glass of champagne. Jessi had it halfway drained by the time she got three steps away.

She was utterly wowed by the space. Soaring ceilings, and fans with blades that resembled airplane propellers rotating lazily. Large windows at the roof level would flood the room with light during the day, but right then it was lit with a golden glow at the walls, and the showcase spaces for each of the projects they had on display perfectly highlighted the gleam of curves and edges of a car or motorcycle. The floors were gorgeous honey-toned hardwoods with customized tile work.

Whoever designed it all was worth every penny.

Jessi scanned the crowd. She'd seen a picture online of Mick and the other two guys who started Twisted Steel. He hadn't changed that much on the outside, but the shadows in his eyes made her heart ache.

Adam was there. She'd have known it the moment she walked in, even if she hadn't seen his car outside. His energy seemed to hum from him like a live wire. He was nearby.

Growing up he'd been intense, but the way he'd felt the last time...

In the last few years, she'd seen Adam three times. Once she'd thrown a drink into his face. Once she'd burst into tears and run away, and the last time, she'd ended up in a dark corner of her parents' basement with him fingering her to climax while people were just upstairs at a party.

A blush heated her face. *At her parents' house.*

He'd kissed her and when she'd gotten back upstairs after a few minutes of pretending they hadn't been in the basement making out, he'd left!

Jessi tapped the woman next to her as they'd been looking at a '34 Ford. "I need an honest opinion."

The woman grinned. "Okay."

Jessi motioned at herself. "How do I look? I mean, if you had foolishly dumped me several years ago, would you look at me tonight and think about how stupid you were?"

"Give me the three-sixty so I can see it all."

Jessi did and the other woman nodded. "He will *totally* be worried he was so dumb. You look great. I'm PJ." She held out her hand for Jessi to take.

"Jessi. Thanks for the opinion."

"How do you get your hair so smooth and sleek? I had a long bob like that for a while, but the humidity makes it curl up all the time."

"There's no way I could get it to look like this daily. Are you kidding me?" Jessi laughed. "I went to a salon earlier and they did it all. Once I wash it, it'll be curly again."

"I really like that you just admitted that. And that you're not so perfect you can get your hair like that regularly. Okay"—PJ looked around the room and back to Jessi—"who are you looking for? I might know him. I do a lot of paint for Twisted Steel—and full disclosure, I'm with Asa Barrons, one of the owners—so I'm around here a lot."

"Oh." Obviously she'd know Mick. "Uh, you do know him. Mick Roberts."

PJ's brows went up and then she leaned in. "I *knew* you'd be gorgeous."

"Me? What? You did? He talked about me?" Holy crap, she needed to find a sentence and go with it instead of word vomiting.

PJ waved a hand and rolled her eyes. "He's a dude so he hints at lost love. You didn't hurt him, did you? I'm pretty protective of my dudes, you know."

Jessi snorted. "I'm sure we hurt each other lots of times, but that break was him."

"He's wearing a suit tonight. They all are. So handsome I made them let me fuss over them extra long." PJ's grin was sort of infectious.

"I'm not sure I've had enough to drink yet for that. Mick in a suit is pretty impressive," Jessi said quietly.

"That's easily remedied. There's a bar station right over there. It's also next to the mini tacos. You should have some of those too. For strength."

This PJ was all right. Jessi liked her pretty much immediately as they headed toward the bar.

Just a few feet away, a wall of incredible-smelling male stepped into her path and she bumped straight into him.

Careful hands took her upper arms to save her from falling. She took a deep breath and looked up into Mick's face for the first time in far too long.

"Jess . . ." He smiled and she smiled, and the love she'd felt for Mick Roberts since they'd been fifteen tumbled through her heart, making her a little dizzy.

"I got the invitation. I figured it was a sign."

His smile softened, went sideways. "You and your signs." He hadn't let go and she made no move, just content to take him in.

"Well. Here I am, looking at you. So I was right. You look very handsome." He'd always had a filter on when he was in public. His eyes were hard, but it was a front. He'd been so pummeled emotionally over his life, his only real defense had been to keep people far enough away from his heart that they couldn't hurt him.

But the real Mick, the one so very few people got to see, was the one he showed to her just then, and it brought a lump to the back of her throat. She shoved it away, choosing joy instead.

"I guess so. It could have been the invitation, though."

That made her laugh. "I'm really glad to see you. I've missed you so much." This time she'd say all the things she should have been plainer about before.

A rush of emotion played over his features right before he pulled her into a hug.

It had been so long since she'd felt like this. Totally happy. A sense of rightness of place and energy. He was the part of her that had never healed over when it was ripped away.

Jessi held on, soaking him in, knowing it would need to end soon because they were in public and standing near the bar. It was his party after all. After one last sniff, she loosened her arms a little, as did he, until they finally broke apart.

That was when she got the full impact of Mick in person. He wore a pale gray pinstripe suit with a dark blue shirt and a skinny tie.

He had ink on his knuckles—*Fists Up*—and red roses peeked from the edge of his shirt cuff at the wrists.

Dangerously handsome.

She knew what was beneath the suit pants. Her nipples beaded at the memory.

Quickly—but not so fast he hadn't noted her attention on his cock—she shifted her attention up to his face and got stuck. His beard was the same caramel brown as his hair when he didn't wear it shaved. He kept it a little long, but not anywhere near *guy-who-has-a-manifesto* stage. She liked it. A lot.

Like the hair. That had been a new thing, when he'd come back from Iraq. Not a smooth shave, because he had a perpetual stubble. It was just clipped very close.

She wanted to touch it. Wished she had the right.

Mick had sent them both invitations on a whim and they were both there. Both looking at him the same way they always had, and it was simultaneously the best moment and the worst because he'd left them both behind.

He hadn't seen Jessi in nearly four years. Gone was the long dark braid she'd worn daily, replaced by one of those haircuts women made look effortless but probably had to be redone every six weeks. The back of her neck was bare—he'd noticed when they'd hugged—and he'd bet it was downy soft.

The dress was...wow. Something he'd never seen her wear before. At first glance it seemed like a classic cocktail dress. It came to her mid-calf and wasn't cut low in the front. But it had these panels on the sides that offered tantalizing glimpses of one of God's finest things, side boob.

She had ink and a nose ring. It looked good on her. He wondered what she had going on under the dress. Given the fit, he could see there was a large back piece that wrapped around her biceps and shoulder. She had ink, she didn't wear a bra, and she was even more irresistible than she'd ever been.

"I missed you too. So..." He waved a hand indicating the space. "What do you think?"

"I think this place is absolutely fantastic. I'm so impressed."

"Thank you." Pleasure that she approved hummed through him. "Want a tour?"

He held his elbow out and she took it. Before they walked away, Jessi glanced over her shoulder and waved.

"You know PJ?" he asked.

"I met her a few minutes ago. She was helping me locate you after we had a drink."

He took two flutes of champagne and handed her one. Guiding her through the building, pointing out the bells and whistles, he tried to pretend he wasn't keeping an eye out.

"So, you really think this showroom is done well?" Mick had always trusted her eye. And her opinion.

She nodded. "I know a thing or two about staging for an audience. This showroom is really fantastic. I read the thing in the paper about Twisted Steel and how you've been named a third partner. I'm pleased things are going so well for you."

He wanted to kiss her. Wanted to sling an arm around her shoulders and pull her to his side like he had dozens upon dozens of times over the years. There was a hesitancy between them now that there'd never been before and it was his fault.

Instead he blurted, "So you don't hate me?"

Startled, her eyes widened and she took both his hands in hers, pulling him to the side. "I could never hate you, and if I did, I wouldn't be here. I'm here because I've always been here, just waiting for you to remember that."